The Education
of Madeline

The Education of Madeline

BETH WILLIAMSON

KENSINGTON PUBLISHING CORP.
http://www.kensingtonbooks.com

BRAVA BOOKS are published by

Kensington Publishing Corp.
850 Third Avenue
New York, NY 10022

All Kensington titles, imprints, and distributed lines are available at special quantity discounts for bulk purchases for sales promotion, premiums, fund-raising, educational, or institutional use.

Special book excerpts or customized printings can also be created to fit specific needs. For details, write or phone the office of the Kensington Special Sales Manager: Kensington Publishing Corp., 850 Third Avenue, New York, NY 10022. Attn.: Special Sales Department. Phone: 1-800-221-2647.

Brava and the B logo Reg. U.S. Pat. & TM Off.

ISBN-13: 978-0-7582-3469-8
ISBN-10: 0-7582-3469-4

First Kensington Trade Paperback Printing: March 2009
10 9 8 7 6 5 4 3 2 1

Printed in the United States of America

Chapter One

Plum Creek, Colorado, May 1872

They were getting ready to hang a man. The whispers flittered through the saloon, the general store, the barber, the blacksmith, and finally to the bank.

Madeline Brewster heard snatches of conversation here and there. She usually tried to ignore the gossips. After all, most of the time, they were gossiping about her. But today was different. This time she heard "horse thief" and "hanging," and her interest was piqued.

There was nothing Madeline hated more than a hanging.

"Mr. Cleeson, come here, please," she called to the nearest teller.

He looked up in surprise and then shuffled over to her office door. His thinning blond hair and watery blue eyes darted around the room, yet he never looked directly at her. He was dressed in his usual white shirt, bow tie, and black trousers. His scruffy black shoes hadn't been changed since the day she'd hired him two years ago.

"Yes, Miss Brewster?"

"What is all this about a hanging?"

She could almost see him rubbing his hands together with glee to impart the juicy gossip to her.

"Well, I heard that the sheriff caught this Irishman red-handed with Old Clem's horse. They knew it was his 'cause of the blaze on his nose. Judge Martin ordered the hanging."

Madeline tapped her fingers on the large oak desk. "I see. And when is this event taking place?"

"Any minute now, Miss Brewster. I expect they're just looking for a sturdy rope."

"And the Irishman? Does anyone know him?"

Mr. Cleeson shook his head. "Came into town a few weeks ago. Was working out at the Double R as a wrangler."

So, a drifter and apparently a horse thief.

"And his age?"

Mr. Cleeson just looked at her with a blank stare.

"How old is he?"

"Oh, about thirty or so, I guess."

He sounded perfect. Now all she had to do was get to the old maple at the edge of town before they hung him. Madeline snatched up her reticule and stood, startling Mr. Cleeson.

"I'm leaving early today. I will be back for my usual afternoon hours tomorrow. Be sure to follow proper procedures all around."

Mr. Cleeson nodded and scurried back to his chair. He was apparently eager to impart the questioning to his coworkers, because as soon as he sat down, he leaned over to Mr. Bryson and started whispering madly.

Madeline pinned on her hat, tugged on her gloves, and swept out of the bank with her head high and her heart pounding. She was about to go meet the man who might change her life. She walked down the wood-planked boardwalk purposefully. Most people nodded a greeting to her, but no one spoke. They rarely did.

Her heeled boots clacked along without slowing. Even so, the walk to the edge of town took more than ten minutes. By the time she got to the tree, a group of twenty men had gathered. In the midst of them, perched upon an old draught horse, was the biggest, filthiest man she had ever seen.

He looked to have black hair, although the dirt and twigs

caking it made it hard to tell for certain. His clothing was matted and wrinkled. There was no way to tell what color it had been originally. His legs hung down past the horse's belly. Everything about him was big, from his hands to his feet and everything in between.

Apparently the incompetent sheriff and the drunken judge had put the man on a horse too small to hang him.

Wrapped around his neck was a thick noose of the sturdiest hemp. He had at least a week's worth of whiskers on his face. His bright eyes glanced through the crowd, searching. When they landed on her, the only woman present, he cocked his head to the side and lazily ran his gaze up and down her.

A flush stole over her cheeks at the perusal. Never, *not once,* had any man ever looked at her as a woman. And what does she do when one does? Blush like a schoolgirl!

Madeline had been right to come. With a long bath, a razor, and several bars of soap, he would be perfect.

"Excuse me, gentlemen," she said.

A hush fell over the crowd as the entire group, which had been pointedly ignoring her, turned to look at her. The Irishman's eyebrows rose in surprise.

"I would like to know what the charges are against this man."

Judge Earl Martin walked over to her with his silly bowler hat perched atop his shining head. His suspenders looked to be holding up nothing but the thumbs he'd hooked in them, as his pants were tight against his round belly. He stopped three feet away—his usual habit because she was at least six inches taller than he. He regarded her with his bleary brown eyes over his mottled red nose and muttonchop sideburns.

"Now, Miss Brewster. You know this ain't no place for a lady."

Someone in the crowd snickered.

"A hanging is man's business. Why don't you go on back to the bank and take care of things there. Your pa wouldn't have wanted you to witness this."

Madeline raised one eyebrow and looked down at the judge. "Fortunately my father has been dead two years, Earl. And unless you find a much bigger horse, there is no way you're going to be able to hang that man."

Mumbles and curses emanated from the crowd.

"We were just working on that problem, Miss Brewster. But like I said, this ain't no place for a lady."

"What are the charges?" she insisted.

The judge took off his hat and ran his hand down his face, a sheen of perspiration evident on his bald pate.

"You ain't going back to the bank, are you?"

"Not without the information I've asked for."

The sheriff was holding the reins of the horse. Jackson Webster was a pompous braggart who couldn't find his ass with both hands. Madeline and Jackson had been in school together until she reached the age of twelve and had to stay home with a private tutor.

Jackson had always been a bit of a bully, and the silver badge pinned to his shirt gave him all the authority he needed to exercise that bad habit.

She grudgingly admitted that he was a good-looking man, well built, with dark blond hair and blue eyes. Unfortunately he was as dumb as he was handsome.

"Sheriff Webster?"

"He stole Old Clem's horse, Madeline. We've got an eyewitness."

"Is this the horse?" she asked, eyeing the creature in question.

"Yup, this is Bud. Been Old Clem's horse for years and years."

"And the eyewitness?"

"Arnie Jones saw him leading it into town, pretty as you please." He looked up smugly at the Irishman. "Danged fool didn't even try to hide it."

"Did you ask him how he came to be in possession of the horse?"

The group was silent for a moment.

"Of course we did. He said he bought it at the hostelry over in Coopersville." Jackson snorted a laugh. "As if we would believe that."

"Why not?"

"Old Clem would never sell Bud. Never! So obviously this here fella took him."

Madeline controlled herself, just barely, from rolling her eyes. "And have you spoken to Old Clem?"

"No, he's not at his house. Pete says he went to visit his daughter in Denver for a month."

It was worse than she thought. They were all a bunch of incompetent fools.

"Sheriff Webster, you cannot hang that man."

A collective groan rose from the crowd.

"And why not? You're not going to stop another hanging with your fancy words. Horse thieving is a *hanging* crime."

Madeline nodded. "I understand that. But you have not proven that he committed a crime. Simply because he had the horse does not mean he stole it. There must be corroborating evidence."

"Corrobo—what?"

"Evidence that proves conclusively he stole the horse. I suggest you wait for Old Clem to return to determine if Bud was indeed stolen, and send someone to Coopersville to check whether or not Bud was sold to this man."

"What do we do with him in the meantime? He wouldn't last one hour in that tiny jail cell, much less a month." Jackson actually had doubt on his face.

Yes, oh, yes. It was working out exactly as she hoped. Madeline walked toward the horse, and the crowd parted like the Red Sea.

"Put him in my custody. He can work for me for a month taking care of some repairs I need completed at the house."

She couldn't, *wouldn't* look the Irishman in the face. It all hinged on this. Convincing them to give him to her.

"He's a big man, Miss Brewster," said the judge. "If'n he gets a mind to run, even a woman of your size ain't gonna stop him."

Madeline let the insult slide past her. She was so close.

"You need not be concerned about me or my safety. I'm sure the gentleman will not harm me. I'm saving his life."

The judge scratched his sideburn and looked up at the man. "He's pretty dirty. Likely get the house dirty, too."

"He'll sleep in the carriage house. And we do have soap and water. And a razor."

Another snicker wafted through the men.

"Any objections?"

There were some side conversations and some murmuring, but no one protested. Madeline's heart was beating so fast she was certain they could hear it. Her palms were clammy in her gloves, and a bead of perspiration slithered down her back.

"All right, then. We'll put him in your custody until Old Clem gets back," Jackson said and then scowled up at the Irishman. "You're lucky Miss Brewster took it in her mind to save your sorry ass."

"I'm much obliged, ma'am. I tried to explain to the gentlemen that I bought and paid for the horse legally. Your intervention is most appreciated," replied the Irishman.

His voice was deep and rich, sliding over her like warm honey. And he was obviously educated. She repressed a shiver with a great deal of effort.

"Remove the noose and help him off the horse," Madeline said without a quaver in her voice.

The sheriff complied with the help of a few of the other men. Within a minute, he was standing, actually towering, over the rest of the men. He had to be well over six and a half feet tall. Finally, a man taller than her own six feet, and he was *hers*. For a whole month.

Her plan was nearly complete.

* * *

Teague O'Neal looked around the group of men as they tipped their hats, nodded, and walked away. The men who had been ready to hang him now acted as if nothing had happened. Unbelievable.

"You listen to Miss Brewster now," the sheriff said to him. "I'll have your ass back up on a bigger horse in ten minutes if you don't." Teague nodded dutifully. "I'm going to keep Bud with the blacksmith until this is over," he continued as he took the horse's reins and started to walk away. "Be careful, Madeline."

His savior inclined her head at the sheriff but did not respond. What kind of town was this?

Stupid question, really. He already knew the answer. To top it off, they'd left him in the custody of a woman.

Alone.

With no protection whatsoever.

Madeline was tall, probably around six feet, with rich mahogany hair that hung in a thick braid down her back. Perched on top of that glorious hair was the most god-awful hat he'd ever seen—with a long green feather that hung down past her shoulders and little dangling things all around the brim. Her eyes were very dark, almost black, and full of secrets. She had large breasts and plenty of womanly curves that could keep his hands and his mouth occupied.

This job was going to be more interesting than he had thought. It was clear Madeline was something different. Intelligent, manipulative, and used to getting her own way. It also sounded as if she really did hold power over the town.

She was looking him over as she walked around him in a circle. Like a horse at auction.

"See anything you like?"

"As a matter of fact, yes, I do." She held out her hand like a man to shake his. "I'm Madeline Brewster."

He looked down at her hand and then held up his for

scrutiny. As dirty as a pig in a wallow. He shrugged, rubbed his hand on his equally dirty pants, and shook her hand. She had a surprisingly strong grip for a woman.

"Teague O'Neal."

"Let's get started on back home. After you've had a bath and a shave, we can talk. I have a business proposition for you." She turned and started walking away without another word.

Teague bit his tongue to keep from snapping at her. She had just saved his life. He didn't want to seem like an un-grateful ass. She walked a few feet away and then turned back to look at him with her sensual eyes.

"Are you coming, Mr. O'Neal?"

He wanted to say no. But he couldn't. She had a business proposition for him. That meant money. Teague would do just about anything for a buck.

Teague took all kinds of jobs that put him in harm's way, from bronc busting to transporting dynamite. He didn't care about the money. He pissed it away on whores and booze anyway. Every day he started with empty pockets, and he fin-ished each day the same way.

With her stiffness and the way she ordered him around like he was some sticky-faced kid, and the way it made him want to wring her pretty little neck, working for Madeline could be his most dangerous job yet.

He stomped along until he caught up to her and gestured for her to proceed. She nodded regally and continued to walk. He felt the urge to stick his tongue out at her. Instead he stared at her ass when she walked. No bustle or anything to detract from the natural curves under the green dress. And the braid swung back and forth, caressing her with each pass. Unbelievably, he felt his lust stirring. Without being drunk. Without imagining she was Claire.

He reached up and slapped his cheek hard enough to bring tears to his eyes. Madeline turned around to look at him with her curious dark stare.

"Everything all right?"
No. Everything's not all right.
"Just dandy. Lead on."

Jackson met up with Earl after the near hanging. He waited behind the jail, smoking a cheroot and feeling like he'd just bagged a ten-point buck.

Earl was a shitty judge; everybody knew it. But somehow he kept getting elected or appointed or whatever the hell it was that got him the job. He drank and whored with the best of them. That made him easy pickings when Jackson needed something done. Like a fake hanging.

Earl came around the corner, his eyes darting left and right like he was expecting an Indian attack.

"Relax. Nobody can see us, fool."

Earl stuck out his chest, which unfortunately just made his big belly poke out like a woman expecting a family.

"Guard that tongue, Jackson. I can have you on a horse with a noose around your neck, too." Malice dripped from Earl's words.

Jackson grinned at him. "Same goes for you, old man."

After a minute of staring each other down, Earl lowered his eyes and scuffed the ground with the toe of one shiny shoe.

"Does he know what to do?"

"He'd better. We pounded it into him all night. He surely did want that five hundred dollars."

Earl grinned and snapped his suspenders with his thumb, making a dull *thwack* against his girth.

"Excellent! Within one month, this town will belong to us."

Jackson took a long drag of his cheroot and let the smoke out slowly.

"One month, and she'll be mine."

Madeline was nervous. A condition she almost never dealt with. As she walked along with Mr. O'Neal behind her like an oversize dog, she tamped down the giddy pleasure welling up inside her. It was almost too easy, the way he had fallen into her lap. Now all she had to do was convince him.

They reached her house within fifteen minutes. Fifteen silent minutes. Mr. O'Neal had not asked one question about what kinds of repairs he would be doing. Or where he'd be living. Or even why she would step in to stop the hanging. Perhaps he wasn't the curious type.

The house was two stories high, with a large wraparound porch and a swing that danced gently in the breeze. It was enormous by any standard, and for just one person, it was simply too big. She'd painted it the brightest blue she could find and turned it into a boardinghouse of sorts. Whenever a stranger came to town, provided they were a good sort, she offered them a place to stay for a night.

Madeline never expected money for it. She already had enough to last her two lifetimes. No, she'd started doing it for the company, to give back some of the blood her father had drained from the world.

Then it became a way for her to thumb her nose at the judgmental town that never even gave her a chance. She bore the brand of being a Brewster and all that it entailed. Her father's life had stolen her future, so she lived for the present.

They walked up the three steps to the front door, which opened to reveal Eppie, her housekeeper, cook, and friend.

"Madeline! Are you crazy, girl? You can't save everyone!"

Eppie was a young mulatto who had been Madeline's first guest a few weeks after her father's funeral. As a freed slave, Eppie had drifted from place to place until she ended up in Plum Creek. A lasting friendship was born immediately. She had been living with Madeline ever since. A scarf tightly wrapped her dark hair, and the bright purple dress accented her coloring. She always wore bright colors, said it made each day a little better.

"Good afternoon, Eppie. This is Mr. O'Neal. He's our new guest."

Eppie gaped. "Are you sure there is a man under all that dirt?"

Madeline smiled. "We'll find out, won't we? Let's start by letting him come inside."

Eppie frowned at her, but she went back in the house. Madeline turned to Mr. O'Neal. She was surprised to find him inches from her back. A wave of awareness swept over her, leaving a trail of goose bumps behind.

"Welcome to my house, Mr. O'Neal."

He looked at her for a moment and then at the house. "Quite a house. Is it just you and the girl?"

"And you. For now."

He opened his mouth as if to say something else but closed it and gestured with his hand for her to lead the way.

After an incredibly awkward moment in the foyer, Madeline sent Eppie to the general store to see if they had any clothes that might fit Mr. O'Neal.

Madeline brought him upstairs to the bathing room, and after explaining how to use the running water, left him with two cakes of soap, three towels, and her father's shaving gear.

Eppie came back with a pair of trousers and one shirt she had bought from Mr. Hansen at the mill. He was about the only man in town as large as the new houseguest. She'd also made arrangements with Brenda Monahan, the seamstress in town, to come by and measure him in the morning for new clothes.

After delivering the new clothes *outside* the bathroom door, Madeline went downstairs and waited for him in the sitting room. It was her favorite room because it had been her mother's and had sat untouched and unused for twenty years.

After her father died, Madeline had opened it up, aired it out, and claimed it as her sanctuary. She had all her precious books in the shelves on the walls. Books were her greatest passion. She was never without one or two or even three lying around, waiting for her to get back to them.

She picked up *Sense and Sensibility*, usually one of her favorites, but found herself reading the same passage over and over. Just as she was about to get up and go check on her guest, he appeared in the doorway.

Madeline had initially thought he was an average-looking man, albeit a big one. She was unprepared to find out she had been *very* wrong. He was anything but average.

Underneath the grit and grime was a man with thick, wavy black hair and a rugged face nearly hewn from granite. He had incredible cheekbones and a strong jaw with full lips. The clean clothes hugged him like a second skin, accentuating the sheer size of his chest, shoulders, and arms. She couldn't bring herself to look any lower than that or she might embarrass herself.

"Mr. O'Neal."

"Miss Brewster."

His deep voice vibrated through her. She wanted to press her ear against his chest and *feel* his voice.

"Please sit down." She gestured to the large sofa that sat across from the fireplace. As he walked toward the sofa, she found her eyes straying to his behind. His perfectly formed behind. When he sat down, she almost asked him to stand up again.

Stop it! Business first!

Madeline sat up straight in the wingback chair and pressed her hands together on her lap. She looked at his feet.

"I have a business proposition for you, Mr. O'Neal. Please listen to its entirety before you give me a yes or no answer."

"I can do that," he responded.

She took a deep breath and continued. "First, let me say that you are welcome to stay in the house for as long as you need to. My house is always open for those in need. In addition, I am willing to pay you to teach me certain skills I am lacking."

Mr. O'Neal nodded.

"As I'm sure you gathered, I am unmarried and . . . untried by a man. My marriage prospects are virtually nonexistent, and I . . . I want to learn everything you can teach me about the intimacies between a man and woman."

She let loose a shaky breath and finally looked him in the eye. He didn't look shocked. In fact, he looked almost amused.

"You want me to bed you?"

"Not just bed me, Mr. O'Neal. Teach me everything there is to know, or at least to the extent of your knowledge. And I am willing to compensate you five hundred dollars after a month's . . . work."

She had thought she was nervous before, but now an entire colony of butterflies was dancing in her belly. He smiled. Then he chuckled.

Madeline almost lost her composure. She stood abruptly.

"I see that your answer is no. I won't bother you again about it, Mr. O'Neal. Please be kind enough not to mention it to anyone."

She held herself together with sheer will as she turned to leave the room. A large hand on her arm stopped her. She turned to look up into Mr. O'Neal's face. He no longer looked amused. In fact, his pupils had widened in his incredible blue eyes, and his mouth had compressed into a thin line.

"I didn't say no."

Chapter Two

Madeline's heart was pounding so hard, she thought it might burst from her chest any second. She found that her voice had deserted her, and her mouth was as dry as cotton.

He didn't say no.

But that didn't mean yes, either.

"Please sit back down, Miss Brewster." He gestured to the chair and waited until she sat before he sat back down on the sofa.

"I thought at first you were joshing me. Trying to see how much trouble a drifter could get into. Then I realized that you wouldn't do such a thing to a man you had just saved from a hanging." He looked at her with a serious expression on his face. "You are a pretty woman, Miss Brewster. Why would you throw away your virginity on a no-account drifter like me?"

Madeline cocked her head and regarded him for a minute before answering.

"Pretty? I think you mean that, Mr. O'Neal."

It seemed odd to be so formal after what she had just proposed, but it seemed to be the only way to keep her sanity together during this strange conversation.

"I'm thirty-two years old," she said. "Now, don't look shocked. You can tell I'm not a girl in the first blush of womanhood. There are no marriage prospects in this town for a woman like me, and circumstances tie me to this town sure as Excalibur was stuck in that stone. I admit to being curious about . . . what goes on between men and women. I've read textbooks, but that's just the scientific explanation. Just once, I want to experience true physical contact with a man while I'm still young enough to enjoy it."

It all came out in a rush, but after she was done, it was as if a great weight had been lifted off her shoulders. She was finally able to take a deep breath.

"Just once?"

His softly worded question brought a flush to her cheeks, even more than her own bawdy proposition.

"I don't expect more than that."

Oh, but that was a lie, and she knew it. Deep down where her dreams lay gathering dust, a long-ago wish rumbled to life. She tried to stuff the wish back into its hiding place, but it scratched and wailed, refusing her the chance to ignore it.

I want more. I want it all. I want a husband and children.

"And you said you would pay me for a month's wages?"

Madeline had to mentally shake herself to focus on Mr. O'Neal's question.

"Yes, I also have repairs that need to be made to the house. I'm willing to compensate you for all your . . . work." She swallowed a lump and kept her gaze locked with his.

He finally looked down at the floor and leaned his elbows on his knees.

"I realize this is out of the ordinary," she said. He croaked something between a laugh and a snort. "And I appreciate that you are considering my offer," she continued.

He stood and wandered over to the window overlooking the backyard. Her eyes strayed to his wide shoulders, powerful arms, and back. A man worked hard to get muscles like that. Mr. O'Neal obviously worked *very* hard.

His back tapered down to a waist that led down farther to

that perfect derriere. His behind was well shaped and as firm as the rest of him. A tiny shiver of longing erupted from within. Longing to run her hands across those shoulders, down those arms. To feel the sinews and bone that made up that perfect specimen of man. Her palms actually itched, so she flattened them against her knees.

"I am more than willing to make any repairs you need, and I truly appreciate the offer of room and board."

Madeline sensed there was more coming, and she was going to be disappointed with the rest of it.

He sighed and leaned against the window frame. "But I can't say yes to the rest of your business proposition."

All the hope that had been building collapsed like a house of cards. It was okay. Really. She hadn't expected more. Really. But she had so *wished* for more.

"Yet."

That one word stopped her crashing spirits. *Yet.*

"When do you think you might ah . . . that is . . . make a definite decision?"

"I'm not sure, Miss Brewster, but maybe we can agree to wait a week." He finally turned to look at her, and the absolute masculinity in this man struck her again. His black hair had dried into waves that looked as soft as silk. His eyes were pools of azure that shuttered his secrets from the world.

"A week is perfectly acceptable to me. Thank you, Mr. O'Neal."

Teague walked over and pulled her to her feet. His hands were calloused and hard, practically engulfing hers, which were not a petite, feminine size. She tilted her head to look up into his eyes—something she hadn't done for nearly twenty years to another human being.

"I'll stay here and work for you on two conditions. First is that you call me Teague."

"Teague." She repeated the name, and it felt . . . perfect on her tongue. "As long as you call me Madeline."

"Agreed. And don't thank me. I should be thanking you for saving my life."

Madeline nodded her head, not willing her voice to speak. It was all so unreal. She had hoped, *prayed* for so long to find a man to fulfill her plan. Here he was. In her house. Willing to consider being her teacher.

"You're most welcome . . . Teague. What's the second condition?"

He closed his eyes and shook his head slowly.

"I can't believe I'm going to say this. . . . If I agree to the rest of your deal, you must never tell anybody I did. I don't want to be known as a whore."

The word slammed into Madeline like a kick from a horse. *Whore.*

It was an awful, spiteful word applied to women who sold themselves for money. She'd never even considered that people would consider Teague a whore, because she paid him a month's wages.

"I don't plan on shouting it from the rooftops. This is a private agreement between you and me and involves no one else. As to the money, let's agree that I will only pay you for the repairs and improvements to the house."

It sounded so cold. So impersonal. But wasn't that what she wanted? Wasn't that how she'd explained it to him? Yes and no. It wasn't what she wanted, really. It was how it had to be.

Teague nodded his agreement. The deal was acceptable. Now it was up to him whether or not it ever went any further than a conversation in the sitting room.

Teague joined her for his first official meal at what Eppie called "The Last-Chance Hotel." When they walked into the dining room, Madeline inwardly cringed at the ornate quality of the room. A black walnut table with twelve chairs sat in the center of the room, a large brass chandelier with dangling prisms hanging above it. A blue tablecloth with match-ing napkins, two place settings of their everyday china with glasses, and a plain vase with bluebonnets in the middle sat upon the table. There was a breakfront on one wall, with del-icate Wedgwood china lined up like a carnival booth. On an-other wall was a huge bay window that overlooked Plum Creek, which ran behind the house. Lastly, there was a liquor cart, which now stood with empty crystal decanters, the bourbon and whiskey long since dumped.

On the floor was a Persian rug of intricate design that was one of her father's prized possessions. The mixture of blues, greens, and purples accentuated the rose wallpaper and the light walnut wainscoting.

All in all, it was a room out of a rich man's mansion (which it was)—a fact Madeline tried to ignore. However, it was hard to ignore it when you had a man behind you scrutiniz-ing the room down to the cream-colored damask seats on the chairs.

"Nice room."

Madeline almost choked on her own spit. It was anything but a nice room to her.

"This was one of my father's decorating endeavors."

She walked over to the chair next to the head of the table, and was as surprised as she could be to see a hand pull the chair out for her. She murmured a thank you and sat down. Teague sat down across from her instead of at the head of the table. He pulled the place setting in front of him.

"Why did you sit there?" she blurted.

He raised one dark eyebrow. "Is this seat taken?"

"No, of course not. It's just . . . well, most men would have sat at the head of the table."

He shrugged one massive shoulder. "Not my house, not my place to sit there."

Madeline watched as he placed the napkin on his lap and waited patiently for Eppie to bring the food in. Obviously well brought up and well mannered, his actions stirred her curiosity. Never a shy person, Madeline didn't try to curb it.

"Where are you from originally?"

Teague glanced down at the empty white plate in front of him. "Is that a job requirement?"

"No, of course not. In this house you are free to keep your secrets, and free to share your dreams."

He nodded and looked out the window. It felt decidedly odd to sit down to supper with a man Madeline had just made an indecent proposal to. She hadn't picked him for his manners or his etiquette or the cut of his clothes (most especially). She'd picked him because he was a man who didn't know her or her family secrets, and, well, in truth because he was big. Madeline was no petite, delicate dumpling. She was not only tall, she also was big and curvy. The man to fit her had to be as big or bigger.

Teague certainly fit the "bigger" description. All over. She had to stop herself from staring at him. She had never experienced a rush of heat looking at a man before, but this one was apparently different. She reminded herself that this was still a business arrangement even if she was lusting after her proposed partner like an animal in heat.

Madeline had to change the subject in her brain, or she was going to embarrass herself. Like a savior, Eppie breezed in with a platter of fried chicken and a bowl of mashed potatoes.

"Here you go. I'll be right back with the green beans and lemonade."

Eppie set the platter down in front of Teague and the mashed potatoes between them. She shot Madeline a look of disbelief after a good look at Teague all cleaned up. Her eyebrows rose nearly to her hairline. Madeline shook her head slightly and frowned. Eppie just grinned and left the room.

"Smells good."

"Eppie is a wonderful cook. She was made to work in the kitchen from the time she was a young girl. Now she does it because she loves to."

Madeline was babbling. She mentally pinched herself to stop being such a fool.

Eppie came back in with a bowl of green beans and a pitcher of lemonade. With her brown eyes dancing, she smiled widely at Madeline and set the bowl in front of her.

"Lemonade?" Eppie asked Teague.

"Yes, please," he replied.

"Such nice manners on your man, Madeline," Eppie teased.

"He's not *my* man, Eppie. Now stop it."

Eppie poured Madeline's glass and then Teague's. As she set the pitcher on the table, she winked at Madeline.

"I'll leave y'all alone so you can talk business."

With a little giggle, she pranced out of the room. The sound of her tinkling laughter floated back to them as she dashed back to the kitchen.

"I'm sorry. Eppie is . . . a free spirit."

"She's a sweet girl."

"Yes, she is. Eppie is my best friend. My only friend."

After she said it, Madeline wanted to tuck the words in her pocket and hide them. She sounded so pitiful. One friend in the whole world.

"I used to have a friend myself. A best friend like your Eppie."

Teague reached forward, speared a piece of chicken, and put it on his plate.

"What happened to him?" Madeline heard herself ask.

"He died in my arms. At Shiloh."

Well, that certainly put a damper on things. Madeline just couldn't stop her mouth sometimes. She put a spoonful of mashed potatoes on her plate and held the bowl out to him.

"Potatoes?"

He took the bowl and slid the platter of chicken toward her. Madeline took a drumstick and tried to force herself to feel hungry. Teague took a healthy portion of potatoes and green beans.

"I'm sorry I said that. It wasn't right to bring it up at our first meal together."

Madeline looked up at him in surprise. Teague's blue eyes shone with sincere regret and a hint of ancient pain.

"We'll start over, then. Could you pass the green beans?"

He handed her the bowl and held on to it as she moved to take it.

"I don't know what to make of you, Maddie."

Maddie.

Her mother had called her Maddie, but no one else ever had. Her father had forbade it after her mother had died. He had always hated the name and insisted she be called Madeline, as her grandmother had been called.

Hearing the name again after all these years brought a rush of memories filled with a myriad of emotions. Sweet Lord, how she missed her mother and the affection she'd given as freely as her smiles. Without her, life had become a stolid, rigid place filled with shadows and duties.

Maddie.

It was as if a door had opened into a dark room. Her heart felt lighter than it had in a long time. All the good deeds she had done over the past two years had felt hollow. Until now. Until she heard the magic word that unlocked life again.

"Maddie?"

Teague was calling her. She must be sitting there with a foolish expression on her face, looking like she had lost her mind, hanging on to the green beans like a lifeline.

"I'm sorry. I was wool gathering! I'm not usually so . . . scatterbrained."

"I didn't think you were."

He finally let the bowl loose, and Madeline set it down next to her plate.

"You are a very charming man, Teague. I think there is a lot more to you than you let on."

He shrugged again and tucked into his food as only a hungry man would: with single-minded determination. Madeline picked at her food and simply watched him. He was obviously very hungry but still used his fork and knife and wiped his mouth occasionally on the napkin.

"I was born and raised here in Plum Creek. I've never traveled anyplace else."

Teague looked up at her with surprise clearly written on his face. He finished chewing the bite in his mouth before he spoke.

"You've never left Plum Creek? Not even to go to Denver?"

She shook her head. "No, my father traveled frequently, but he never took me with him."

"Why not?"

"I think he was trying to engrain a sense of home and the purpose of a woman to keep that home for her man. Not that he ever let any man near me. I guess he was too busy allowing me to run his house." That sounded good. Might as well let all the ghosts out of the closet. "My father was not an easy man to like, Teague. In fact, most people hated him. He was cruel, selfish, and rich as Midas. He owned half this town and half the people that live here. They were beholden to him for loans and favors so deeply he choked the life out of some of them, like a big, vicious weed in a garden. Everyone attended his funeral, but my impression was that they came to gloat that he was dead."

Teague nodded. "And all that money and property, and indebtedness, transferred to you?"

Madeline grimaced. "Unfortunately yes."

"You know, Maddie, most people would give their right arm to live in a house like this and be up to their noses in money."

He sounded angry.

"I'm sorry; I don't mean to sound like an ungrateful, spoiled child. It's just . . . I didn't want it. The town painted me with the same brush, and no matter what I've done to change my color in their eyes, nothing's worked. I am as black-hearted as he was. My only redeeming quality is my money and what it can do for this town." Madeline couldn't keep the bitterness out of her voice.

"Don't expect me to feel sorry for you."

"I don't. I just wanted to let you know what you were getting into working for Rufus Brewster's daughter. They call me the Black Widow, you know."

He chuckled. "You? Why?"

"Some people think I smothered my father to get his money. And because I'd been acting as his hostess for almost twenty years, well, there you have it. The Black Widow."

The corner of his mouth twitched. "Do you have a red mark on your belly?"

Said belly suddenly felt very heavy, as did the rest of her below that. Heavy and very aware of the image of Teague examining her belly. Her naked belly.

Madeline forced a small laugh. "No, no red mark on my belly."

Teague started eating again, apparently undeterred by the airing of the Brewster family dirty laundry.

"You're likely to hear the gossip, perhaps be the target of some of the nastier ones if you stay here and work for me."

"I can handle it."

Madeline nodded and picked at her chicken again. Her appetite had vanished. She was itchy, restless. Like something was nibbling at her that she couldn't quite scratch.

Eppie came into the room to check on them. "You folks about finished?"

Madeline nodded her head and handed her plate to Eppie. She frowned at the food left on the plate. "You need to eat more than that."

"I'm not hungry. Don't nag me, Eppie."

"You don't get any pie if you don't eat your meal."

Madeline rolled her eyes, and Eppie giggled.

"Looks like Mr. O'Neal is going to finish off all this food and get a pie to himself for dessert."

He put the last bite of mashed potatoes in his mouth, chewed, and then wiped his mouth.

"Pie?"

Eppie smiled at him. "Peach pie. One of the trees in the orchard was ready last week."

Teague rubbed his flat belly and made a silly face. "I don't know if I can eat one more bite. But because you went to the trouble to make it, I'll force myself to be polite and have some."

Eppie played along with him. "You are truly a gentleman, sir." She curtsied and took both plates with her as she left the room, still smiling.

"Didn't you like your supper?"

Madeline shrugged. "It was good. It always is. I just . . . My appetite is suffering."

Teague raised one dark eyebrow and took a long drink of his lemonade. He licked his lips and then looked straight at her with hooded eyes.

"Feeling hot and achy?"

She nodded, wondering how he knew that.

"Maybe your stomach is fluttery?"

She nodded again. He reached across the table and took her hand in his. His big thumb caressed her palm slowly. She watched it slide back and forth, experiencing a rush of pleasure from the simple contact.

"I feel it, too, Maddie."

"Feel w—what?" she stammered, definitely off-kilter.

"This. Whatever it is between us. There's a connection there."

He pulled her hand toward his mouth, and she watched, fascinated, as he gently bit the pad of her thumb. A pinch of desire squeezed her so tightly she lost her breath.

"It makes things easier. At the same time, it makes it more complicated."

Madeline couldn't think about easier or complicated. She

was thinking about him gently biting other parts of her body. Parts that were currently tight, aching, or throbbing. He kissed the palm of her hand and then let it loose.

Eppie came in with the pie, breaking the sensual spell woven by Teague's mouth. Madeline knew she was in for a lot more than a simple education if just that small touch of his lips wreaked havoc on her.

Chapter Three

It was a long week. The most excruciatingly long week of Teague's life. When Madeline made her indecent proposition, he'd almost said yes immediately. Almost. The idea that she may have asked any man before him pricked his conscience. So his second reaction was to say no. Almost.

In the end, he asked her to give him a week to decide. That was before he had stared at Maddie across the dinner table, nibbling at her food, her luscious pink tongue licking her fork and then at the grease on her lips. It was all he could do not to grab her and throw up her skirts on the table. Fortunately she apparently had other places to be during the day, so there was at least a small reprieve while she was gone.

Maddie was a passionate, sensual woman trapped inside the body of a thirty-two-year-old spinster who hadn't experienced life yet. A woman trapped like a butterfly in a glass jar all her life. Never knowing what was beyond it. It wasn't uncommon for folks to stay in the same town all their lives—most times it was due to lack of money for traveling. But it wasn't common for a rich man's daughter to never leave. They obviously had money to burn. Yet her father had kept her here. It was *how* he kept her here that puzzled Teague.

She was obviously a strong woman, used to getting her way and ordering others around. Then, on the other side of that, she was kind to him and to Eppie, the young mulatto who apparently lived and worked in the house.

It was as if there were two of them. Maddie and Madeline. Maddie was the woman who yearned to break free of the confines she lived in. Madeline was the rich banker's daughter who snubbed the world for being less than she was. One was kind and generous. The other was bossy and argumentative.

She was a conundrum. She was also driving him mad. Each morning, she had breakfast with him. Maddie had a weakness for cinnamon rolls, so Eppie made them every day. It was sheer torture to watch her eat a cinnamon roll with near passion. Watching her lick the stickiness off her fingers with that pink tongue each morning distracted him for hours afterward. During the day, she brought him cold lemonade or water as he worked on repairing the barn and corral. Her smile was dazzling, and her tits were mouthwatering.

He'd said a week, and he meant a week, but damn it all to hell, after two days, he wanted to beg her. He didn't. Instead he focused on finding out Maddie's secrets and what lurked behind those dark eyes. He wasn't sure if he was doing it for the money or not.

Madeline was sitting in the parlor with her tea, staring out the window at the blue sky. She needed to get to the bank, but her mind refused to cooperate. Two days had passed, and Teague hadn't mentioned her proposition yet. She was worried he was going to say no. The thing was, she was beginning to like him. Really like him. He was funny, smart, and could be charming.

Eppie came to the parlor.

"Someone here to see you." Her eyes were hostile as her glance flicked behind her to the man in the shadows.

Jackson walked in with his usual swagger, hat in hand. He was dressed in a freshly pressed blue shirt, denims, and those sharp-toed boots he favored. His smile was bright and meant to be devastating.

"Morning, Madeline."

"Good morning, Jackson. What brings you by?"

He twirled the hat in his hands and peered out the window.

"I'm checking on the prisoner. Has he given you any trouble?"

For some reason, the sneer of his lips made the hackles snap to attention on her neck. He could always find a way to get her goat.

"Mr. O'Neal has been nothing but a gentleman. Polite, mannerly, and a very hard worker."

"Is he sleeping in the barn?"

"Excuse me?" Madeline felt her face flush at the question.

"I'm sorry. I shouldn't have asked that. I know you well enough, Madeline. You would never do anything improper."

Her flush turned into an all-out fire on her face. Little did Jackson know what improper things she *wanted* to do but hadn't. Yet.

Madeline stood, intent on getting this windbag out of her house.

"Is there anything else, Sheriff?"

He couldn't mistake the cold crispness of her words for anything but a dismissal.

"No, thank you kindly for your time, Madeline. I'll just stop on by and chat with the prisoner on my way out."

He put his hat on and tipped it to her and then swaggered through the door with one last wink in her direction.

Madeline shuddered. The visit left a bad taste in her mouth. It was like chatting with a rattlesnake. She wondered what he could possibly want to talk to Teague about.

She walked to the kitchen, took a glass from the cupboard, and poured a glass of water from the pitcher on the table. As she took a gulp, she saw Jackson talking to Teague. She couldn't hear what they said through the window, but she could watch.

Eavesdropping was another sin her father used to rap her knuckles about. She wasn't eaves*dropping*; she was eaves-*watching*.

Take that, old man!

Teague shook his head, and Jackson poked him in the chest with two fingers. Teague pushed his arm away and shook his head again. Jackson poked him again and then pushed his shoulder.

It was like pushing on a tree. Teague didn't move. His expression was stony.

What in the world?

She was going to go outside and find out what was going on, but Jackson shook his finger at Teague and stomped away.

Teague looked after him with enough fury to nearly form daggers with his eyes. The old adage was true—if looks could kill, Jackson would have been dead.

It was the third day of his residence, and she was slowly going mad.

Watching Teague had become an obsession. The first day he was repairing the corral, Madeline went out to bring him a glass of water and ended up dropping it on her foot. He had taken off his shirt and was half naked in her yard!

Oh, sweet Lord above! She was wrong. A cold marble sculpture could never compare to the muscle and sinew and pure fire that was Teague's body. Just looking at him nearly burned her eyes. He swung a sledgehammer down, driving the post far into the ground. The swing of that instrument in his hands was like a symphony of human beauty. Everything rippled and sang together as an orchestra might. The raw masculinity made a tune her body hummed along with.

Teague was a gorgeous man. Maddie could barely keep her hands to herself. She walked within three feet of him before she realized her hand was outstretched, ready to caress the sun-bronzed god who had stumbled into her life. She whirled around and ran back to the house for another glass.

She made excuses to herself to visit him during the day when she was home. The hours at the bank gave her time to cool herself off, but then there were the times she was home and temptation was within reach. Each time, no matter if he wore his shirt or not, her heart and her body reacted as one. Reaching for him, wanting him. Needing to know what it felt like to touch him. What it felt like for him to touch her. Her experience was limited to simple kissing and hugging, but she could imagine quite a bit more. Especially with the help of the medical texts she'd read. Although none of them quite explained the exact details of fornication, she was fairly certain she had figured it out.

Now she couldn't wait to try it. If only she hadn't agreed to give Teague a week to decide. A week was too long. Far too long. She should have given him one day. No more. She had to find some way to distract herself from *thinking* about bedding him. An idea struck her.

"Do you play any games, Teague?" Maddie asked as they left the dining room after supper.

He didn't answer, so she turned to look at him. A mischievous grin played around those beautiful lips, and one eyebrow arched over humor-filled eyes.

"What kind of games?"

Madeline felt a bit flustered, and she hoped it didn't reflect in her cheeks. She didn't want him to know her self-control was melting like an icicle in July.

"Checkers, chess, backgammon. Those kinds of games."

When his grin turned into a full-blown smile, Madeline gripped the doorjamb to stay upright. She thought she was prepared. She was so very wrong. That smile was devastating. It lit up his whole face, made his eyes crinkle at the corners, and turned her into a puddle of unrequited passion.

"No, but I play a mean game of poker. Do you play?"

Madeline shook her head, disappointed. That canceled her distraction idea.

"Would you like to learn?"

She felt an urge to blurt, "No!" but grabbed it before it could be let loose. The proper lady wasn't going to make the decisions this time. Proper ladies may not play poker, but Maddie Brewster was going to learn.

After searching for thirty minutes, they found a deck of cards in her father's old desk. Teague suggested they play in the kitchen, as it was in the back of the house and relatively private.

When they settled at the table, the lamplight threw a cozy glow over the room. Madeline watched Teague's hands, fascinated by how quickly he shuffled the cards. His fingers were lithe and strong at the same time. She wondered how those fingers would feel on her skin, making her temperature rise degree by degree.

Teague explained a game called five-card stud. The rules were a bit complex, but Madeline understood most of them. He let her play a couple of practice hands, and then they started to play in earnest.

Madeline lost five hands in a row before she started to really enjoy playing the game. She won the next hand. Teague actually looked surprised.

"Very good, Maddie. You're getting the hang of it."

Madeline smiled. "I think I understand why gamblers like to play this so much. Can we gamble, too?"

Teague threw back his head and laughed. It was the first time she'd heard him laugh, and the rough, raspy sound of it did something strange to her equilibrium.

"Don't you think gambling is the root of all evil?"

"No, I don't. I've seen the root of evil, and it's definitely not poker."

He looked like he wanted to respond, but he didn't. He shrugged. "I don't have money to play for."

Madeline watched his hands as he shuffled the cards again.

"How about we play for truths?" he said without looking up.

"Truths?"

"Yes, each time one of us wins a hand, we get to ask the other a question, and the loser must tell the truth."

His hands shuffled faster. By the time the cards started flying off the deck, his fingers were a blur of motion. In a few seconds, five cards lay in front of her.

"I'll play for truths. There isn't much I've got to hide anyway."

Madeline lost the first truth hand.

"Are you ready for the first question?" he asked with a small grin.

"Yes, I'm ready."

"Why did you paint your house blue?"

It was her turn to laugh. "I thought you were going to ask me what color my bloomers were."

His eyebrows rose. "Now you've spoiled it. That was my next question."

"I painted it blue because it was my favorite color, and I wasn't allowed to wear anything that bright. After my father died, I indulged myself."

He nodded. "That answers why it's so damn bright."

She laughed and waved her hands at the cards.

"Deal again, Teague. I'm itching to ask you a truth question."

This time, Madeline won. She pondered her question for several minutes, earning a sigh and rolling eyes from the sore loser.

"Why didn't you say no to my proposition to bed me?"

He clearly hadn't been expecting a personal question like that. The cards he'd been shuffling fell out of his hand like an explosion, raining down all over the table and floor.

"I had to stop myself from saying yes too quickly."

Heat pooled low and insistent in her belly, and a throbbing began between her legs.

"Does this mean you're saying yes to my . . . proposal?" she asked. Her mouth felt as dry as cotton. "I mean, it sounds as though you're going to say yes."

He stood abruptly, and she could see the outline of his penis clearly in his pants. My, oh, my! That certainly was a large-looking organ. Much larger than ones in the drawings in the book.

Teague let the rest of the cards fall from his hands and came around the side of the table. The primal way he walked was enough to make her nipples pucker. He clearly wanted her. *Her*. Madeline Brewster!

When he reached her side, he knelt down on the floor next to her and cupped her face in his big hands.

"Why me?"

She shrugged, somehow. "I need a big man. I'm not . . . petite or feminine like most women. I didn't want my teacher to feel embarrassed by the size difference if I was bigger. You . . . You're bigger than me. And . . ."

"And?"

"Just looking at you makes my body hum."

His pupils widened, and he licked his lips.

He's going to kiss me!

Madeline closed her eyes. She expected his lips on hers. What she didn't expect was featherlight kisses along her brow, down her nose, across her cheekbones, to her chin. Small, jittery kisses that made her ache that much more.

"Hurry up and kiss me," she demanded.

He chuckled against the corner of her mouth. "If you want me to be your teacher, you're going to have to be the student. Can you hand over the reins, Maddie girl?"

Madeline thought long and hard about that question. It wasn't a matter of being under his thumb like her father. It was trusting that he would teach her what she wanted to know without doubting or interfering in his methods.

"Yes," she breathed.

She felt him smile. "Good. Now just close your eyes and feel. This is lesson number one."

"Wait! Does this mean yes?"

"Yes," he said, and then he pressed his finger against her lips. She had the absurd notion to lick it and almost giggled.

She felt his hands in her hair, and suddenly it was tumbling down around her shoulders. She wanted to stop him, to say no, but didn't. Lesson number one.

Teague ran his fingers through her hair, gently massaging her scalp with incredible tenderness. She leaned into him, letting the languid motion lull her.

"Your hair is magnificent. Whenever we're having a lesson, you will have it free like this, understood?"

Madeline nodded.

"Good girl."

His fingers traced the outline of her ears and then down her neck. His lips brushed across her cheekbone until he reached her lips. His tongue traced the seam of her lips ever so lightly until she shivered.

He nibbled the corners of her mouth. She wanted so badly to kiss him. This waiting was torture! But it was sweet torture . . . oh, so sweet. The anticipation was heightening her arousal. She could feel it.

Suddenly his lips were on hers, a slow, moist kiss that felt like a decadent dessert. She leaned into him, and a mewling sound erupted from her throat. His thumbs rubbed her neck as his lips captured hers again and again.

Teague's tongue lapped at her lips.

"Open for me, Maddie."

She opened her mouth, and his tongue plunged in like a conqueror. The twining serpent taught her how to dance with it even as her thighs grew wet with moisture. The roughness of his tongue scraped deliciously around her teeth. He sucked her lower lip into his mouth and gently bit it.

With sweet, slow kisses, he taught her about the inside of

her mouth. How sensual the roof of it was, how tingly her teeth could feel, how fast her heart could beat without bursting from her chest.

He kissed her hard and then pulled back.

"Look at me, Maddie."

She opened her eyes, and it took her a moment to focus on his face. His eyes were heavy lidded.

"That was lesson one. How to kiss. You did very well."

He stood, and she was suddenly at eye level with his erection. Her hand itched to feel it, test the length and breadth of him.

"Is that all?"

"For today."

"When is lesson number two?" she asked, anxious to continue.

"Tomorrow after dinner."

"Can we do them every day after dinner?"

He chuckled and pulled her to her feet. He kissed her again, this time pressing his body fully against hers.

Holy Mary! He was as hard as an oak tree from top to bottom. She was positively sizzling from the heat between them. He pulled away and turned to leave.

"I'll see you in the morning, Maddie."

With that, he was gone. Madeline was left standing there pulsing, pounding, *throbbing* without her teacher. She was frustrated and hoped lessons would move along more quickly so she didn't have to go to bed so . . . unfulfilled.

Teague walked out to the carriage house with a dick hard enough to hammer nails. He wanted to kick his own ass for giving in to his urges and kissing Maddie.

Kissing her? Ha! He wanted to throw her on the table and fuck her. To make matters worse, he had agreed to her proposal. He could have stayed his month here, found out what he could, and then left for places unknown. But, no. He gave in and said yes!

He pounded one fist onto his thigh until it grew painful. He was not only betraying Claire, he was betraying his vow to never be with another woman. He'd broken that vow three times in seven years, and all with whores.

This was different. This scared the bejesus out of him. She scared the bejesus out of him.

Three days. He lasted three goddamn days before he touched her. He reached the carriage house and pounded up the stairs to the small room at the top of the stairs. He yanked off his shirt and shucked his pants in rapid-fire succession.

When he was naked, he lay down in the bed and tried to ignore the throbbing hard-on that lay heavily on his belly. It didn't work.

Instead his hand, seemingly of its own accord, crept down his chest to wrap around his hardness. He closed his eyes and sighed in relief as his hand began squeezing, moving up and down rhythmically.

Faster and harder he pumped. His balls tightened as he felt his release coming. Pleasure coursed through him in waves until he groaned with the ultimate pleasure.

Teague was distressed to realize it was Maddie's face he had seen when he came and not Claire's.

Chapter Four

Madeline woke with an ache inside her. An ache that seemed to have taken over her body. Insistent, impatient, and unceasing. She hoped Teague would move along quickly with her lessons because she didn't think she would last two hours, much less two days.

She was just brushing her hair when Eppie flew into the room with her usual fluttering.

"Oh, Madeline, I tried to tell them it was too early, but they wouldn't listen."

Madeline's stomach did a funny flip-flop.

"Who?"

"That witch Matilda Webster and her coven."

Her stomach flipped again. Matilda was the sheriff's wife as well as a beautiful, petite blonde. She was also a pain in the rear end who took pleasure in pointing out all Madeline's flaws. Preferably in front of lots of onlookers, for the fullest effect.

"Don't you go looking all pitiful now. You let them wait while you finish with your hair. Let them stew in their own juices for a while. They came to your house unannounced."

Madeline nodded. Eppie was right. It was just so . . . intimidating to have them in her house. She always felt out of place and awkward.

After Eppie left, Madeline sat at her small vanity and took

great pains donning one of her nicest dresses, one of deep blue, and then put her hair up into a chignon at the base of her neck. She pinched her cheeks to put color into her pale skin and then scowled at her reflection.

Why couldn't she be even slightly pretty? Being plain was hard. Being plain and big was doubly so.

She stood and smoothed her skirt and then headed downstairs. By the time she reached the bottom, she could hear them chattering in the parlor. Thank God Eppie hadn't put them in the sitting room. They didn't ever belong in there.

Her palms were wet with sweat, which she quickly wiped on her hanky and tucked it back up her sleeve. She entered the room with as much grace as she could muster.

Matilda sat with her two best friends, Virginia Ralston and Beatrice Adams. Their husbands were prominent businessmen in Plum Creek and, as such, they considered it their duty to stick their noses into everybody else's business.

Matilda sat on the settee, flanked by Virginia on the left and Beatrice on the right. All three were petite, ranging in hair color from blond to blonder, with stunning blue or green eyes and flawless skin. They were like the triplets from hell. If Madeline hadn't known their parents, she'd swear they were spawned from the same evil source.

They all smiled prettily with their white, razor-sharp teeth, like blond, overgrown rats.

"Good morning, Madeline. I see with a man around the house you can keep late hours," Matilda said.

"I've been up for hours. I was in the middle of balancing the household accounts and didn't want to lose my place," Madeline lied as she sat on the wingchair across from them.

"Oh, household accounts? Jerome takes care of all of that kind of thing," tittered Beatrice. "I wouldn't know the first thing about it."

"That's too bad, Beatrice. What if something were to happen to Jerome?"

She gasped, and her hand flew to her chest as if wounded. "Why would you say such a thing?"

Madeline shrugged. "I like to be able to take care of myself."

"Then it's lucky you never married, so you can follow through with that," said Virginia with a smirk.

"What can I do for you ladies?" Madeline asked, holding her temper in and her pride up with forcible effort.

"Why, Jackson told me about the criminal you are allowing to stay in your house. I thought it was my civic duty to come over and make sure you were all right."

"He's not a criminal. He is a man accused of a crime. Innocent until proven guilty."

"I heard he had the horse and taunted the sheriff right there in town," said Beatrice.

"I heard they tried to hang him, and Madeline jumped on the horse to stop them," said Virginia.

"Ladies, I did no such thing, and neither did he. Yes, the horse was in his possession, but until the judge or sheriff speaks to Old Clem, no crime has been committed." Madeline felt like she was talking to twelve-year-old girls.

"Hmph," said Matilda. "I heard—"

The door swung open, and Teague looked in. And my, oh, my, was he looking captivating in his too-tight shirt and trousers. He was a hell of a man, and he was *hers*.

She glanced at the three women, who wore identical shocked expressions. Shock mixed with interest, and was that envy?

"Good morning, Miss Brewster." Teague's deep voice reverberated through the room.

"Good morning, Mr. O'Neal."

"I see you've got company. I'll speak to you after you're finished."

With that, he shut the door, but not without a surreptitious wink at Madeline. Eppie! She must have run out and told him to interrupt the pecking party.

"W—was that him? The criminal?"

Madeline stood. "That was Mr. O'Neal, and he's not a criminal. Now if you ladies have nothing further to discuss, I have a lot to do this morning."

They couldn't ignore a dismissal even if they wanted to. With a few grumbles and squawks, they were out the door, and Madeline gratefully closed it behind them.

Eppie poked her head out from the kitchen and grinned broadly.

"Are they gone?"

"Yes, you evil girl, they're gone. What possessed you to send Teague in there?"

Eppie stepped out into the hallway and put her fists on her slender hips.

"When a man looks that good, he scrambles stupid women's brains like eggs." She shrugged. "He didn't mind."

Madeline shook her head.

"It definitely scrambled their brains. I never saw Matilda so flustered."

Before she could stop it, a giggle burst out of Madeline's mouth. Eppie laughed right along with her.

"What did they want?"

Madeline sighed. "To be nosy and sanctimonious."

"Sancti-what?"

"She means they think they're better than Maddie and me and you, but they're wrong." Teague's voice joined the conversation from behind Eppie. Madeline nearly jumped out of her shoes. How could a man that big be so silent?

"Yes, that's exactly it."

"That's the gospel truth. There were never three more wrong women in the world."

Madeline's heart began to pound a little harder as she stared at Teague across the hallway. He stared right back.

"I'll just go back to the kitchen," she heard Eppie say.

"Good morning, Maddie."

His voice unnerved her. The echoes of lesson number one

danced up and down her spine. She felt her body respond like an instrument longing for its master musician.

"Hello, Teague."

"Did you sleep well?" he asked with a small tilt to his mouth.

"No, I'm afraid I didn't. I was . . . restless."

She wanted to pinch herself for telling him, but she wanted to be completely honest with Teague always.

"I was restless, too."

She found herself walking toward him as if in a trance. Her nipples strained at her dress, rubbing delightfully against her chemise. When she stood a foot from him, she breathed in deeply. He smelled of soap, sunshine, and man.

"Lesson number one?"

Madeline felt bold this morning. Ready to snatch what was in front of her. In this case, literally. "Will there be a repeat of it? I believe I need a refresher course."

Teague made a sound, low and deep in his throat that reminded her of a cougar. Feline, primitive, and raw. An answering feminine creature within her howled.

He grabbed her and was in the dark of the linen closet before she could blink.

"Teague?"

"Shhhhh . . ." His hands cupped her cheeks, and his thumbs ran across her lips. The familiar quality of it heightened the experience.

His hands moved to her shoulders and down her arms until his hands grasped hers. He laced his fingers with hers and pulled her flush against his body.

She let out a shaky breath and opened her mouth to ask a question when his hot mouth descended on her. There were no gentle kisses this time. It was raw masculinity at its very finest. His tongue plundered her mouth even as he backed her up against the shelves. She could smell the starch Eppie had put on the sheets, and she could smell Teague.

His mouth was as insistent as it was strong. She kissed

back as best she could. Her heart hammered in her chest; pressed against him, she could feel his heart, and they were nearly in tune with each other. He groaned and pressed his hardness into her softness.

His erection felt like a log, it was so firm. She found herself grinding against him in small circles. Much to her delight, pleasure began to radiate out from the contact until her mons became wet with need. Her nipples were aching points of desire that rubbed against his rock-hard chest.

It was a riot of senses that nearly overwhelmed her. She wondered what she'd do when they were naked. The very thought made her groan loudly.

"Shhhhh . . ." he said again.

He lapped at the inside of her mouth like a cat with a bowl of cream. Like she was delicious and he couldn't get enough of the treat.

Her breath caught in her chest like a fluttering bird trying to get out. She felt like she was drowning, gasping with pleasure as intense as anything she'd ever felt.

He finally let her mouth go and pressed his forehead against hers. His breath rasped out and flew into her mouth. She breathed him in even as her own breath filled his mouth. She felt dizzy and so out of control of her own body.

She loved every second of it.

"Jesus Christ, Maddie."

"I think . . . I'm going to enjoy these lessons. Lesson number one was . . . stimulating."

He chuckled huskily. "Lesson number one? I think I'm going to be dead before lesson number three."

"Madeline?"

She could hear Eppie's voice through the closed door.

"Where did you get off to?"

Madeline had to hold in a giggle. Twice in one day! She felt ten years younger.

He held her against him for another minute until Eppie's

voice faded away. Then he kissed her softly, gently sucking on her lower lip, before he pulled away.

Without a word, he let her go and opened the closet door. The brightness of the morning brought tears to her eyes. When she was finally able to focus, she realized Teague was gone.

She was alone, standing in a closet, looking thoroughly kissed, she was sure. Madeline smiled and walked out of the closet to find some breakfast.

Madeline sipped her tea and munched on a piece of toast. She could not stop thinking about that kiss. Lesson number one.

Sweet Mary. She couldn't believe her luck. Choosing Teague had been the smartest thing she had done in a long time. He was a very skilled teacher. Very skilled.

Eppie came in from gathering the eggs with her basket and raised one brow at her.

"Are you gonna tell me what you were doing in that closet with him?"

Madeline felt her cheeks flush. "Eppie!"

"What?" She laughed as she set the basket on the counter and unfolded the towel. "I knew you were in there. I'd be a fool if I didn't."

Madeline tried not to laugh at Eppie's antics. But she was feeling so happy she couldn't keep it in.

A knock at the front door interrupted her.

"I swear, it's like a social party here today. I wonder who that is?"

"Don't swear, Eppie."

Eppie stuck her tongue out at Madeline and headed for the front door. Madeline sipped her tea again and listened to the murmur of voices. The door closed again, and she could still hear Eppie talking. She was bringing someone to the kitchen.

Madeline stood up and saw a young Negro man with

Eppie. She was grinning from ear to ear, and he was holding his hat in his hands, shuffling from foot to foot.

"Miss Madeline, this here is Isaiah. He heard you let folks stay on that needed a place to sleep for a spell."

Madeline could clearly see that Eppie was delighted Isaiah had shown up on her doorstep.

"Of course. We have plenty of room, Isaiah. It's very nice to meet you."

Madeline walked toward him and held out her hand. With a look of disbelief, he tentatively reached out and shook her hand ever so briefly.

"Welcome to my home. Are you new to Plum Creek?"

"Yes, ma'am. I heard tell there was good work in the mines in the mountains, so I'm on my way."

"That's hard work, Isaiah. I'm sure there's plenty of work for a good man in Plum Creek if you're inclined to stay."

He nodded. "It's a right nice town."

Madeline smiled. "I think they're hiring down at the sawmill if you want to check there first. I'm sure Eppie would be happy to show you the way."

Eppie nodded. "Of course I will."

"You're welcome to stay here as long as you need to."

Isaiah looked at her, his dark eyes full of disbelief mixed with wonder. "I appreciate it, Miss Madeline."

"Can I take him now?" asked Eppie.

Madeline was delighted to see the sparkle in her eyes.

"Of course. Dinner isn't for hours, and there isn't much else that needs tending right now."

Eppie smiled at Isaiah, who smiled back at her. The two of them left, side by side, quietly chatting.

Seems like life was changing for everyone this week.

Madeline cleared her dishes to the sink and then rinsed out her teacup. That's when she realized she was alone. No, not just alone, alone with Teague. Her heart galloped in her chest as she imagined what lesson two would be like.

Her hands were shaking when she set the teacup on the

counter by the sink. Taking a deep breath, she tried to calm herself, but it was no use. She had to find him. Right then. It was nearly . . . urgent. This feeling she had. Urgency. Yes, that was it.

Madeline dried her hands quickly on the towel hanging beside the sink and then walked out the back door into the yard. She couldn't stop the twinge of disappointment to find it empty. She headed for the barn to take a look in there.

She peeked her head in the barn and the carriage house, but they were both empty. She sighed and then called herself a ninny for expecting another lesson in the same day.

Teague must have gone into town for supplies at the store. She had the overwhelming urge to find out more about him. He was a man with haunted eyes. She was curious about his ghosts.

Looking around like a guilty child, she slipped into the carriage house and tiptoed up the stairs. When she got up to the loft, she wasn't surprised to find it neat. The bed was made, and no clothes lay on the floor. Not that he had but one extra set to wear.

The clothes, which Eppie had scrubbed until she complained her shoulders hurt, were hanging on a hook on the wall. The only other possession in the room was a small bag on the floor under the cot. The mattress was stuffed with straw and was probably not the coziest thing to sleep on, and he was such a big man, his feet must have hung off the end.

A small mirror was hanging on a nail by the window. Next to it on the sill lay a razor, strop, and a bar of soap perched in a cup. The smell of sandalwood was faint but unmistakable. It was a manly scent that reminded her of Teague immediately. She tried not to stare at the small bag under the bed, but her eyes kept returning to it.

Don't look inside it.

But I want to.

An inner battle raged between her devil and her angel. In the end, she found herself sitting on the edge of the bed, peering under at the small brown sack. It was no bigger than a loaf of bread, and there didn't seem to be a lot in it. He must have had it in his pants pocket when she found him with a noose around his neck.

Madeline watched as her hand reached out and picked up the bag, placing it on her lap. She stared at it for a minute or two before she reached in and felt for the contents. She touched something cold and metallic and pulled out a small picture frame.

In it was a much younger Teague standing beside a petite woman holding a baby. They stood in front of a small house on a flat prairie. Teague was smiling with his arm around this woman. His wife, more than likely. It seemed like it was a happy day. A long time ago, for sure. He not only looked young, but his eyes were young.

She stared into his eyes. There were no ghosts or shadows lurking in their depths. So whatever existed there now probably had to do with what had happened to this woman and child.

She set the picture frame on the cot beside her and reached into the bag again. This time, she found what felt like a stack of paper. She pulled out letters, tied in some tired-looking twine. There had to be forty letters, carefully held together so neatly. All addressed to Teague O'Neal in a woman's flowery script. Madeline assumed it was the woman in the picture. They were postmarked from Missouri during the war and addressed to a Union Army camp. So he had fought for the Union, and he was from Missouri.

She didn't want to read the letters. They were too private to open. The letters joined the picture frame on the cot. Madeline reached in again and pulled out a small Bible. It was well worn and looked to have a bloodstain on the cover. She opened the cover and found an inscription that read: *To my darling husband, Teague. Keep the faith and keep yourself safe. Love, Claire.*

Claire. So that was the woman's name. Very feminine and

pretty. Madeline tried to squelch a spurt of jealousy. She had no call to be jealous of Teague's wife. He was her employee, not her boyfriend.

She set the Bible down with the other items and reached into the bag one last time. There was only one thing left in there that made her hands shake when she took it out. It was a lock of light brown hair and a lock of light blond hair. They were woven together to form a ring that would fit on Teague's wrist.

Hair from his wife and child. A piece of them to carry with him, likely into war. She stared at the hair in her hand and knew, just knew deep down, that they were dead. They had died while he was off at war. Somehow, someway.

Madeline felt her eyes prick with tears. He carried only four things with him, and they were all a part of his wife and child. He obviously loved her and still did. A small stab of disappointment lanced her heart. There wasn't any room in his life for another woman. Claire still owned his heart, even from the grave.

She reverently put the hair back in the bag and then re-placed everything else as well. As she put the bag back under the bed, she heard footsteps downstairs.

Teague couldn't find anyone in the house or outside, so he went in the backyard to look. The door to the carriage house was open, so he figured Madeline or Eppie was in there.

As he stepped in, he heard someone upstairs. *In his bed-room loft.* A surge of annoyance went through him. What the hell would either one of them be doing up there?

He took the steps two at a time and found Madeline stand-ing in the middle of the room, looking flushed and guilty.

"What are you doing up here?" he asked.

"Looking for you," she answered.

"You're lying, Maddie."

She looked as if he'd slapped her. "I beg your pardon?"

"You're looking like a kid with her hand in the cookie jar

right before suppertime, so don't tell me you were looking for me. I was obviously not here."

He felt angry and a bit of something else he couldn't identify to find her there. He glanced under the bed and realized his bag had been moved.

White-hot anger took over annoyance.

"Were you looking through my things?" he shouted. "You have no right!"

"I'm sorry!" she said as she wrung her hands together. "I am a horrible person. I . . . I can't help myself. I get these impulses and . . . I'm so sorry, Teague!"

"Get out."

She nodded and went to leave the room. She stopped to touch his arm, and he flinched.

"You're an admirable man, Teague. A better person than I am. You have my deepest apologies."

She left with a whiff of lavender. Teague's hands clenched into fists, and his breathing became irregular. He hadn't expected his emotions to come roaring back into his life. But they had with the force of a twister. Slamming him around like a wind he had no control over.

Damn Madeline for snooping. And damn his soft heart for caring about what she thought of him.

Chapter Five

It was late—after midnight. Madeline couldn't sleep a wink. Her body was anxious, hungry. She felt like ants had landed on her body and were making her jump to their tune.

She had thrown the covers off hours ago. She lay in her bed staring out the window. It was a clear night, and the moon and stars were both staring down at her. The crescent moon was as bright as a new coin.

A cool breeze ruffled the gauzy white curtains. They moved gently toward her, reaching. The cool air felt wonderful against her heated skin. Her nipples puckered under her nightgown to painful points.

Her hands crept up and brushed across her breasts. A tingle of pleasure radiated from the contact. She closed her eyes and pictured Teague's handsome face. Remembered his hot, wet kisses. Soon her hands were rubbing back and forth across her nipples, faster and harder.

Madeline pinched one, and a jolt went straight like an arrow to the moist heat between her legs. She imagined that being with Teague would be like this, only more intense. She moaned in anticipation of it.

The small sound echoed through the bedroom and came back on her like a gentle rain. Her own pleasure was as arousing as thinking of Teague.

She pulled up her nightdress and exposed her heat to the

cool breeze. Her legs slowly slid apart, and one hand landed between them. Her fingers stroked the swollen folds over and over as her hand continued to tease her nipples.

Back and forth, pleasure seeped through her body from head to toe. She wound up tighter and tighter. Her hands moved faster and faster.

Soon she was crying out in release as she reached her peak. The throbbing between her legs continued as her hands dropped away to land at her sides.

Her rapid heartbeat slowed as her heated blood cooled. Soon she shivered, and goose bumps broke out over her skin. She pushed her nightgown back down and pulled up the sheet.

Sleep crept over her finally. Her body relaxed into the feather mattress, and she drifted off into dreams of Teague and his entrance into her bed.

Madeline went outside in the morning with a fresh mug of coffee for Teague. She was going to apologize again for her behavior the day before and hoped he would still agree with her proposal. She knew she would never be able to approach another man about it, so it was Teague, or it was never.

The bright sunshine pricked her eyes. She wiped at them with the back of her free hand as she walked across the grass toward the carriage house. As she reached the door, it opened suddenly; startled, she raised both hands to ward off a broken nose or black eye. Instead, she tipped the hot coffee all over her chest.

She screamed in pain as the scalding brew burned her skin beneath her cotton dress. She dropped the mug on the ground and tried to pull the hot material away from her skin.

"Oh, shit, Maddie, I'm sorry!" Teague said as he stood there like a bump on a log.

"That . . . was what . . . I was coming to . . . say," she huffed out as the pain grew to a crescendo.

"Let's get you in the house so Eppie can get something on that burn."

Madeline just nodded and bit her lip. Who knew Eppie made the dang coffee so boiling hot? Her breasts and the top of her chest were throbbing in tune with her pulse. Over and over. It was worse than she thought. She was almost sure blisters were forming on her skin.

The two of them burst into the kitchen and scared Eppie, who was washing the table.

"Lord Jesus! What are you doing?"

Teague scowled at her. "She's been burned, Eppie."

"Burned?" Eppie's eyes widened. "Burned by what?"

"Coffee."

"What are you doing with coffee, Madeline?"

"Never mind," Madeline hissed. "Just get some cold water and baking soda."

Eppie jumped to the sink to start pumping water.

Teague led her to the table and sat her down gently. He reached for the buttons on her dress, and she stopped him.

"What are you doing?"

"We need to get that dress off you."

Madeline almost smiled. "Something I hoped to hear from a man someday but not in my kitchen."

Teague scowled deeper. "This isn't funny, Maddie." His dark eyes were full of concern.

Madeline's heart skipped a beat. He was worried about her. That must mean he cared, at least a bit. How absolutely marvelous.

He started unbuttoning her dress with his big hands, and she wished she could have enjoyed it. When he saw her lacy white chemise, his mouth tightened perceptibly. His eyes flicked up to hers. She felt a pulse of heat shoot down to her mons. How could she possibly be thinking about bedding him? She was in agony, yet her body responded automatically to being near his.

"Eppie, go get something dry for her to wear."

Eppie set down a pitcher of cool water and a rag and then dashed out of the kitchen.

"You'll pardon me," Teague said right before he ripped her chemise right down the middle. Then he stared at the exposed skin.

It was another moment she desperately wished she could enjoy.

Madeline couldn't force herself to look down at her skin. Afraid of the damage.

"How bad is it?" she asked.

"Not too bad," he said as he dipped the rag in the cool water and then wrung it out. When the cloth touched her skin, she hissed a breath in.

"Sorry, Maddie. I'm trying not to hurt you."

"It's . . . okay," she managed to say around the pain.

"What were you doing out there anyway?" he asked.

After a moment, the coolness felt good, and she did her best to ignore the abrasiveness of the cloth on the tender skin.

"I was coming to apologize again."

"To me?"

She rolled her eyes. "You know anyone else living in my carriage house?"

"No need to apologize. You already did."

She shook her head. "Not properly. I ran like a coward from my own mistake. I really am truly sorry. I . . . It was very wrong of me to snoop through your belongings. I hope you can forgive me."

He glanced up at her, and his blue eyes were measuring. "You had no right to look through my things, but because it's your house, I suppose you do. I don't forgive easily anymore. I know you didn't mean any harm. I just ask that you not do it again."

He dipped the cloth again, wrung it out, and continued his ministrations.

She sorted through his words before replying. "Thank you, Teague. I promise I won't do it again. Being nosy is one of my vices—one of many, actually."

The corner of his mouth kicked up in a small grin. "Oh, I doubt you have that many vices, but I can teach you one or two."

The idea of what vices he was willing to teach her was enough to set her imagination and her pulse fluttering again.

Eppie bustled back in the kitchen with her robe. "Mr. Teague! What are you doing? Madeline's half naked, and you're looking at her . . . at her skin!"

"It's okay, Eppie. He's only helping."

Eppie grumbled as she wrapped the robe around Madeline's shoulder. "Helping himself to an early dessert is what he's doing."

Madeline felt a smile playing around her lips and met Teague's gaze. His eyes were dancing in amusement.

"I'll leave her in your capable hands, then, Miss Eppie."

"Better mine than yours, mister. You go on now and do what you're getting paid to do."

Madeline had to bite her lip from laughing. What Teague was getting paid to do did involve her skin and his hands. With a salute at Eppie and a wink for Madeline, he went out the back door.

Eppie shook her head as she glanced at Madeline's skin. It was tight, throbbing, and painful.

"Only a couple welts. Mostly just angry looking. Let's get some baking soda on that and lay you down in bed for a spell."

Eppie led her upstairs to her bedroom and then ran back to the kitchen for her supplies. She made a poultice out of baking soda and some other ingredients Madeline didn't want to know about and then left her in her bed.

Alone again.

Madeline could hear Teague hammering somewhere outside and wished he was lying beside her. She felt her nearly sleepless night kick her gently, and the rhythmic sound of the hammering lulled her into slumber.

Teague wiped his arm across his forehead. The sun was warm, giving a hint of summer heat. He stared at the boards he'd repaired in the front fence, but he was seeing Madeline. Madeline with her dress open and her dark eyes full of want and longing.

He wanted to quench that thirst, fulfill her needs. When had it happened? When had he started forgetting about Claire? What was it about Madeline that pushed Claire out of his thoughts?

He threw the hammer down in self-disgust. He'd vowed never to let another woman touch his heart or his soul. Madeline, in less than a week, had made him forget that vow.

"You okay, mister?"

Teague looked up to find a young Negro man standing at the fence.

"Can I help you, son?"

"No, sir. I'm staying at the house. Miss Madeline gave me a room till I can find a place of my own."

Teague shook his head. "Miss Madeline has a big heart."

"Yes, that she does. Miss Eppie does, too." His brown eyes lit from within.

So that was the way of it. He was sweet on Eppie.

"You work here?"

"I'm working for Miss Madeline for a month, fixing up things and whatever else she needs done."

The man nodded. "I wish I could find a job like that. I asked at the mill, but they ain't hiring my kind."

Teague felt a spurt of anger over how people treated Negroes. He'd never owned a slave, never thought they were beneath him in any way, and treated all folks the same. He was sick and tired of other people's attitudes.

Too bad he wasn't supposed to care. Damnit all to hell. Now his emotions were popping up right and left.

"Maybe Miss Madeline has something she can hire you on to do."

His eyes looked hopeful. "You think she needs to hire someone else?"

Teague shrugged. "I'll be here only a month. She probably needs help with that garden out back behind the barn and likely with the milk cow in the barn. There's a few hens out back scratching the ground, too. Lots to do."

The other man nodded. "I'll go speak to Miss Madeline directly. Much obliged. . . ."

Teague held out his hand to shake. "Teague. Teague O'Neal."

"Isaiah Harper."

After the other man left, Teague blew out a breath and headed for the well. Maybe a dunk of cold water was what he needed. He was just pulling a bucket up when Eppie came out the back door. She eyeballed him suspiciously before she marched over with a bucket.

"Going to milk the cow?" He inclined his head in greeting.

Eppie nodded. "You sent Isaiah to talk to Miss Madeline about a job?"

"I won't be here long. She'll need someone full time to help around here. There's much more work to be done than I can do in a month's time."

Eppie nodded. "Not doing it out of charity, then?"

"No, ma'am. He looks like a strong worker." He shrugged. "And someone that won't cheat or take advantage of her. I expect people try to do that all the time."

"Yes, Mr. O'Neal, they do. But not when I'm around. I take care of her."

"I can see that."

"Just so we understand each other."

Teague thought he'd just passed some kind of test. What test, however, he hadn't the foggiest clue.

"How is she?"

"She's resting now with a poultice I put on her. It won't

scar, but she'll be paining some the next few days. She won't be able to go to the bank neither. Not that she's been there in the past week for her usual hours anyway. She's taken way too much time off."

Eppie started to walk away.

"Bank? What do you mean bank?"

She cocked her head at him. "Didn't you know? Miss Madeline owns half this town, including the bank. She's a right important person, if only I could make her see that."

Eppie was like a little philosopher. She looked young and innocent, but behind those chocolate-brown eyes beat the heart of an old soul. She saw Madeline struggle with her guilt over what her father had done and knew she could do something about it but didn't. Madeline had to stand on her own two feet by herself.

Teague's estimation of this young girl was way off. She was not only Maddie's friend, she was the wall behind her. Ready to help her when she got up off her knees.

"We'll be having ham sandwiches for dinner. In about an hour or so. Come on in the house after you wash up, and I'll have it ready."

"Thank you, Miss Eppie."

She giggled as she walked toward the barn. "Calls me ma'am and Miss Eppie. Crazy man."

Teague contemplated her retreating back. Eppie was a formidable foe in this town. He was glad he knew that before he stepped on her tail to get to Maddie.

"What did that girl want with you?"

Teague turned to find the sheriff behind him, staring at Eppie as she went into the barn.

"Nothing. She was just talking to me. People do that sometimes."

"Don't get smart with me, O'Neal. You are mine for the next month, or the noose goes back around your neck."

Teague's hands tightened on the handle of the bucket until

he felt a warm trickle of blood on his fingers. "What do you want?" he snapped.

"Are you doing what we told you to do?"

"I am doing my part."

"Good," said the sheriff as he slammed his hand down on Teague's shoulder. "Without you we won't be able to follow through with this. If you fiddle with us, and the plan fails, you won't need to worry about the noose. You'll be buried out behind the saloon in a shallow hole before anybody misses you. Understand me, boy?"

Teague felt sick to his stomach. How the hell had he sunk so low as to get involved with an ass like this?

"I said, you understand me, boy?"

"And I said I'm doing my part."

The sheriff stared at him for another minute. Teague itched to wipe the dust from his shoes with this pompous son of a bitch.

"Well, get busy doing what you need to do."

Chapter Six

The morning after the coffee incident, Madeline was itchy and grumpy. She wanted to wash off the hideous poultice Eppie had put on, but she daren't go against the girl's instructions. She'd done that before and never wanted to do it again. Eppie could be formidable.

She sat at the kitchen table with a cup of tea and shot glares at her friend when she wasn't looking.

"You are a bad patient."

"You are a mean nurse."

Eppie burst out laughing. "If your Teague could only see you now. Acting like a little girl."

"He's not *my* Teague. And I'm not acting like a little girl." Madeline heard the whine in her voice and hated it.

Eppie harrumphed at her and turned back to the bread dough she was kneading.

"When can I take this concoction off?"

"Tonight, if you're a good girl. I'll run you a warm bath, and your skin should be almost good as new."

Madeline grumbled under her breath a bit more and then stared into her tea. If she was being honest with herself, she was grumpy because the injury prevented lesson number two. A lesson Madeline looked forward to. With great anticipation. She couldn't wait for her bath.

She spent the day in her robe, trying to read and catch up on the household accounts. It was no use; she couldn't concentrate, and it wasn't the injury.

She could focus on only one thing. Teague. His hands, his mouth, his body. Her natural curiosity was like a bunch of screaming bells going off. Madeline was miserable and achy. She supposed it was unfulfilled desire. She'd never felt it before, so she could only surmise that's what it was.

She was in the sitting room, staring out at a yellow butterfly as it flittered past the window, when Teague's voice interrupted her. It was as if she'd conjured him from her imagination. Immediately her body tightened and groaned with hunger.

"Good afternoon, Maddie."

She was horrified to remember that she wore only a robe and, with her hair down, probably looked like last week's washrag.

"Hello, Teague."

He leaned against the doorjamb, looking like a Greek god come to life in a new blue shirt and brown trousers that had been delivered that morning. "You feeling better today?"

"Yes, I am. Eppie says I can wash her poultice off later. It smells a lot worse than it feels."

He grinned. "I'll take your word for it."

"Believe me, I can't wait to take a bath and get clean."

His eyes darkened. "A bath? Sounds . . . inviting."

Her pulse sped up, and the ache intensified within her. She was nearly glad for the robe so he couldn't see how hard her nipples actually were.

"Yes, inviting." Her voice was husky, aroused.

"Do you think you'll be ready for another lesson after your bath?"

Oh, yes, yes, yes!

"Perhaps," she said, amazed she was actually flirting with him. "Will you be ready to teach?"

Teague sauntered toward her with his predatory gait, like a great big cat stalking its prey. A shiver danced up her spine.

He was so big, so . . . masculine. Thank God Madeline had found him. Thank God he was hers for a month.

He leaned down and brushed his lips lightly across hers like the wings of the butterfly she'd been watching. She closed her eyes and savored the brief contact, inhaled his scent, his essence.

"I'll be ready."

With one last searing glance, he walked back out of the room. Madeline couldn't help but stare at his behind. It was firm, round, and her hands itched to feel its contours, touch his skin.

Madeline couldn't wait for her bath.

Eppie put rose petals in the bathwater. It was as if she knew something was going to happen that night. Something Madeline needed to smell pretty for.

Eppie chattered on and on about Isaiah and how wonderful he was. Madeline was excited to see her friend truly smitten with a man. She deserved to be happy. She finally left Madeline alone with soap and a washrag, which she put to good use immediately.

After the poultice washed off, she finally got a good look at her skin. It was bright pink but had no blisters or scarring. It felt a bit tight and a little sore, but she was sure the damage would have been much worse had Eppie not worked her magic with her concoction.

Madeline forced herself to take a long, leisurely bath. Eppie had to help her rinse her hair. It was so thick and long it was nearly impossible to get all the soap out alone.

After her hair was squeaky clean, she laid back in the bath and daydreamed of Teague. Her body grew heated even as the water cooled. She felt like she was teasing herself by waiting. The anticipation was building like steam in a pressure cooker.

When she stepped out of the bath, she dried herself slowly, rubbing the towel over and over her skin. By the time she was dry, she was wet between her legs, and her nipples seemed permanently erect.

She slipped on a white cotton nightgown with short sleeves and a lacy collar Eppie had made. Sitting on the stool next to the tub, she used the towel to dry her hair as much as she could. Then she took the brush and ran it through her hair.

"Can I do that?"

Teague should have surprised her, but he didn't. It was as though she was expecting him to come into the bathing room. Wanting him there.

"Yes," she answered a bit breathily.

He stepped up behind her, and she felt his body heat meld with hers. She held up the silver-backed brush that had been a gift from her mother when she turned eight. His thumb touched her hand as he took the brush; the calluses sent a bolt of heat up her arm straight to her breasts. Her nipples almost shivered with longing.

God how she wanted Teague to *touch* her.

His big hand gently touched her head. She closed her eyes as the brush slowly slid from the top of her head to her behind.

"You have beautiful hair. Like a dark waterfall."

Teague stroked her hair again and again. Each stroke built on the last. Like a symphony of music playing in her body. The notes echoed through her.

Madeline heard the brush settle on the floor. His hands ran through her hair.

"So soft."

He lifted her hair to expose the back of her neck. She felt a wisp of a breeze right before his lips landed on her nape. They were soft and hard, hot and demanding. His tongue licked her lightly. She arched toward him. Eager, wanting, aching.

"Are you ready for lesson two?" His voice skittered across her skin.

"Oh, yes," she replied on an exhale.

Madeline felt a cloth go over her eyes, and she stiffened.

"You said you were ready."

She relaxed, ready to learn whatever Teague wanted to teach.

The cloth settled lightly around her head, and she was in darkness. She could only feel. And touch. And taste.

He slipped her nightgown off her shoulders, leaving the entire top part of her body exposed to him. She felt embarrassed by her nudity, and her arms immediately came up to cover herself. His hands stopped her.

"Don't hide yourself from me. I want to see you. *You*. All of you. You're beautiful, Madeline."

Beautiful.

He must have needed spectacles because she was nowhere near beautiful, but she surely *felt* beautiful at that moment.

His fingertip grazed her forehead, down her nose, across her cheekbone and her lips. The finger slowly moved back and forth across her lips. She gave in to the urge and kissed his finger. He pressed against her until she opened her lips, and he slowly slid the finger into her mouth. His finger was clean and slightly salty. He pulled it out and then stuck it back in again.

She felt the primal rhythm and sucked at the digit. He hissed in a breath and pulled his finger out completely. He wiped it back and forth across her lips, wetting them with her own saliva. Then he blew on her lips. The combination of the cool and hot made her entire body pulse.

Then he kissed her. The kiss was long and hard; his tongue moved like a snake, charming her into following it. He wasn't touching her other than with his mouth, but she felt like her whole body was against him.

Teague's kiss nearly stole her soul. His lips finally left hers and traveled across her cheek to her ear. She sucked in a shaky breath. He gently nipped her earlobe, his breath gently tickling. His tongue outlined her ear before he blew in it, again giving her the hot and cold sensations that caressed her body.

He kissed his way down her neck, sucking and nibbling on her skin as he traveled. She moaned when his tongue dipped into her collarbone.

"You smell like roses."

"Mmmm . . ." She could barely speak.

Madeline felt him kneel in front of her and pull her knees apart. She resisted his hands until his hand cupped her cheek.

"Trust me, Maddie. I won't hurt you."

She allowed him to spread her legs, and she felt his body slide between them. She immediately clenched in anticipation of more.

The fabric of his pants rubbed against her tender skin, eliciting sparks that sizzled up and down her. His hands traced her breasts in large circles. Her breathing became irregular as the circles grew smaller and smaller. He was getting closer to her nipples. The aching, hungry points that begged him to touch them.

Just before his fingers reached the sensitized points, the circles reversed and grew larger. She moaned in frustration.

"Patience, Maddie, patience."

"Please touch me, Teague. I can't . . . I need . . ."

He kissed her softly. She tried to lean toward him, but he set her back on the stool.

Teague took the ends of her hair and ran them back and forth across her nipples, teasing, tantalizing her once more. She was ready to tear off the blindfold and demand he touch her.

"Do you know what I see?"

"A desperate woman?"

He chuckled as he dropped the hair and ran his fingers up her arms to her collarbone and then to her neck.

"An incredibly sexy woman full of passion. God, Maddie, you have so much passion, more than any other woman I've known. Your skin is like a pink rose, with that pretty flush. Your nipples are like raspberries, succulent, ripe ones begging for my tongue. Your lips are parted, waiting for me to return."

As Teague spoke, Madeline grew more and more aroused. Her body was ready to simply explode. He was a sensual poet who wove a spell of ecstasy with only words.

When his mouth closed over one nipple and tugged, she cried out as sensations raced through her. His hand closed on the other nipple, and she thought she was going to die right then and there.

His other hand slid up her thigh to her moist center. She was too far beyond reasonable thought to even want to stop him. His fingers brushed her swollen lips, and she opened her mouth to beg him again.

A finger slid inside her as his thumb circled her nubbin of pleasure. She felt the thin membrane of her virginity tear as he explored untouched territory. There was a pinch of pain, and then it passed under his pleasurable assault. Around and around it went as his finger, then two, pushed in and out of her. His mouth suckled greedily while his hand tweaked and pulled at the other nipple.

Within minutes, she reached her peak with the force of a thousand bolts of light. Her body jerked against him as he plunged his fingers deeply inside her. The waves rolled through her, over and over. Her eyes almost rolled back in her head as the most powerful sensations she'd ever felt racked her body.

He gentled his suckling and rubbing as her body slowly floated back down to earth. Tears pricked her eyes as the enormity of what had happened hit her.

Teague had pleasured her beyond her wildest imaginings—and there were many imaginings in Madeline's cold, lonely bed. He kissed her gently and then stood.

"That was lesson number two."

With that, she heard him walk toward the door, open it, and then close it behind him.

That's when she realized she had never even seen him the entire time he had been in the bathing room with her. She had only felt and touched. Her heart would never be the same. Neither would her body.

Teague walked out of the bathing room in a daze. His body was as hard as an iron bar, but it was his head and his heart that were completely off-kilter.

What had he done?

Ever since Eppie had told him Madeline was taking a bath, he had been anxious. More than anxious—ravenous for her. She wanted lesson two and had even teased him about it. He couldn't deny his hunger any longer, and he'd snuck into the bath.

She'd smelled like a field of flowers. Her skin was beautiful like fresh buttermilk. Somehow he'd seduced her into allowing him to live out a fantasy he'd always had. Pleasuring a woman blindfolded until she came in his hands.

Well, he'd accomplished that fantasy, but the result was unexpected. He thought it would quench his desire for it. He was dead wrong. In fact, Teague could barely keep from tearing back to her and finishing what he'd started.

He stood at the door for more than a minute until a movement in the shadows brought him back into consciousness. He peered at a door down the hall as it closed. Maybe Eppie or Isaiah.

He pushed away from the door with forcible effort and stalked down the hallway to the stairs. He brought his hand up to his nose and inhaled. God, her arousal was intoxicating. He couldn't stop himself from licking her taste from his fingers. When he did, he almost fell headfirst down the stairs but fortunately caught the banister in time.

She was delicious, arousing, and tempting. He was stupid, horny, and in way over his head. His dick had certainly never been this hard before, even when he was a teenager and all he thought about was said organ. He tried to adjust it to a more comfortable position, but it was no use. There would be no comfort until it lay deeply inside Madeline Brewster.

Teague realized that not only was he a whore, but that he was a well-paid one who was slowly but surely falling in love with his client.

In the smoky back room of Bart's Watering Hole, Sheriff Jackson Webster played a game of five-card stud with three other men. Strangers mostly, boys who worked the range on various ranches.

He didn't care. He was winning and had nearly two hundred dollars more than he'd come with. The air was thick with the scent of cigars and cigarettes. Jackson was puffing on a fat cigar he'd purchased at the store that day just in case a tempting poker game got going. He had a glass of good whiskey—Bart kept a supply for special customers like him. He sipped at the potent brew as he contemplated the three jacks he had in his hand.

"You in or not?" asked the man to his right who had a permanent sneer to his lips due to the scar that ran from the corner of his mouth to his ear. His hair was inky black, and Jackson saw a ghost of Injun in the man. He thought his name was Rafe or something like that—couldn't be more than eighteen but was as hard as the floor under his feet.

"I'm in," said Jackson as he tossed ten dollars into the pot. "Call."

Each of the three men who still had cards in their hands laid them down. Jackson was not happy to see that Rafe's straight beat his hand. As the boy scooped his winnings toward him, Jackson opened his mouth to accuse the pup of cheating when the door opened abruptly.

"Sheriff."

He turned around to find that young Negro boy at the door, twisting his hat in his hands and looking around the room like they were going to string him up.

Too bad it wasn't gonna happen that night. Jackson excused himself from the game, pocketed his winnings, and left the room to talk to the boy. He promised himself to play poker with Rafe again. Perhaps he could catch him cheating and be able to get back what he'd lost.

He led the boy up the back staircase to Bart's private office. It was a pigsty, but it was empty.

"What did you find out?"

The boy took a deep breath. "Mr. O'Neal, he went in the bathing room while Miss Madeline was taking a bath."

Jackson sat in Bart's squeaky leather chair behind the desk

piled high with papers and smiled at the boy through his cigar smoke.

"Sit down. What was your name again?"

"Isaiah, sir."

He gestured widely. "Tell me more, Isaiah."

Chapter Seven

Madeline went to work at the bank in the morning. She walked with a spring in her step and a smile on her face. She was a woman who had spent the previous night receiving incredible pleasure, and it showed. She looked in the mirror that morning and was surprised to see a flush to her cheeks and a sparkle in her eye.

Madeline was afraid to admit to herself that she was falling in love with Teague. It was too soon. She barely knew the man.

On the ten-minute walk to the bank she decided she would have a private dinner with him that evening and try to get him to open up a bit. Perhaps about what had happened to his wife and child, or maybe about his childhood. She was insatiably curious about him and wanted to gobble up every crumb of information she could find.

Madeline passed Matilda Webster on the sidewalk by the barber, and Madeline smiled. Actually smiled at her! Matilda looked like she'd seen a ghost as her blue eyes opened wide in shock.

Perhaps she had. The ghost that lived inside Madeline had come back to life. All thanks to Teague. Well, him and Madeline's outrageous proposal that had changed her life. She was wearing her favorite purple dress with a jaunty hat that had little cherries that bounced as she walked.

Madeline reached the bank fifteen minutes before nine o'clock and used her key from her reticule to let herself in. The morning sunshine shone through the windows and onto the dark wooden floors. Her heels clicked across the shiny surface as she walked toward her desk.

She let out a yelp of surprise when Mr. Cleeson walked out of the back room where the safe was located. She clutched the corner of her desk, and her pulse jumped like crazy.

"Miss Brewster!"

"Mr. Cleeson! What are you doing here so early? You nearly scared me to death!"

His eyes widened like saucers, and he looked like a small child caught filching cookies. He pulled the door closed behind him and looked at her with eyes laced with guilt.

"I must confess something, Miss Brewster. Last night . . . last night I left without double counting the cash in the safe, so I came back this morning before the bank opened to finish it."

Madeline frowned. "What made you neglect your duties?"

He shuffled his feet a bit before he answered. "I had a dinner engagement with a young lady I've been seeing. I was late and . . ."

He trailed off, and Madeline's temper rose. She handselected her employees as her father had—for their loyalty, hard work, and attention to detail. Not completing their assigned duties was so unheard of because of the caliber of the employees at the bank.

She'd never had to deal with an employee shirking their duties, especially one she trusted to act as manager in her place.

"Mr. Cleeson, this behavior is most unusual and both surprises and distresses me."

"I'm sorry, Miss Brewster. I promise you it will never happen again."

She set her reticule down on the desk and considered her options. "I'm going to have to think about this incident and then speak of it further with you."

"Of course."

She sat down behind the desk and looked at him. He still stood there until she prompted him. "Mr. Cleeson?"

He jumped like she'd pinched him and headed toward his desk across the bank.

"You will return your key to me until I decide what to do."

He stopped, and she saw a fleeting glimpse of anger in his eyes. That was a definite problem.

"Yes, Miss Brewster." He took the key from his vest pocket and laid it on her desk.

She nodded and took the key, dropping it into her reticule on the desk.

Madeline tried to concentrate the rest of the day until three, but she kept finding Mr. Cleeson's gaze on her. He'd turn away quickly, but she still felt it.

Something was wrong in the bank, and it bothered her that she couldn't quite put her finger on it. Mr. Cleeson had sounded honest, but it was all just so odd.

Madeline was never so glad to see the end of the day. She and Mr. Allen double counted the cash in the safe together and then locked up. By three-thirty, the spring in her step was less obvious.

The incident with Mr. Cleeson still nagged at her. She needed to stop thinking about it and focus on something else. Unfortunately that something else turned out to be someone.

Reverend Mathias.

He had known Madeline since she was a young girl and preached a bit of fire and brimstone from his pulpit. Madeline had never liked his sermons and stopped going when her father died. That had been two years ago. Another reason the town could point a finger at her and call her names.

The reverend was a tall man with a shock of white hair as thick as summer grass on a riverbank. He had cold blue eyes and wrinkled jowls that shook when he spoke. He had a belly made from Sunday dinners and gravied biscuits. He was wearing his customary black accoutrements and currently stood in the middle of the sidewalk staring at her. She either had to stop and speak to him or cross the street simply to avoid him.

Madeline decided she would be the adult and face her problem head-on.

"Good day, Madeline." His voice was still as powerful as it had been twenty-five years earlier when she had first heard him. It was deep and resonant in the ear and in the soul.

"Good day, Reverend."

Madeline tried to step past him, but he stuck out his arm, and she had no choice but to take it. It was hard yet brittle, and the cloth was abrasive beneath her wrist. Thank God she was wearing gloves, or her hands would be feeling it, too.

"It's a beautiful spring day. I thought it would be nice if we strolled together as you walked home."

"Of course," she answered while inwardly cursing like Teague.

"It's come to my attention that there are two strange men living in your house again, Madeline. You know we've had this discussion before."

She sighed. "Yes, we have, and my answer remains the same. My house is open to anyone who needs a place to lay their head."

He sighed and patted her hand. It was all she could do not to yank it from his grasp.

"This time you've gone too far, though. A colored boy and a criminal are no company for a genteel lady like yourself. I don't like that mulatto serving girl, either. Miscreants and ne'er-do-wells surround you. You must think of your immortal soul, Madeline."

"I am, Reverend, which is why I open my house to people. Have a good evening."

Madeline pulled her arm free and walked briskly away from him. She was wound up as tight as a watch spring now.

How dare he judge her and her friends? Small-minded folks did not belong in cleric's clothes and certainly shouldn't be judging other people.

She heard him sputter behind her and call her back, but Madeline simply waved and kept walking faster. By the time she reached her front porch, the bright blue a welcoming sight, she was almost panting with effort. A trickle of perspiration slid down her back, dampening her purple dress.

As she walked up the steps, the weight of the day lifted off her shoulders. When she saw Teague sitting on the porch swing smiling at her, her spirit lifted, too. His dark hair was damp as though he'd just washed it. His beautiful eyes were smiling, along with his sexy mouth. He was wearing his own threadbare clothes, which stretched just a bit tightly across his massive chest and shoulders, not to mention his legs.

"Hi, there."

His voice never failed to send shivers up her spine.

"Hi, there, yourself. Are you waiting for me?"

"Yes. Eppie told me not to fetch you and walk you home, so I thought I would wait here for you instead."

Madeline walked over, pulled off her gloves, and sat on the swing next to him. It swayed gently back and forth, and the welcoming breeze cooled her heated skin. She felt comfortable sitting next to Teague.

"Thank you for welcoming me home."

Teague's hand took hers and laced their fingers together. His was one of the few hands that could make hers feel small. She sighed.

This. *This* was what she wanted. To have a husband, a partner to sit quietly with and share her day.

"You looked tense, Maddie. Something wrong?"

"Nothing. Well . . . one of the bank employees left without finishing his duties yesterday. He snuck in early to finish it, and I caught him."

Teague tensed slightly beside her.

"Did he take anything?"

"Take anything? No, no. I don't think he'd ever take anything."

"You'd be surprised what people will do."

Madeline shook her head. "I don't think I'd be surprised. You forget I'm the Black Widow, Rufus Brewster's daughter. I've seen the worst in people for a long time."

His thumb started stroking the back of her hand, sending delightful sparks of pleasure up her arm.

"Something else is bothering you."

How could he see inside her so easily? She supposed they shared a connection now. Linked by their shared physical closeness.

"Reverend Mathias tried to poke his nose in my life again."

"Local preacher?"

"He preaches hell and damnation for everyone but Matilda Webster and her band of witches." She gasped and covered her mouth with her hand. "Did I actually say that out loud?"

Teague chuckled. "You did, and I agree with you. She probably carries a broom with her. Does she have a cat?"

Madeline smiled and looked into his eyes. For a moment, she saw who Teague could be if he threw off the cloak of self-hate and grief that surrounded him. He allowed her that small glimpse before the walls slid back and his eyes were again unreadable.

"You're a puzzling man, Teague O'Neal."

He shrugged one big shoulder. "I'm a simple man, Maddie. I eat, I sleep, I work. There isn't much more to me."

"But there used to be."

It popped out of her mouth before she could stop herself.

Instantly his face hardened, and his jaw clenched. "What do you mean?"

In for a penny, in for a pound.

"In the picture I saw in your bag, you looked . . . so happy, content, like a man who enjoyed life and his family. I expect you did more than eat, sleep, and work."

He broke her gaze and looked out at the yard. She heard a bee droning near the rosebushes that had just blossomed by the front gate. She waited with just enough patience that she didn't shake him.

"Life was different then, Maddie. Before the war."

She squeezed his hand and willed him to continue, but he remained stubbornly silent.

"The war didn't touch us much out here."

"It destroyed everything I had, including my heart. Don't expect it to come back to life, Maddie. We're together for only a month, and then I'm moving on."

He stood abruptly, stomped down the front steps, and then headed for the side of the house. Madeline cursed her wayward tongue. With another sigh, she rose.

A hot bath would be most welcome, and perhaps she could persuade Eppie to make a special dinner for Teague tonight.

Then maybe lesson three might happen. Madeline had no idea what that lesson entailed, but hoped a blindfold and more intense pleasure was the beginning.

Eppie made a beef stew and dumplings for dinner, which turned out to be one of Teague's favorites. He sat across from Madeline in the dining room and ate without saying much. She was content to watch him. Although they had ended their conversation earlier a bit abruptly, the silence in the room was comfortable.

Madeline decided it was because they'd been intimate. Well, she had yet to actually touch other than his lips, but he had touched her nearly everywhere. In fact, she could hardly wait to get her turn at Teague.

"Will I get to touch you soon?"

His spoon clattered into his bowl, and a smattering of beef stew landed on the tablecloth.

"You sure don't believe in beating around the bush."

He glanced at her with heat in his eyes. Heat that ignited an answering flame inside her.

"No, I guess I don't. Things won't happen unless you ask for them. That's how I found you."

He licked his lips, and Madeline could barely take her eyes off that incredible tongue.

"You want to touch me, Maddie?"

Her stomach clenched with a fluttering of anticipation.

"Oh, yes. I can hardly think of anything but touching you."

His eyes burned brightly. "You certainly know how to turn a man's head."

She shook her head. "I've never been a woman to turn a man's head."

"Don't doubt yourself, Maddie. You're beautiful, especially when you're naked and aroused."

She froze like a deer near a hunter. His words were meant to tease her, test her, tantalize her. It was working perfectly.

"Take your hair down."

Without thinking about it, Madeline reached behind her and released the pins holding her chignon together. Her hair fell down in dark waves, brushing her cheeks with a soft caress. Her nipples hardened in anticipation of what was yet to come.

"Take me to your bedroom, Maddie."

Chapter Eight

Teague felt like a piece of hay in a twister. Swirling around and around, nearly out of control. His pulse was thrumming so fast he was afraid he'd get dizzy from all the blood rushing to his cock.

He walked behind Madeline up the stairs. Her incredible ass was at eye level. Her hair was swaying back and forth across it as she walked up the steps. He had to physically restrain himself from biting her.

Teague had never been this aroused or lost such a grip on himself over a woman. With Claire, it had been sweet and loving, never snarling and elemental—like Maddie was his bitch, and he was the hound getting ready to mount her. He could almost smell her arousal through the purple satin dress she wore.

His dick was straining at the leash, and all he wanted to do was lay her down on the bed and fuck her until neither one of them could move.

It wasn't as though he had promised her anything except to teach her how to be intimate. So far all he'd done was tease her and end up pleasuring himself every night because he had a permanent hard-on.

They finally reached the top of the stairs and headed down the hallway. He could see light shining from the doorway on the right. The same one he'd seen someone step into when he left the bathing room. A shadow moved beneath the door. Someone was listening.

He started walking on his toes to try to minimize the amount of sound he made. Looked like a houseguest—he wasn't sure if it was Eppie or Isaiah, but his money was on the boy—was enjoying watching and listening to Madeline's education. Well, that was about to stop. No one needed to know anything that went on in or out of his pants. Shit, now he had to be really quiet.

They reached Maddie's bedroom, and she turned her dark eyes on him. The pupils were wide, and he felt as if he'd fallen straight into them. He was drowning in her and had nothing to stop himself from falling. His mental hooks grabbed on to nothing.

He leaned down and gently pressed his lips to hers, but one taste was not enough. He scooped her into his arms and entered the room, pushing the door shut behind him with his foot.

"Lock it." He growled in a whisper.

She reached behind, and he heard the snick of the key turning in the lock. Her eyes flew back to his.

"You carried me."

"This is only the first ride of the night, darlin'. Hang on."

He captured her mouth again as he walked over to the bed, trying not to notice the girlish quality to the room. Maddie was not a girl, even if she had pink furniture and white, lacy canopy shit on her bed, or dolls on the window seat.

She was a woman.

When he reached the bed, he let her slide down his body until she stood, her softness rubbing nicely against his hardness.

"Oh, my," she breathed as her feet touched the floor. "You're so hard. Like a tree."

He chuckled. "That I am, and bound to get harder."

Teague twined her hair around his fist like a satin rope and pulled her close to him until they were chest to chest, groin to groin. He tugged on the hair, and she leaned her head back. He stared down into her eyes.

"This is lesson three, Maddie. There isn't any going back after this. By morning, you'll know what it feels like to be with a man. Are you sure you're ready?"

She licked her lips, and his cock bellowed like it felt that tongue already.

"I've been ready for fifteen years, Teague. All I needed was to find you."

He tried to ignore the way her honest response plucked at his heartstrings. Maddie was not his wife, nor would she ever be. He liked her. Truth was, he liked her a lot, and even more, he respected her. He was in a tight spot here, between a rock and a hard place. Being in Maddie's bed was complicating matters, but he was that piece of straw in the twister. Helpless to stop. So instead of fighting the wind, he flew with it.

Teague kissed her hard and then released her hair.

He took off his boots and sat down on the edge of the bed.

"Take off your clothes for me, Maddie. Start with the petticoats and drawers."

Madeline pulled up the bottom of her dress long enough to grab the petticoats and drawers and push them down. She stepped out of them, and they disappeared somewhere behind her.

"Now the dress."

He could see her hands shaking, but she began unbuttoning the hundred tiny pearl buttons that trailed down the front of her dress. As each one popped free, he felt an answering spark inside his chest.

He could see the white chemise beneath her dress and told himself she needed colored undergarments. A woman as sexy as Maddie shouldn't wear white under her clothes. She was too passionate.

The last button popped free, and the dress gaped open nearly to her pussy. He could see the faint shadow of it as the dress opened wider when she pulled it off her shoulders.

"Slowly."

She nodded as the dress slid down her arms to her waist. As she pulled her hands free, she shimmied it down those long legs to the floor. It pooled around her feet until she stepped out of it and pushed it aside with one foot.

"Now the chemise . . . slowly, darlin'."

She swallowed hard, and beneath the nervousness, he saw excitement in her eyes. An arousal that lit from within. Madeline liked him to tell her what to do.

"Should I pull it up or push it down?"

Teague ran his gaze up and down her body. Her nipples stood erect, begging for his attention. Her skin nearly glowed with arousal as a pink flush crept over it. His dick grew another inch inside his already tight pants.

"Push it down."

Madeline slipped the straps off the chemise and pushed it down her chest until her breasts sprang free. The raspberry-colored nipples were darker in the centers, like fruit waiting for him to pluck. Her skin slowly came into view in the candle-light, causing Teague to start rubbing himself through his pants. He couldn't help it. He was so horny, and it had been so damn long since he'd been with a woman.

"I like that."

He looked in her eyes. "Like what?"

She licked her lips, and his dick twitched.

"What you're doing with your hand. It makes me . . . achy."

"Me, too."

For a virgin, she surely did not hold back what she was thinking. She pushed the chemise all the way off and then took off her stockings and garters.

"Are you going to get undressed?"

Teague shook his head. "You're going to do it."

Her eyes widened, and he saw a small smile playing around her lips. She walked toward the bed, and it was all Teague could do not to throw her on the bed and pump into her.

She pushed his knees open until she stood between them.

"Vixen."

Her long fingers unbuttoned his shirt slowly.

"I want to kiss you. Touch you."

"I'm all yours, Maddie."

She nodded again, as if receiving instructions. As his chest appeared in the opening of the shirt, she leaned forward and planted a kiss. Then did it again and again. When it was completely unbuttoned, her finger trailed down the path of hair that led from his belly to his dick. Then it went back up to his belly button and gently caressed it.

Madeline slipped his shirt off and tossed it behind her. His breathing was as labored as hers, and they hadn't even really started yet. Her hands ran up and down his shoulders and arms and then down his chest. When her fingernails lightly scored his nipples, he hissed.

"I've wanted to do this from the moment I saw you," she whispered huskily as she bent forward to lick one nipple and then the other.

That, as they say, was the straw that broke the camel's back. Teague stood abruptly, tossed her on the bed, and then yanked off his boots and trousers in record time.

Madeline lay on the bed, looking at him with a mixture of fear and excitement in her eyes. When her gaze dropped down to his cock, she swallowed and licked her lips. Teague groaned.

"You're gonna make this be over before it starts."

"I don't mean to."

"Hang on, because it's going to get a little bumpy."

He lay down on top of her, and his entire body sighed with relief. Skin to skin, they fit perfectly. Her softness melded with his hardness. Her thighs opened, and he slid between them to nestle in the softest of havens.

"Oh, Lord, Teague. I . . . I . . . that's incredible. It's like heaven."

Secretly Teague agreed with her. It was like heaven. He lifted his head up and smiled.

"Not quite, but we're getting close."

He kissed her hard while his hands roamed up and down her body, pinching, teasing, and caressing. He thrummed and ached to take her, but he wanted her first time to be perfect. She had, after all, paid for it with good money.

He rocked back and forth against her mons until her slickness told him she was nearly ready.

He kissed her across her jaw to her ear, and then, after a few nibbles, he moved to her neck. She smelled and tasted of lavender and woman. He licked the crook of her shoulder and then moved to his ultimate goal, her pouting nipples.

He captured one pert point in his mouth while his hand rolled and played with the other. Continually rocking against her, he built up the tempo until he could tell she was close to reaching her peak.

"The first time will hurt," he murmured against her breast.

"I don't care. Oh, please, Teague, I need . . . I need. Please."

"Open for me."

Her legs slowly spread, and he was flush against her. She was so hot and so wet, he nearly came at the first touch of skin. With rigid self-control, he pushed into her an inch and felt the squeeze of an untried pussy. He was sweating and hanging on by a thread to his sanity.

In. In.

He ignored his inner demons and pushed in a smidge more.

"Oh, yessssss," she said. "That's what I want."

Again he slid forward in a bit more and nearly lost it right then and there. Oh, Jesus, she was so tight.

So good.

"Are you ready, Maddie? There's no going back after this."

She spread her legs wider and grabbed his ass with both hands, pulling him forward so quickly into her wet heat he was helpless to stop her. But, goddamn, once inside he wondered what had taken him so long. She was not only tight, hot, and wet, she was clenching around him over and over.

"You okay?"

"Mmmm, yes. Can you penetrate me again and again?"

He would have laughed if he hadn't been a hair's breadth away from coming his brains out.

"You need to stop reading textbooks, Maddie."

He pulled all the way out and then pushed in. His rhythm picked up, and so did hers. Together they rode the twister, bucking and fucking like two pieces of straw twined together.

"Teague, it's happening again."

He drove into her harder, deeper. So close, oh, so damn close.

She screeched his name as her body convulsed around him so hard. He slammed his lips down on hers to muffle the sound. He came with enough force he saw stars. He pumped into her deep, deeper, deepest. She clawed at his back as her tremors continued.

Teague was breathing like a bellows against her shoulder. Her heart was fluttering in her chest, and he felt tingles from one end of his body to the other.

"Holy shit."

He kissed her and rolled off, sliding easily against her sweaty body.

"Sweet heavens."

"I like mine better."

Madeline raised a shaking hand, pulled a hair from her cheek, and then leaned over and kissed him softly on the lips. Her lithe tongue darted out to lick his bottom lip playfully. Her dark eyes were sparkling with mischief.

"How long until we can do this again?"

He gauged his body's readiness and grinned.

"Half an hour?"

"It's a date."

He glanced at Maddie and saw the most beautiful sight a man could see. A woman he loved, well sated and glowing from their lovemaking.

His stomach cramped with the realization of his thoughts.

A woman he loved?

Not happening. He did *not* love Maddie. He *liked* Maddie. It was absolutely, positively not love.

Teague woke her in a few hours. His big hands cupped her breasts and lightly pinched her nipples until she arched against him. His hardness pressed up against her backside, and she rubbed against it, an answering wetness began to gather between her legs.

"Are you ready for another lesson?"

She smiled into her pillow. Who knew sex was going to be so amazing and incredible? She imagined it to be messy and awkward. No, sirree. It was far beyond that. It was . . . bliss.

"Yes, professor."

His hand slid down her leg and lifted it at the knee. He slid into her easily, and she sighed at the feeling. She was full, complete. He was big but not too big. She was actually quite amazed it fit. Teague had a very large member, as was expected. He was not a small man anywhere.

"God, you feel good, Maddie."

"So do you."

They moved together slowly. Teague never increased his pace. Just in and out over and over. He pulled her hands up to her breasts.

"Touch yourself."

His hand slid between her legs and started caressing her nubbin of pleasure. With a bit of embarrassment, she circled her nipples with her fingers. After a few minutes of his hand, his cock, and her own hand, the embarrassment disappeared. She pinched and rolled her nipples with abandon.

"Yes, that's it, darlin'. Feel me fucking you? You are so damn tight. I could do this all day."

His naughty words just served to excite her even more. She thrust against him, silently willing him to go faster, harder.

More, please.

"Don't get too pushy, Maddie," he growled in her ear and then bit her lobe.

Just when she thought she'd go insane from his pace, he pinched her clit and thrust deeply. Her body fell over the precipice of pleasure, and she squeezed her own nipples as the waves rolled through her. Over and over. She heard him whisper her name as he thrust in deeply again, reaching his own orgasm.

Madeline released her nipples as she tried to come down out of the clouds. Her body was throbbing and humming with satisfaction. She knew it was a feeling she'd never find with anyone but Teague.

Chapter Nine

The next morning Madeline found herself alone in her bed. The covers were mussed beyond belief, and the room had a distinct musky odor. She stretched lazily, and many muscles were yelling loudly at the movement. That's when she realized she was naked.

Madeline was no longer a virgin.

She smiled into the empty room and forced herself to rise. The sun was brightly shining in through the window. It was late, probably midmorning. She slipped her nightgown over her head and opened the window. The sounds of the world drifted in on the soft breeze. Madeline breathed deeply of the fresh air.

She felt wonderful. More than that, she felt as if she were ten years younger. A woman in love.

Where is Teague?

He had probably slipped off before dawn to save her some embarrassment with Eppie or Isaiah. He needn't have. She didn't care if they knew Teague had been in her bed. Madeline had to restrain herself from running down the street and shouting it to the world.

She stared down at the street and saw Sheriff Webster riding toward her house on his big bay horse. She grimaced. There was no time to take a bath, but she'd better wash the scent of Teague off her skin. Something she didn't want to do but had to.

After a quick wash with tepid water, Madeline fixed her hair and then slipped on a demure brown dress with a high collar and lace at the cuffs. The dress felt wrong somehow. She wanted to be wearing something colorful to match her spirit.

Smiling, she went downstairs to see Eppie standing with her back against the front door.

"Madeline! Where have you been? That fool sheriff won't go away."

"Eppie! You need to stop calling him names."

Eppie frowned. "Even if it's true?"

Madeline shook her head and bit back a grin. "What does he want?"

"He wouldn't tell me. I's just a po servant."

"Stop it!" Madeline admonished. "You'll make it worse by acting stupid."

Eppie shrugged and headed for the kitchen. "I'll go put water on for tea. Oh, and by the way, you might want to pull the collar up a bit higher. You got a good case of whisker burn from your man."

Madeline felt her cheeks heat, and she yanked on the collar until it touched the bottom of her jaw. Whisker burn? What was that?

She opened the door to find Sheriff Webster leaning against the column by the front steps.

"Good morning, Jackson."

"Hello, Madeline."

She stepped outside and closed the door behind her. "What brings you by?"

He hitched up his trousers and bracketed his hands on his hips.

"Well, I heard that man you took in was getting to be a problem."

Madeline felt her annoyance blossom. "Who told you that?"

"It makes no never mind. Fact is, I was worried about it

from the moment you convinced us to hand him over to you."
He waved his hand in the air in dismissal. "I want to know if
he's been trouble."

She squared her shoulders and prepared for battle. Madeline
had learned from the best how to be stubborn, intractable, and
immovable. Now was the time to put those skills to the test.

"I don't know who told you he was trouble, but it isn't
true."

"Then he didn't tear your dress open in the kitchen?"

Madeline felt her mouth open and snapped it shut immediately. How could he know about that?

"I was burned by hot coffee, Jackson. Eppie was there
helping me, as was Mr. O'Neal. It was all perfectly innocent."

He nodded and pulled at his chin.

"I also hear he kicked you out of your own carriage house."

"No one kicks me out of anywhere. You know that. Who
is telling you these exaggerated lies?" Her heart was pounding, and her palms felt clammy. What kind of person would
deliberately do this?

Jackson took off his hat and scratched his thinning blond
hair. "You know that's confidential information. I've had
someone keeping an eye on you and that horse thief."

"He is not a horse thief!"

"So you say, but I reserve my judgment."

"You don't have to judge him at all. The evidence will
prove it."

He stepped toward her and put his hands on her shoulders,
looking at her eye to eye. Not many men in Plum Creek
could do that.

"I am worried about you. He is not a man to be trusted.
Let's face it, Madeline, you don't have much experience with
men. Somebody with a silver tongue could take advantage of
you."

She tried to step away from him, but he held her firm.

"Let go of me, Jackson. Now."

He released her arms, but a dangerous glint of something

flew from his eyes. She felt it hit, and her uneasiness increased tenfold. Jackson was up to something. Something that didn't bode well for her or Teague.

"I appreciate your concern, but there is no need for it. I've told you before, Mr. O'Neal is a perfect gentleman. I won't keep you from your duties."

It was a dismissal. He knew it, and it stuck in his craw. He nodded and put his hat back on his head.

"Be careful, Madeline," he said as he walked down the steps and headed toward his horse.

She knew he wasn't just talking about Teague. His words spoiled her perfect mood as a gray cloud covers the sun. She shivered and hugged her arms to her chest.

She watched the sheriff's horse until he turned the corner into town. The sound of the creek behind her house should have been soothing. Instead it sounded like a melody of warning.

Teague took a break from working on the roof of the carriage house and wiped the sweat from his forehead with his discarded shirt. From up there he could see all the way to town. He saw the sheriff ride up to the house and then ride back into town half an hour later.

God only knew what he'd been talking to Maddie about for half an hour. Teague was most assuredly not that curious and definitely not jealous. Madeline was not his woman. She was his . . . well, hell, he didn't know what she was. What he did know was that he didn't trust that sheriff for a second. The only thing he served was his own interests.

Teague went back to hammering and saw a horse and buggy pull up to the house. It was as busy as a train station at Maddie's house. A natty little man in a bowler hat and a pretty suit hopped out and went in the house.

Teague tried to focus on the roof, but his eyes kept straying to the house. He wondered who the man was and what he was doing with Maddie.

He smacked his thumb twice with the hammer and then dropped some of the boards off the edge of the roof. Cursing in Gaelic and English, he climbed down the ladder to retrieve the boards. By the side of the house, Isaiah was standing in the shadows, peering through the window.

Wasn't that interesting.

Teague walked up behind him silently. He was good at being silent, one of the many skills he'd learned in the war. Most of them he was not proud of. He stood only a few feet from Isaiah and tried to figure out what he was doing.

He heard Eppie humming through the open window. So, the young man liked to peep. That was definitely not polite.

Teague grabbed him by the throat so quickly he didn't make a sound and then dragged him back to the carriage house and slammed him against the wall. The force echoed through his arm, and he was pleased to see fear in the other man's dark eyes.

"What did you think you were doing?"

"I . . . I was . . . only . . ." Isaiah croaked out.

"You were spying on Eppie. She is a good girl, and I won't let you turn her into something cheap you can find at any saloon. You understand me?"

Isaiah nodded and pulled at Teague's arm. It didn't move so much as an inch.

"I didn't mean no harm."

"Doesn't matter if you meant harm or not. You did harm just by looking at her when she didn't know it. That's the last time you're going to do it, too, isn't it?" Teague bared his teeth in a feral smile.

"Yes. I swear. I won't never spy on her again."

"Good. I'm glad you agree with me. Now, aren't you supposed to be taking care of weeding the garden today?"

He let Isaiah's throat loose and stepped back. Isaiah rubbed his throat with one hand and looked at Teague like he was an avenging angel.

"I finished. I was fixing to ask Eppie what else she needed done, and I . . ." He trailed off and looked at the ground.

"You can start weeding the flowers in the front, then. Get busy, Isaiah, before I stop being nice to you."

Isaiah ran for the front of the house like a swatted fly. Teague was glad he was scared of him. No man should ever take advantage of a woman. Ever. He punched the side of the building and winced as a blister popped on his hand from the force.

There were too many secrets in the house already. Isaiah just added another unexpected layer that forced Teague to rethink what he was doing.

After Mr. Finley left, Madeline felt exhausted. The attorney had had so much information for her to review and approve it had simply drained her. Not to mention the fact she had been up half the night learning. Lesson number three had been worth the wait.

She stretched out on the settee in her mother's sitting room and looked out the window. The gurgling water in the creek was soothing now, pulling her closer and closer to sleep. Her eyes drifted closed.

Teague was going down to Plum Creek to wash. Sweat, dirt, and sawdust coated his skin from his work on the roof. It wasn't summer, but the sun was hot enough, especially when you were working your ass off in it.

He grabbed a towel and soap from the pile Madeline had left. The sound of bees humming, birds chirping, and squirrels chattering were soothing, in a way. It brought back the normal quality of life. God knew his life hadn't been normal for years. He breathed deeply of the Colorado air. It was a bit thinner here in Plum Creek, not as bad as Denver, though. The air was so thin in the Mile High City, he was dizzy for days when he got to town.

He followed a well-worn path through the woods and almost salivated at the sound of the water. He needed to get clean and cool in the worst way.

Teague reached the bank and shucked off his clothes in a blink. Laying the towel and his clothes on a nearby rock, he walked into the water. The cold water shriveled him up and cooled him off right quick. This was likely melted snow from the mountains. But, damn, it felt *good*. Surprisingly the creek was about twenty feet wide, and his feet just touched the bottom. Big creek. When swollen with rain, he had no doubt it was deadly. The current gently tugged at him, but his feet found firm purchase on the sandy bottom.

He ducked his head under and wet his hair. Coming up he was startled to find Eppie standing on the bank, her hands fisted on her hips and a scowl on her face.

"What did I do?"

She pursed her lips. "You touched Miss Madeline, that's what."

"That's not your business, Eppie." He started lathering himself up and tried to ignore her.

"It is so my business. My life wasn't worth spit until she found me. I love her like she was my sister. I won't let no drifter horse thief break her heart."

Teague just kept on lathering and gritted his teeth. Life always got so fucking complicated.

"I don't plan on breaking her heart. What's between us is not your business. Leave it alone."

She stamped her foot, which caused her to slide into the water. She started screeching like a banshee. With a sigh, Teague dropped his soap and swam toward her. He grabbed her and towed her back to the edge. She climbed up, chest heaving and yelling, "Lord have mercy!" over and over.

She stood and wrung the water from her dress.

"That water is devil cold, Mr. Teague. I don't know how you're in there buck naked in it."

"Go home, Eppie."

She took his towel and started drying herself with it. Teague tried vainly to get some of the soap from his head to scrub the rest of his body, but it was no use. And his soap was probably halfway to Utah by now. Well, there was always sand. Not his favorite way to wash, but effective.

"Not until you promise to leave her alone."

He started walking toward her. "If you don't head on home now, I'm gonna give you an eyeful of man."

She squeaked and dropped the towel, running through the trees toward the house. Teague dove back into the water to finish washing himself, cursing the fact that his now wet towel was lying in the mud.

Madeline woke and gazed around her, disoriented. It was her mother's sitting room. She must have fallen asleep. In the distance she could hear Eppie shouting something out by the creek.

Madeline stood and walked to the window in time to see her stomping out of the woods soaking wet.

What in the world? Eppie didn't know how to swim! What was she doing down by the creek, and why was she wet?

Within minutes, Teague came strolling out of the woods with his hair wet and his chest bare. In fact, he was wearing only his trousers, and they were half buttoned.

Madeline's stomach sank to her knees as she pondered the possibility of why Eppie and Teague were both wet and in the creek together. She couldn't come up with a plausible reason, and her heart squeezed tighter and tighter as a pain ripped through it.

Teague was supposed to be hers. For a month, anyway. How could he be with Eppie when they had just had the most incredible, pleasurable experience of her life less than twelve hours before?

Her tea threatened to come back to haunt her as her stomach rolled. A tear snuck out from her eye. She snapped it away angrily and headed for the kitchen.

Eppie was not there. Madeline stomped to her room instead and pounded on the door.

"Eppie!"

The door opened, and Eppie stared out at her in surprise. "Madeline?"

"Why . . . what . . . how could you, Eppie?"

A sob burst from Madeline's throat, and she clamped her hand over her mouth to stop it, but it was too late. Her heart was already on her sleeve.

"Oh, Madeline," said Eppie as she pulled her into her room and shut the door. She stood in her chemise, which was wet, and hugged Madeline. She shook like a newborn foal as she felt the first pains of love tear through her.

"I fell in the creek because I was yelling at your man. He saved my life."

Madeline barely heard her through the roaring in her ears. "What?"

"I didn't do nothing with that big ol' Irishman. He's too big and too white for me. I wanted him to leave you alone. Oh, Madeline, I was afraid this would happen. He's already breaking your heart!"

"You tried to scare him off?"

"Yes, I surely did! He wasn't budging though. Stubborn cuss."

Madeline stepped back from Eppie and started to laugh through her tears. He hadn't been with Eppie at all. She was trying to warn him away from a relationship that Madeline had paid for. Eppie, of course, had no idea. The idea that she'd tried to warn him away sent Madeline howling with laughter.

"It ain't that funny!"

Madeline laughed and hugged her friend again. "Oh, Eppie, what would I do without you?"

Eppie started to laugh, too, and both of them nearly hurt themselves. Madeline got a stitch in her side and had to sit down on the bed.

"You want to keep him?" Eppie asked as she changed into dry clothes.

Madeline wiped her eyes with her sleeve.

"I would love to keep him, but he's mine for only a month,

Eppie. And I'm going to savor every minute of it. It's all I'll have for the rest of my life."

Eppie looked at her doubtfully.

"Please just let me have this time with him. I promise my heart won't be broken. Bruised, yes, but I won't let it be broken."

Eppie nodded. "I think you're bug-eyed crazy, but it's your life, so it's your choice."

"Thank you."

Madeline hugged her one last time and then left the room. After a quick wash of her face, she was going to find Teague. It had been far too long since last night. She needed to feel him, taste him, touch him.

Love him.

Chapter Ten

Teague was damp and irritated. By the time he got back to the carriage house and his room, his feet and the bottom of his clean pants were as muddy as the towel. He walked up the stairs, leaving dirty footprints, and threw his dirty clothes and the towel in a pile on the floor.

Glancing down at himself, he yanked off his pants, wiped his muddy feet on them and threw them in the corner, too. That left him with one set of clean clothes for the week. And it was only Tuesday.

Naked, he padded over to the hooks on the wall that held the clothes Maddie had bought for him.

"If I ever doubted the existence of a God, I could never do it again after seeing you like this."

Maddie's voice should have startled him, but it didn't. It was as if he knew she would be there. Unashamed, he turned to face her. She stood at the top of the stairs. For some reason, her dress had wet splotches on it. It was a hideous shade of brown to begin with and made her look like a dull bird.

"You need to wear brighter colors." She nodded and walked toward him. "Thanks, by the way. I didn't know me being naked would bring thoughts of the Almighty to your head."

She smiled, and Teague felt his temperature spike. Maddie was beautiful. She couldn't help but see the evidence of his arousal. It literally pointed right at her.

Two feet from him, she stopped, hesitation clearly on her face.

"I want to touch you, but I don't know how. Teach me, Teague."

He closed the distance between them. Her body heat mingled with his. He breathed deep and smelled her unique scent again. All woman, all Maddie.

"Lesson number four," he said.

Madeline's knees were knocking together, and her heart was pounding. Her hands literally itched to touch all that flesh. *All that flesh.*

Sweet heaven, but he was a beautiful man. Covered in taut, tanned skin from his rugged face, down his broad shoulders and chest. His arms were strong and covered in the same dark whirls of hair that kept that massive chest warm.

His stomach looked like a washboard, and it had an arrow of that dark hair that pointed straight to his cock. Lord, but the man was huge. Much larger than the pictures in the book and much, much harder. The pictures in the book showed it limp and hanging to one side. Aroused, Teague was a sight to send even the birds twittering.

His legs were long and muscled. Even his feet were perfect.

Teague was beautiful. And he was hers. Like a little girl on Christmas morning, she couldn't wait to touch him.

He took her hands and brought them to his chest.

"You did pretty well last night. Just start where you were and do whatever comes naturally. There isn't anything that's wrong between two people who—who are enjoying each other. The only rule is if you don't like something, say so."

Madeline nodded and swallowed back her cowardice.

"Touch me, Maddie."

Taking a deep breath, she ran her hands around his chest. His small nipples pebbled almost instantly. She ran her fingertips around the flat circles. They weren't as soft as her own, but they were much softer than the rest of him.

She moved her hands in wide circles around his chest, the crisp hair sliding beneath her skin. She remembered how it felt against her skin and shivered. His skin was slightly tacky from his bath in the creek, and he smelled of fresh air and man.

Her hands followed the curve of his shoulders and probed the muscles in his arms. He stood as still as a statue, but she could hear his breathing and feel his pulse racing. Her eyes strayed to the ever-growing member between them.

"You can touch it."

Madeline licked her lips, and she saw it jump. Her eyes flew to his. The pupils were wide with arousal, and his nostrils flared as he breathed. She did that. She was responsible for making this man aroused. The power of that realization gave her courage she would not normally find.

One hand cupped his balls while the other closed around his shaft. A shaky breath burst from his throat. His skin was soft here like his nipples, but he was as hard as a block of wood. His balls were large and covered with lighter brown hair than his chest. They were firm and warm in her hands.

He swayed slightly on his feet when her hand tightened on him.

"Can you get on the bed?"

He nodded and then stumbled over to the bed and lay down. She looked at six and a half feet of man waiting for her, and a pulse of arousal beat so strong it made her completely wet between her legs, made her nipples pinch up harder than Teague's cock, and took her breath away.

He was better than any Christmas present. He was *hers*.

"Get undressed," he commanded.

Without acknowledging the order as such, Madeline undressed to her chemise and stockings. She pulled off the chemise and saw Teague's eyes widen.

"Where did you get red garters?"

She smiled. "A woman has to have her secrets." She leaned down to take them off, but Teague stopped her.

"Leave them on."

The idea of having sex with Teague in her stockings and garters was more than exciting. She actually felt a trickle of her own arousal slide down her thigh.

Madeline walked over to the bed and looked at him with a question in her eyes.

"Straddle my legs and kneel on the bed. You can touch me as long as I can take it."

She did as he bade. The cool air caressed her heated core. Her hands moved up his thighs to his cock again. She examined him from top to bottom, touching, caressing, and measuring. As she explored, his balls grew tighter and tighter.

"You're going to have to stop now, Maddie, or this will be over before we start."

She didn't quite understand that but immediately removed her hands.

"Now move up and take me inside you. You're going to learn to ride me."

Madeline hadn't realized women could be on top, but the thought was as tantalizing as it was exciting. She moved herself up until she was just over him. His eyes were nearly black, and a sheen of perspiration dotted his brow.

"Take my cock and put it inside you."

She spread her legs a bit wider and took him in her hand. When the head of his cock met with her skin, it jumped in her hand.

"Oh, my God, you're so wet. Put it in, Maddie. Ride me, girl."

He slid in slowly, inch by inch. She wasn't sure how to do this, so she did it slowly.

"Your nipples are begging me to touch them." His hands reached up and began rolling the nipples between his fingers. She clenched deep down inside, and he groaned.

"Yes. Yessss. . . ."

She finally had him entirely inside her, and the feeling was indescribable. She was not only full, she was as aroused as she had ever been in her life.

"Now move."

Madeline looked at him helplessly. She was finding it hard to focus, with the pulses of pleasure radiating throughout her body.

He grabbed her by the waist and pulled her up slightly. The friction between his cock and her pussy echoed through her.

"Up and down, darlin'. Up and down."

She understood the rhythm immediately. When she started moving up and down, the pleasure was intense. He pulled her down, so she braced her hands on either side of his head. As she rode him, he captured a nipple in his mouth.

His teeth grazed and teased while his tongue laved and lapped at it. Her rhythm grew faster as the pleasure built inside her. Teague switched nipples and bit down hard. She moaned and slammed down on him as a wave of pleasure washed over her.

She clenched and convulsed around him. She was blind and deaf to everything but the pleasure that had taken control of her body. As if in a cloud, she heard him shout her name and grab her hips to thrust in deeply. That thrust started her pleasure all over again. Stars danced in front of her eyes as she felt him spill his seed inside her.

Madeline fell forward to land on his chest. His big arms closed around her. She snuggled into him and clutched his shoulders.

"Hell, Maddie, you sure are good at this for a first-time rider."

She chuckled against his skin. "I'm only as good as my teacher."

"Oh, darlin', that's not true. You are passion come to life. All I did was wake it up."

Madeline didn't know if that was true or not, but it made

her feel ten feet tall. He thought she was passion. Her. The Black Widow. The Spinster of Brewster House. Madeline "Too Tall" Brewster.

"Thank you."

"You're welcome. You know, Eppie is a very protective friend."

Madeline sat up and swayed at the sudden movement. He caught her shoulders, and his eyes were full of concern.

"You okay?"

She nodded. "Eppie is a very good friend. She doesn't know anything about our . . . arrangement, and she won't ever know."

His thumbs caressed her skin. "You inspire people, Maddie."

Madeline realized he was still inside her, and he was still hard. She tightened around him, and his eyes widened.

"You're playing with fire, you know."

She grinned. "I am an eager pupil. I love to learn."

In a blink, she was lying on the narrow cot with Teague above her. He slowly slid in and out, gentleness replaced by the fevered dance from their first joining.

As the sun sank into the horizon, Teague and Madeline explored each other's bodies again until they were both too tired to move.

Madeline was spooned up against Teague, sated and exhausted. Twinges of sore muscles dotted her body. One big arm curled over her waist, and he was lightly snoring in her ear.

This was bliss. Complete and utter bliss. Madeline explored his hand as he slept. His fingers were long with blunt ends, the nails clipped. Small patches of dark hair sat on the skin between the knuckles. Calluses upon calluses were thick on his fingers and hands. He was so different from any man she'd ever known.

Was that the appeal? Was that what drew her to him? Perhaps initially, but that wasn't all of it. There was more. Now her heart was involved.

She had lied to Eppie. She would be heartbroken when he

left. No doubt about it. But it was worth it. More than worth it.

Being with Teague was the best thing that had ever happened to her.

With a sigh, Madeline slipped out of bed and dressed quickly. She kissed him on the brow and then left the carriage house.

Eppie scowled at her when she entered the kitchen. She knew her hair looked mussed, and her lips were no doubt as red as her cheeks.

"I sure hope you don't catch yourself a baby."

Eppie's words dropped like a stone in a dry well.

Baby?

The thought had never entered her mind. First and foremost because, at thirty-two, she figured she was too old to have a baby. But even if she did "catch" a baby, she was more than prepared to love and raise a child. Especially one made with Teague.

"I'm too old, Eppie. Don't be worrying about it."

Eppie shrugged and went back to stirring a pot on the stove. "Miss Merriweather came by to drop off a pie for you."

Madeline spotted the apple pie on the counter and smiled. "She didn't have to do that."

"She wanted to say thank you kindly for what you did for her after her brother died. No one thought she could manage the store on her own, but you helped her prove them wrong."

Candice Merriweather was a spinster like herself, only about five years older. She had run the general store in town with her brother until he'd died six months ago. The reverend and the sheriff had put pressure on her to sell the store and live off the proceeds.

Madeline had known Candice since they were children and had felt it her duty to assist her. So she had. She taught Candice how to balance books, how to contact suppliers, and how to negotiate the freight and price with wagon haulers.

Every week since, Candice had sent a pie to Madeline. She was truly a good friend, and a visit was long overdue.

"What did you tell her?"

Eppie smirked. "I told her you weren't here but thanked her for you."

"Thank you, Eppie."

She walked past her with her head held high and then ran up the stairs to the bathing room. She smelled like Teague and hot, joyful sex. Eppie surely had smelled it, and no doubt anyone else would, too.

Teague woke up alone. He could still feel her next to him. He pressed his nose into the pillow and breathed in her scent. Madeline was getting under his skin. He tried desperately to stop it, but each time they were together, whether in bed or not, it got worse.

He recognized the symptoms. He'd had them once before, with Claire. It seemed like a hundred years ago. He didn't remember it being as intense as this, though. This need to be with her, protect her, and touch her.

His cock twitched to life, and he groaned. Not again today. He wouldn't be able to walk tomorrow. He washed up quickly and put on his clean clothes. Grabbing the soiled ones, he walked down the stairs, ready to wash them himself. Because, sure as hell, Eppie wasn't going to do it.

Teague didn't expect it. The beating, that is. It was dark, and his senses were still full of Madeline. He was blindsided with a block of wood across his head. Two men then proceeded to beat the ever-loving shit out of him. He couldn't get his bearings, and blood was dripping into his right eye.

He tried to fight back, but it was no use. He was dizzy and weak from the blow to the head. With a final fist to his stomach, he dropped to the dusty ground.

"You do what you're being paid to do, drifter. Stop fucking the bitch and find out the information we need."

Teague groaned and tried to rise. One boot slammed into his chest, and he fell back.

"You understand, boy?"

He recognized the voice. That bastard Jackson Webster, sheriff of his own domain. Teague didn't answer, not that he thought he could. His mouth was full of blood and a few loose teeth, not to mention the dirt they'd kicked in there.

"You were hired to find information. Find it."

That bastard kicked him in the balls with what felt like lead shoes. The pain was excruciating, and he was glad when he blacked out.

Chapter Eleven

It was Wednesday, and that meant she was at the bank all day. Madeline stared across her desk at Horace Bindle. He had come into the bank to ask for an extension on his mortgage payment and was currently telling her why he needed that extension.

She tried, truly she did, to focus on what Horace was saying. He was an older man with frizzy gray hair, a heavily creased face, and bright blue eyes that blazed when he was excited about something. He had a small farm just outside town and provided fresh vegetables, fruit, eggs, and milk to Merriweather's Store.

Try as she might, Madeline's body had other ideas about what she should think about. She found herself envisioning Teague lying on his bed, naked, waiting for her. All sorts of interesting ideas on what to do with him swirled and whirled until she actually found herself wiggling—*wiggling!*—on her chair.

"Miss Brewster? Are you all right? You look mighty flushed all the sudden."

Madeline smiled as best she could at Horace. She flushed even brighter, this time with embarrassment instead of arousal.

"I am feeling a bit warm. Summer is coming quickly, isn't it?"

"That it is," he said as he nodded sagely.

"I will give you an extra week on your payment, Horace, but no longer. I've already extended you three weeks. This will make it a month, and that is the most we can offer." Madeline tried to keep her head on bank business.

Horace thanked her profusely, shook her hand with his knurled, clammy one, and then left the bank. She stared at the pile of paperwork in front of her and pinched herself on the arm. No more daydreaming.

Two hours later, Madeline was ready for the midday meal. She glanced at Mr. Cleeson and found him staring at her. She nodded and stood. When she started walking toward him, she saw him slide the papers on his desk into his top drawer.

How odd.

"Mr. Cleeson, I'm going to walk home for dinner. I should be back within the hour."

He nodded, his flyaway blond hair waving in the wind.

"Make sure Mamie and Bernard have sufficient funds in their till."

"Yes, ma'am."

"Mr. Cleeson, is anything wrong?" Her warning bells were tinkling, and her sense of danger, although not keen, was sniffing like a bloodhound again.

"No, Miss Brewster. That young lady I told you about . . . well, I asked her to marry me, and now I've got to ask her pa. I was checking my bank balance and making sure I could support her and a family." His Adam's apple bobbed up and down when he swallowed.

"Well, good luck with that, then." Madeline took her reticule from her desk and left the bank. She was amazed to find several people saying hello to her—people who *never* talked to her or would probably not bother to spit on her if she were on fire.

Jackson Webster stood outside the sheriff's office on the other side of the road. He spotted her and hurried over, narrowly missing a wagon loaded with lumber. She kept walking at her brisk pace, hoping to lose him before she reached home.

No such luck.

"Madeline!" he called.

She was only six feet away and couldn't pretend she didn't hear him. Especially because two women walking the other direction looked at both of them.

She turned and looked at Jackson. "Yes, Sheriff?"

"I hear your horse thief got himself in trouble last night down at the saloon."

Madeline swallowed the lump that rose in her throat. Teague had not come to supper, and she hadn't gone looking for him.

"Is that so?" she inquired as politely as she could.

"Pretty banged up. I hear he had to be thrown out on his ass—pardon me, on his rear end."

She nodded. "Spirits will drive any man to act like an animal."

He grimaced. "What's it going to take to convince you that man is a criminal and all he needs is a neck stretching?"

"Nothing will convince me of that."

She turned, angry and scared, and walked away from him. She was startled when he yanked her arm. He stared into her face, and Madeline knew a moment of fear. Deep in his eyes she saw anger, greed, and something that looked like excitement. That scared her most of all.

"You best keep your legs closed from here on out, Madeline. The whole town is going to know about it soon. He is not a man to be trusted or to be taken to your bed."

Madeline gasped and wrenched her arm free.

"Keep your filthy mind and hands to yourself, Jackson Webster. You are no longer welcome in my house."

She heard the two women watching them titter and whisper under their breaths. They'd certainly gotten an eyeful to share with the gossips in town.

Pleasantly surprised by how good it had felt to tell Jackson that, Madeline continued walking home. By the time she got there, she was shaking like a leaf. Someone knew she and Teague had been together. That someone had told Jackson and God only knew who else.

Clutching her stomach, she went into the house.

Eppie was ripping old sheets into strips—into *bandages*—in the kitchen. She looked at Madeline with pity and anger.

"Someone beat the tar out of your man, Madeline."

It was true! Jackson had told her he had been at the saloon, but she hadn't really wanted to believe it.

"I found him on the floor this morning, bleeding like a stuck pig. Isaiah helped me get him up outta the dirt so I could nurse his wounds."

"Where is he?" She had to see him. Now.

"In the carriage-house loft. He don't look too nice, now, so don't you get yourself in a tizzy." Eppie sounded like her mother rather than her friend sometimes.

"I don't need another speech. I need a friend."

Eppie nodded and grasped her hands. "I'm sorry. I just cain't rightly believe someone did this right under our noses!"

"What do you mean?" Her heart was pounding in tune with her head, and she clutched Eppie's hands tightly. "The gossips say he was stirring up trouble in the saloon last night."

Eppie scoffed. "He was half dressed, wasn't even wearing shoes! And he had a pile of laundry with him. He wasn't anywhere but here. That man was ambushed."

Teague felt like a dozen horses had run over him. There wasn't a spot on his body that didn't ache, throb, or pound. He was pitiful, and he knew it. Thank God Eppie had found him.

He didn't want to be beholden to that little curmudgeon, but the truth was, he owed her. She'd spent most of the day doctoring him, bringing him broth and water, changing his bandages, and making sure he was all right.

Who knew she could be such a good nurse? He thought she'd want to squash him flat if she could.

He heard the door open downstairs and footsteps running up. That wasn't Eppie.

Maddie.

Teague was mortified to find tears pricking his eyes. He hadn't even realized that he missed her, that he needed her, until he heard her footsteps. She flew into the room in a bright blue dress with her dark braid swinging and her dark eyes etched with concern. She ran over to him and knelt beside the bed.

"Oh, Teague," she said as a tear rolled down her cheek. "I'm so sorry this happened to you."

"Not your fault," he said through cracked, swollen lips.

"It happened on my property, and you are my . . . friend. It's my fault if I want it to be my fault."

She lightly touched his face, and the well of emotion he had tried so hard to ignore came rushing up like a volcano.

"I'm so sorry, Maddie."

She kissed his lips softly. "You have no reason to be sorry."

Tears trickled down the back of his throat as Teague struggled to tell her what he needed to say.

"Yes, I do. There are so many things I did. . . . Not good things, either. . . . Let me tell you what I did."

Madeline stood and pulled the chair over from the small table and sat next to the bed. She took his hand in hers and then brought it to her lips and kissed it.

Teague knew right then and there that he had fallen in love with Madeline. He hadn't meant to, and he sure as hell didn't deserve to, but there it was. All he could do now was pray she could forgive him and try to make it right with her.

"I fought for the Union in the war. I didn't want to go and leave Claire and Christopher, but I had to. I was gone for two years. Two of the most hellish years of my life. I had to walk most of the way back from Virginia to Missouri. When I finally made it back"—he swallowed hard—"I found them both dead.

Killed by bushwhackers or something. They had hung my five-year-old son and raped my wife until she bled to death."

Madeline's hand tightened on his, and he could hear her quietly crying for him. He couldn't look at her yet.

"I just walked away. There was no way I was going to be a dirt farmer on the land that held the blood of my wife and child. I wandered for years. Took jobs when I needed money. I didn't care about anything or anybody, Maddie. I would do anything, *anything* for a buck.

"I drove dynamite up to the mines—hell, even mined for copper for a few years. I did all the jobs most men wouldn't dare do because they could get killed. That's why I did them, though. I didn't want to live, but God apparently wanted me to."

He stared up at the wooden roof and took a deep breath for what he was about to say.

"The night before you rescued me, I'd tied one on and had to walk back to the ranch I was working at. I found this damn old horse wandering, and I took him because my feet were tired. That fool sheriff found me and charged me with horse thieving. When I was locked up in that prison cell, he came to me with a deal.

"I would agree to help him find information to ruin Madeline Brewster so the town could finally rid themselves of the Black Widow. In return, I got five hundred dollars and a free pass out of town."

The room was as silent as a tomb. Teague was afraid whatever Maddie felt for him had just died, so it was an appropriate atmosphere.

"What does that mean?" she whispered.

"I was supposed to try to compromise you, distract you, and find out what you do in this house with all the strangers you bring in. They seem to think it's a whorehouse and you are a madam. A rich madam that holds the town in her tight fist, squeezing as much blood out of it as you can."

Her head dropped to her knees, but he held on to her hand. It felt clammy and cold.

"Sweet Jesus."

"I'm so sorry, Maddie. I didn't know you when I made this deal. The last two weeks were amazing and . . ."

"Stop. Just stop talking."

She stood and walked to the window, her arms wrapped around her waist.

"I'm sorry, Maddie."

She didn't answer. With a jolt of pain that nearly made him black out, Teague rose and limped over to her. He swayed and grabbed the wall beside the window to stand upright.

He forced her to look at him. The naked agony in her beautiful dark eyes undid him. A sob worked its way up his throat, and he wrapped her in his arms. She was stiff and un-yielding.

"Please, Maddie. I want to make this right."

"You told them." She hissed.

"Told them what?"

"Told them about us. How else would Jackson know you'd been in my bed?" She pushed away from him, and he stumbled into the wall.

"I didn't tell them anything. Why do you think they beat me?"

"I don't know. Maybe you weren't moving fast enough for them. Fuck her faster, Teague. Get rid of the old bitch!"

She turned to flee, and he grabbed her arm. She fought against him, but, even injured, he hung on to her until she stopped struggling. He pulled her back against his chest and waited. It started as small hiccups but turned into gut-wrenching sobs. He held on to her and murmured soothing words in her ear.

Teague had no idea how long they stood there before her storm was over. She sniffled and tried to wipe her tears with her hand.

"We'll stop them, Maddie."

She shook her head. "I think it's too late."

"What do you mean?"

"I think the plans are already in place, and they started at the bank."

Her dark eyes were full of pain and misery. Most of which he had put there. He had failed miserably for Claire and Christopher. He vowed right then to make it right for Madeline. Even if it killed him.

Madeline wept until she couldn't weep anymore. Her mind and body were numb, but her heart, oh, her cursed heart was howling like a coyote at a full moon. Howling in pain and misery.

"Who did this?" she asked.

"The sheriff and that fool judge. There are a couple more, too, but I believe those two are the brains behind the plan."

Madeline stepped away from him and finally looked him in the eye. Then felt like crying all over again. Teague's battered face was awash in as much pain as hers. She couldn't trust it was real. What she really couldn't trust was her heart. So she had to think with her head.

"I don't trust you anymore, Teague. I hope you understand why."

He nodded, his jaw clenched tight.

"I want to find out what they're planning. Are you willing to help me?"

"Yes" gushed out of him before she even stopped speaking.

"If this happens, whatever they're planning, I will probably lose everything I have."

She had to face that. Obviously being an independent woman was more than a town full of men could take. A woman with money owning half the town was worse. Leaving her home behind would be hard, but it would be the people she helped who would suffer the most. She shuddered to think what would happen to Eppie. Fact is, most didn't like Eppie. Her outspokenness was one of the very reasons Madeline loved her.

Madeline wasn't going to roll over and die. She was going to fight.

"Do you have a plan?"

"Maybe. If we feed them false information, perhaps it will come around on them."

He touched his split lip. "It might work."

"What kind of information were you supposed to find?"

He sighed and shuffled back to the bed. "Evidence of you squandering money, using it for improper stuff, hording cash here at your house, giving it away to people. Anything odd or eccentric, particularly about money."

"They want to prove me insane." Madeline was getting angrier. "I am one of the sanest people in this town."

"That's the truth. Plum Creek is full of crazies."

Madeline sat down next to him heavily. "You broke my heart, Teague."

"I know. I'm sorry, Maddie. I can't tell you how much."

She bit her lip to keep in any tears. No more crying. "Was it all part of the plan?"

"What?"

"The lessons," she swallowed. "Was it part of the plan?"

"Oh, Jesus, no." He folded her in a hug and rocked back and forth. Madeline cautioned herself against trusting him again, although his arms felt like heaven. They felt so safe and warm.

"I want to believe you, but . . ."

"I understand. I can't even begin to tell you how sorry I am that I found that stupid horse."

"I'm not. Even if my world crashed down around me, the last two weeks were the most alive I have *ever* been in my life. I wouldn't trade it for anything," Madeline confessed.

Teague kissed her forehead. "You'd best get back to the

bank, Maddie. You don't want to give them any more ammunition to shoot you with."

Madeline stood and left the carriage house without another word to Teague. She had to wash her face and try to look as if she hadn't just had her heart broken and her life torn asunder.

Madeline had to get ready for battle.

Chapter Twelve

Madeline used a cold rag on her eyes to bring the swelling down before heading back to the bank. She forced herself to smile and say hello to people, although all she could think of was that they hated her. They wanted her gone by any means necessary.

Her heart wasn't just broken from Teague's part in this. It was also hurting from the town's betrayal. A town she had lived in all her life, contributed to, where she had worked on Founder's Day celebrations and attended Fourth of July picnics. She also helped those in need and did everything she could. It was all for naught.

Madeline was going to be as vicious and grabbing as they were. No more free room and board, no more donations or extensions on loans. They would get what they gave to her. Nothing.

She made it back to the bank about half an hour late. Mr. Cleeson was deep in discussion with Judge Martin, whose jowls were swinging madly as he spoke under his breath to the young clerk.

That answered her suspicions about Mr. Cleeson immediately. Whatever was going on involved him. She couldn't let him know she was aware of his perfidy. She pasted on a smile and walked over to his desk.

"Good afternoon, Earl. What brings you to the bank today?"

The judge looked a bit flustered and fiddled with the chain on his watch while his eyes darted from her face to Mr. Cleeson's.

"Just chatting with the young man here about this and that."

Madeline nodded. "Is there anything I can help you with?"

He held up one pudgy hand and shook his head. "Oh, no, I don't need anything. Thank you for the offer, though. I need to get back to my office."

He tipped his hat to her and scuttled away like the insect he was. Madeline turned to Mr. Cleeson and kept the smile firmly in place. It was amazing what anger and fury could do to your self-control. In her case, it made it rock hard.

"I am sorry I'm a little late. A minor problem at home. How did everything go while I was gone?" She slipped off her gloves and watched his reaction. His little eyes narrowed just a smidge, as if he were grinning inside. She'd like to knock that grin into next week.

"Just fine, Miss Brewster. No problems at all."

"That's good. Thank you, Mr. Cleeson." She turned to walk back to her desk. "Oh, I gave Horace Bindle a one-week extension on his mortgage payment. Please be sure to record that in his record."

"Yes, ma'am."

Madeline made a mental note to check Mr. Bindle's record the next day to see if her suspicions were correct. She had a sinking feeling that all the transactions she requested recorded were never done. All the loans, extensions, and payments she handled were likely in her head.

When she got to her desk, she took out paper and started writing down all she could remember, beginning with that morning and working her way back.

After two hours, she had five sheets and approximately two months' worth of information. There were definitely some holes, but luckily Madeline had an analytical mind, and her memory for numbers was astounding—likely the only reason her father allowed her to be involved in the bank.

The tellers had all gone home, and Mr. Cleeson was the only one left. He kept sneaking glances at her as she wrote, probably wondering what she was doing. She ignored him until he shuffled out the door at four o'clock. After he left, she took out more paper and made a copy of all her notes. She put the copy in an envelope and sealed it. The original went in her desk to see if it would disappear.

She stared at the envelope and tried to decide if there was anyone in town she trusted enough to keep the envelope safe. The fact that she had to think about it just reinforced the fact that she was alone.

Alone again. She had Eppie, but she was a friend and a stranger to the town.

Candice Merriweather might be a good choice, but the crazy thing was, Madeline didn't know if Candice was in on the plan, too. She had no choice but to send the envelope out of town . . . but, no, that wouldn't work, either. No doubt someone watched the mail as well.

Madeline stood, feeling paranoid and alone. There was one person who could help her feel better, and he had broken her heart. The sad fact was she didn't care. She needed him.

Taking the envelope in hand, she extinguished the gas lamps, locked up the bank, and then headed home.

As she was passing the store, Candice came out and flagged her down. Madeline really didn't want to talk to anyone, but she didn't want to be rude. Besides, she needed to keep up the front of being a stupid old spinster who let a town bully her, take her money, and send her to some hospital in Denver.

"Madeline! Oh, it's so good to see you. Please come inside for a few minutes."

Madeline embraced the smaller woman briefly. Candice was a plump redhead with sparkling green eyes and apple cheeks.

She never had a bad word for anyone, and most of the town respected and liked her.

"Hello, Candice. Thanks for the pie—you know you don't have to do that."

"Pshaw! Of course I do! Without you I wouldn't even have this store anymore."

"I didn't do that much." Madeline was embarrassed each time she brought it up.

The store was empty except for the two of them. Madeline had always loved her trips to the store as a child because her mother always let her get a peppermint stick. The store was stocked neatly with sundries, food stuffs, bolts of cloth, canned goods, and other things like books and farm tools. Candice catered to her customers and knew it was important to have on hand the goods they wanted.

She brought Maddie to the back of the store to a small office and sat her down in the chair next to the desk. There were lots of papers on that small wooden desk, but they were all neatly stacked and looked to be in order.

"Tell me how it's going with this horse thief you brought into your house. You need to stop taking in strays." She chuckled.

Madeline shrugged. "He's a good worker, very polite, and always does whatever I ask him to do. I don't think he's a horse thief, by the way. That is Jackson and the judge's supposition, but the evidence doesn't support it."

"You should have been a judge or an attorney. You even speak like one!"

Madeline felt her cheeks redden. Candice couldn't possibly have known she'd asked her father when she was fourteen if she could be an attorney, and he had laughed. He'd laughed like he'd never heard anything so funny in his life. She'd never brought it up again.

"I have enough to do with all the businesses in town."

Candice nodded. "Very true. I don't know how you manage so many when I struggle to manage just one."

"I have help, Candice. My attorney, Mr. Finley, is invaluable in that regard."

"He's also single. I was wondering if perhaps you could introduce us at the next church social."

Madeline agreed but neglected to mention to Candice that she hadn't gone to a church social in years. The reverend made it clear Eppie wasn't welcome, so Madeline didn't go.

"Is he handsome?"

"Who?"

"Your horse thief!"

Madeline sighed. "He's not a horse thief, Candice. Yes, he is handsome and very big, too. I'm sure you must have seen him in town. I hear tell he was at the saloon last night."

Candice tapped her cheek with one finger as if thinking. "I don't believe I've seen him. I wasn't at the saloon, though. What does he look like?"

"Tall, dark hair, blue eyes. About the same height as Mr. Hansen, but a bit broader."

Candice's green eyes widened. "He's a big man, then. Are you sure you're safe?"

Madeline smiled. "Oh, I'm safe. He wouldn't ever hurt me. Mr. O'Neal is a gentleman. Although I think he likes to eavesdrop." Here was the information she wanted to give to see if it came back around full circle to her through Teague.

"Eavesdrop?"

"Mmmm. I caught him a few times. I told him to stop doing it." She shrugged. "I don't know if it worked or not. I guess he's just very nosy."

"That's odd for a man."

"Yes, well, he is an unusual man."

After a bit more chatter, Madeline finally excused herself and left the store. The jingle of the bell scraped on her raw nerves as she turned to say good-bye to Candice. She could see Jackson out of the corner of her eye across the street watching her. She ignored the sorry bastard and headed home.

* * *

Madeline found Teague waiting for her on the front porch again. Tears pricked her eyes as her emotions rolled around inside her, and she started shaking. How did he know she needed him?

He must have spotted something on her face or in her eyes because he immediately hopped up out of the porch swing with a groan and met her on the stairs. Without a word, he led her inside to her mother's sitting room, sat on the sofa, and pulled her onto his lap.

He held her tightly until she stopped shaking. She touched his bruised face and thanked God he was there.

"You made it through the first afternoon."

"I don't know who to trust, Teague. I feel like the whole town is watching me, making notes on everything I do or say. I even thought my friend Candice was part of it."

Teague's big hand stroked up and down her back. "What did you decide to do?"

Madeline sat up and slid off his lap. She took a deep breath and launched into the first stage of *her* plan.

"I told her I caught you eavesdropping. What I want you to do is go to the sheriff with another piece of false information. If he tells you you've been spotted eavesdropping here, I'll know Candice is a part of it."

He looked into her eyes and frowned. "And what do I tell him?"

"Tell him I have a collection of clothes and jewelry that's hidden in a closet in the house. Thousands of dollars' worth."

One dark eyebrow rose. "Why?"

"I have a feeling they are going to make money go missing from the bank and try to blame me. If you give them that information, they'll have a claim to substantiate their false accusations."

Teague frowned. "Why would you want them to think you stole money from the bank?"

"So I can catch them in their own trap."

*   *   *

Teague didn't like it, but he couldn't talk her out of it. Madeline was determined to smear herself in the town's eyes. She had started with her friend Candice, and now with him. By the end of next week, she should be a thieving floozy with illegal slaves and an opium habit.

With a grimace, he stepped out of the carriage house the following morning and walked into town to the sheriff's office. Coming around the back door, he was surprised to find the sheriff buried in a woman. And that woman was not Matilda Webster. She was a young saloon girl with curly black hair, a bright yellow petticoat, and long legs. At least, that's what he could see of her, he thought with a smirk.

"Ahem."

The sheriff ignored him, so Teague leaned against the side of the building and waited. It was noisy, but it was over in a minute. With a final thrust, Webster finished up with his saloon girl. When she pulled her skirt down, Teague was disappointed to see that she was young. Too young to be whoring her way through life. She glanced at Teague with sad brown eyes, took the money from the sheriff, and scooted off down the alley.

The sheriff fixed up his clothes and straightened his tie before turning to Teague. His hat hung on a hook beside the door. He slapped it on his head and leaned against the building beside Teague. His blue eyes were as sharp as any hunting knife.

"You interrupt me for a reason?"

"I came to tell you I got your message."

The sheriff's mouth kicked up in one corner. "I can see that. You look like a bull ran over you. Twice."

Teague knew he was still bruised and swollen, but it was nothing compared to the wounds he had inflicted on his woman.

Maddie.

"When Miss Brewster was at the bank yesterday, I did some looking. That young girl was out picking in the garden, so I snuck inside."

Webster's interest was piqued. He stood up straighter and leaned into Teague. His eyes were hungry, and he licked his lips.

"What did you find?"

"Now, let me start by saying I think Miss Brewster is a nice lady, and she's been right kind to me."

"Who gives a fuck? Tell me what you found!" A bit of spittle flew from the sheriff's mouth to land on his arm. It was all Teague could do not to scrape it off and fling it back at him.

"A closet with things in it."

"What kind of things?"

Teague screwed up his face like he was remembering. "Fancy stuff like sparkly dresses. Lots of those. Some of them looked like they even had real jewels in them. There was a box of jewelry, too. Some big diamonds, rubies, and some kind of stone that sparkled like rainbows."

"Opals?"

"I guess. I don't know what you call them."

Webster smiled broadly. "Anything else in that closet?"

"Lots of papers. I didn't know what they were. And shoes. High-heeled shoes that were all sparkly and had gewgaws on them, too."

Webster slapped his hand on his knee. "I knew it. She's been skimming his money since he died, buying herself all kinds of stuff with the town's money. I knew it!" he crowed.

"I gotta get back before they figure out I'm not there."

Webster shrugged. "Good. You do that."

Teague wanted to smash this man into a stain on the dirt. His hands actually clenched into fists. Webster must have seen something in his face, because he backed up a step and put his hand on his six-gun.

"You remember who can hang you in the blink of an eye.

You get me more information like this, and you can go back to the hole you crawled out of."

Teague nodded, his jaw clenched so tight it popped. He turned to leave, when the sheriff called him back.

"Hey, drifter."

"What?"

"Don't make me remind you again that your life is in my hands."

Teague ignored him and walked away. He could envision the bullet slamming into his back and almost wished for it. Back shooting a man was a crime the sheriff couldn't cover up. But nothing happened.

When he got to the street, he let out a breath all the way from his toes. He had planted the first seed of information in Madeline's crazy garden.

Madeline couldn't help but think everyone was watching her. From the moment she sat down at the desk and realized her list of transactions was indeed missing, she could actually feel eyes on her. She was thankful to have made a copy of the list, which now sat in her reticule that she kept with her all the time.

It was like a colony of bugs had taken up residence on her skin and spent the day crawling up and down. She had to stop herself twice from scratching at them.

She wondered if Teague had met with the sheriff. She wondered if the sheriff had believed him. She also wondered if the information she gave Candice had made it back to Teague.

Too many questions, too many *unanswered* questions. She was driving herself insane with them. She thought about what her father would do in a situation like this.

Well, first of all, he wouldn't be in that situation. But if he were, he'd go on the offensive and not wait for whatever weapons they had to surprise him.

"That's it!" she shouted.

Everyone in the bank turned to look at her. She would have

heard a pin drop if she had one. Fighting back excruciating embarrassment, she pretended to have discovered a missing clerical error in her paperwork. After two very long, incredibly long, minutes, everyone began whispering and shooting furtive glances at her behind her big oak desk.

Inside, she was gleeful. Madeline had a plan.

Chapter Thirteen

Teague did not join her for dinner that night. He might have been meeting with the sheriff. She didn't want to even think about what he might be doing besides that. She hoped he was still recovering from the beating. The gaping wound in her heart was still fresh from his betrayal. Deep down, she still wanted to believe he had feelings for her. God knew she still loved him with every fiber of her being.

After a lonely dinner of potato soup, Eppie ate in the kitchen with Isaiah, and Madeline went upstairs early with a book. It was a new dime-store novel she had been itching to read, *The Marshall's Misdeeds*. The story sounded promising, and she loved a good yarn about a lawman.

She took a long soaking bath and read her book, smiling and trying to keep her mood light. She tried, Lord knew she tried, to *not* think about Teague, but it was hard.

She remembered the last time he was in the bathing room with her, and her temperature started to rise. As the book dropped down to the floor, her hands crept to her breasts, circling the nipples until they peaked. As her fantasy continued in her head, a knock sounded at the door.

Madeline grimaced at the closed door.

"Yes, who is it?"

"It's me, Maddie. Can I come in?"

Teague's voice sent shivers up her spine. She was angry

with him, yet still aroused by the very thought of him. Her pride won out over her hunger.

"No. I don't want to talk to you right now. I'm trying to relax."

Silence met her petulant-sounding response. She hadn't *meant* to sound petulant—she'd meant to sound assertive. So much for her pride. It was her body. The thought of him excited her, and her body was fighting with her mind over possession.

"Please, Maddie."

Why did he have to go and sound so sincere? Now she wanted to fling open the door and throw herself in his arms. Her will reasserted itself.

"I said no. You can wait until after my bath."

Madeline heard his booted footsteps trail back down the hallway. A mixture of disappointment and triumph swirled through her. Was she hoping he'd insist? Or break down the door like a man come to claim his lady?

She snorted. This wasn't a fairy tale, and there likely was not going to be a happy ending. Her bath was over, thanks to Teague's interruption. She just couldn't enjoy it anymore. She let the water out and dried off quickly with a fluffy towel, ignoring the twinges of pleasure when the cotton rubbed against her nipples. "You're going to start believing those stories soon yourself," she whispered.

She yanked on her nightdress and robe and then took the towel and brush to her room. Stomping in, she threw them on the chair by the fireplace. When she turned and saw Teague lying on her bed with his hands laced behind his head, she yelped and jumped nearly a foot off the ground.

"What are you doing here?"

"Waiting for you. You said after your bath, so I decided to wait here."

Madeline's heart leaped at the sight of him. He was wearing his faded blue shirt with the sleeves rolled up and tight brown trousers again. The chest hair she loved to touch peeked out the top of the shirt. His tanned, beautiful arms flexed as he moved. And his pants, they left nothing to the imagination—she could clearly see, and remember, just how big he really was.

Her body instantly heated at least ten degrees. She was thankful she was wearing a bathrobe so he couldn't see how hard her nipples really were or how wet her pussy was. He could likely see her face flush.

"You didn't ask permission. I haven't forgiven you, Teague. Get out."

He smiled, and she felt her knees wobble. Lord above, he had a beautiful smile.

"I wanted to be there when you got home, but Eppie sent me on ten different errands."

Sounded like Eppie. Anything to keep Madeline away from Teague, and vice versa.

"You weren't there for dinner."

She wanted to bite her tongue when that slipped out.

"I know. I missed you, Maddie."

She sniffed. "Get out."

"No."

Madeline's mouth dropped open. "No?"

He got up and walked toward her. She couldn't stop the involuntary shudder that racked her body. He reminded her of a predator stalking its prey.

"I mean it, Teague. Get out." He stopped two inches from her, and she breathed in deep. Big mistake. Not only could she feel his body heat, but she took his scent into her body. A body already aching for his. "I'm paying you, remember? That means I'm your employer, and you . . . you have to listen to me."

Why did she sound like such an idiot?

He grinned, and her resolve crumbled a bit more. "You haven't paid me yet."

"But you agreed to it."

He reached out one finger and trailed it down her cheek. Her eyes closed, and she swayed toward him.

"Don't deny me, Maddie. Your body wants me. I can smell you."

She didn't, couldn't, say a word. It was true.

"Tell me to leave again." His hand trailed to her collarbone and pushed the robe off her shoulder. "Or tell me you're ready for lesson five."

Oh, Sweet Mary, help me.

"I . . . I want you to . . ."

"Yes?"

He kissed her ear, and Madeline felt the scrape of his whiskers on her tender skin.

"Tell me, Maddie," he whispered, and she groaned, throwing her arms around his neck.

He pulled her against him, and she was lost in the feeling of his hard body. His mouth captured hers, and together their tongues dueled and slid in a mating dance. Her robe slipped completely off and fell to the ground. Teague's deft hand slid the shoulders of the nightgown down slowly. His lips followed the path of the cotton.

Kiss. Lick. Kiss. Lick.

"Is this lesson five?" she asked breathlessly.

He grinned against her skin. "Not yet, but we're getting there."

Teague scooped her up, carried her to the bed, and then set her down on the edge as if she were made of china, not flesh and blood.

"Take it off for me, Maddie."

She pulled her nightgown off and threw it on the floor. His eyes roamed from the top of her head to her feet.

"Beautiful."

She tried to cover herself with her hands. He kneeled on the floor in front of her and pulled her hands away.

"You're blind."

"No, I'm not."

"I'm not a small, pretty little thing. I am as big as a man."

Teague grinned and ran his hands up and down her legs. "You are the right size for me, Maddie. I'd be afraid I'd break a little woman."

She didn't believe him. Well, not completely, but she was warmed by his sincerity. He meant it. She could see it in the depths of his blue eyes, the eyes that were devouring her even as her skin heated.

"Now comes lesson five. Are you ready?"

She nodded, unsure what he could teach her that he hadn't already. Medical textbooks never went past lesson three. He gently pushed her back on the bed until her legs dangled off the side. She swallowed as he spread her legs wide.

"Teague?"

"Shhhh, Maddie. Just feel. No more talking. Just feel."

His roughened hands delicately skimmed up her legs, followed by his mouth. He paid special attention to the skin behind her knees, kissing and caressing until she felt wet with need between her legs.

His thumbs circled and teased as his mouth made love to her skin. Kissing, nibbling, and licking as he traveled the path up to her pulsing core. She didn't know what he was going to do, but she had an idea it involved his mouth. The very thought of that made her even wetter.

When he reached her upper thighs, he blew lightly on her hot skin. She clenched and nearly jumped off the bed. The combination of hot and cool was intoxicating.

"You are beautiful, Maddie." His thumbs opened her nether lips as he blew again on her. "Lesson five."

She closed her eyes as he descended on her pussy. His tongue circled her with the lightest butterfly touch all around the edges to the middle. He put one thumb inside her while he gently laved her.

Never, *never* had she known this existed. This incredibly sensual experience that she would have missed had it not been for a stupid old horse that had wandered.

Teague.

He nibbled at her core, and his thumb began to move in and out of her. He licked her over and over, faster and faster. In between licks were bites and sucks. She moved her hips in rhythm with his thumb without even thinking about it.

Her body wanted him. It wanted release. It wanted more.

Teague.

His rhythm grew to a crescendo as her body pulsed beneath his talented mouth. Over and over, licking, sucking, biting at her until she felt a wall of pleasure building and building. Suddenly it crashed over her, pulling her down into a whirlpool of ecstasy. Her body clenched at his thumb as he sucked her pleasure button, prolonging her orgasm. Waves crashing over and over.

Amazing. Intense. Life-changing moment.

"Teague," she gasped as he lifted his head and smiled at her. "I love you," she blurted.

He looked as if she had hit him with a poleax. Stunned and stupefied. She cursed her runaway tongue and her impulsive behavior.

"Forget I said that."

He stood, still looking shocked. Madeline felt her cheeks heat with embarrassment as she tried to close her legs. One big hand stopped her.

He started unbuttoning his shirt. Maddie's heart leaped. His eyes bored into her. Without breaking eye contact, he shed his clothes completely.

The beauty of Teague's body struck Maddie again. Tanned skin stretched over well-defined muscles, topped by a sprinkling of dark hair everywhere—by a patch of dark hair that lovingly cupped his hardened staff and balls.

Teague.

Hers. He was *hers.*

He stepped closer to her. The quilt brushed against her behind as she scooted to make room for him on the bed. As he crawled up onto the bed, the heat from his body came at her like a summer breeze. She shivered and ached at once for him.

"Maddie," he whispered as his skin skimmed against hers. He reached her mouth with his and slammed his lips down on hers, kissing her until she was mindless.

She arched against him, reaching for him even as he slid into her wet, welcoming core.

Yes, oh, yes. That was it. Sweet God! That was *it.*

He sank inside her slowly, inch by inch, until he had buried himself to the hilt. She was full, fuller than she'd ever felt in her life, and not just inside her, but within her heart and soul.

After a moment, his breath gusted across her cheek, and he began to move. His rhythm was slow and measured, in and out, again and again. He kissed his way across her shoulders, up her neck, and then down the other side. One hand kneaded and tweaked her breast in time with his strokes.

Madeline's frustration was building. She wiggled beneath him, willing him to move faster. Deeper.

"Teague?"

"Hmmm?" he asked from her collarbone.

"Can you . . . uh, that is . . .?"

"Lesson six, Maddie. Tell me what you want."

Six? Moved past five already, apparently. Not that five wasn't the most incredible experience of her life.

"I don't know how."

He chuckled. "Yes, you do. Let it out, Maddie. *Tell me.*"

Madeline was silent, wrestling with her entire being. Against everything she'd been taught.

"Tell me."

Teague stopped moving completely inside her. She clawed at his back, but trying to get him to move was like trying to pull up an oak tree by hand. She grew desperate, needful. Finally she tossed her pride aside and went with her heart.

"Please, Teague, I need you. Deeper, faster."

He started plunging into her again, this time deeper. She clenched around him, pulling him in completely.

"Tell me."

"My breasts. I like it when you put your mouth on my breasts."

He immediately suckled her nipple, laving and nibbling at it while his hand tweaked and rolled the other. Her pleasure increased again.

"Yesssss," she hissed. "Oh, my God, Teague."

Although she had reached her peak already, her body was building up to another. Building so hard and so intensely she could hardly keep a breath in her lungs.

Teague's rhythm increased again. Madeline thrust against him, slamming her clit against his pelvic bone. Sensations battered her body as she coiled tighter and tighter around him.

Suddenly the world stopped for a moment as she reached her second peak. Pleasure radiated through her over and over. Teague bellowed her name as he thrust into her one last time, carrying her along on his journey.

His arms were shaking so badly he fell on top of her. After a minute, she realized she could hardly breathe, so she thumped his shoulder. He rolled off and landed on the bed next to her.

Madeline felt like one great big tingle. From top to bottom. Zings, shudders, and shivers raced up and down as if competing for which one could reach an area the quickest.

Teague was breathing hard and staring up at the ceiling. Madeline snuck a peek at him from under her lashes. He looked a bit dazed. She figured she did, too. She certainly felt dazed.

"You okay?" he asked.

"Yes, just . . ." She trailed off, unable to find the words.

"Me, too."

"About what I said . . ." she began.

"I don't think I can talk about that right now, Maddie."

Madeline felt her heart pinch. She couldn't tell from the tone of his voice if he was upset or simply overwhelmed.

"I talked to the sheriff."

Her ears perked up immediately. She sat up and looked at him, forcing herself not to stare down at his nakedness. "What happened?"

"I told him what you said about the closet full of clothes and jewels. He was drooling like a dog at dinnertime." Teague frowned as he met her eyes. His hand reached up and cupped her cheek. "Let's see if he takes your bait."

Madeline dressed in a plain blue dress to go to the bank the next morning for her usual hours. She fixed her hair in a stiff bun rather than her usual braid. She wore her clumpy black shoes and walked down to the bank with a stiff back.

A few whispers, titters, and turned heads met her. Interesting. A bit more gossip than usual. Most times people ignored her, but this . . . was different.

She clutched her reticule, and the crinkle of paper inside comforted her. She still had her list of ledger records. It was a start, but it wasn't enough. She had to collect more information about the sheriff, the judge, and whoever else they were working with.

The key was to ferret out who those individuals were. Obviously there was someone at the bank. Madeline would bet a million dollars it was Mr. Cleeson. His actions recently were suspicious already. Now that she knew someone was trying to ruin her, she would watch him like a hawk.

Madeline walked past the general store and waved at Candice inside. Candice waved back with a friendly smile. She would hate to think her friend was part of the town's conspiracy. She fervently hoped news of Teague's eavesdropping habit was not going to come back to her. She needed to be able to trust someone besides Teague and Eppie.

Madeline arrived at the bank and nodded to Mr. Cleeson, who was busily scribbling on a piece of paper on his desk. No doubt noting what she was wearing today, she thought with a wry grin.

She settled into her desk and glanced at the top of it, noticing things were just a bit different. The inkwell was on the left side, which wasn't possible, because she was right-handed. Someone was definitely rifling through her things. That just fueled her anger all the more. Time to fight.

The day passed with monotony abounding. There were the usual number of customers in the bank. At lunchtime, she went to Clara's restaurant and had ham and potatoes alone. No one spoke to her, but she did get quite a few pointed stares.

After eating, she went back to the bank and finished the afternoon, trying to ignore the people who were ignoring her.

"Mr. Cleeson?"

His squirrelly head popped up, and he scurried over to her desk.

"Yes, Miss Brewster?"

"What happened to yesterday's ledger entries? I know I wrote in several that seem to be missing."

Mr. Cleeson peered at the book and looked confused and then scratched his head. Madeline had to bite her lip to keep from laughing. He looked like a fool at a sideshow.

"I'm not sure what you mean, Miss Brewster. Why, I tallied those amounts myself against the deposit and withdrawal slips."

Madeline nodded. "Yes, I suppose you did. I swear I remember something different, though. I must be mistaken."

Mr. Cleeson nodded his head, greasy blond hair flopping with the movement. "Yes, ma'am."

"Thank you. That will be all."

He slithered back to his desk and stuck his nose back into the papers spread around him. Madeline took the deposit and withdrawal slips and wrote them in the ledger herself. Then made a copy of the ledger page and slipped it into her reticule.

There was money missing. The question was where was it going? She knew someone was going to pin the blame on her. No one was going to accuse her of stealing from her own bank while she had breath left in her body. No one.

* * *

Teague was at the back of the lot, at least five acres from the house, fixing the back fence when Judge Martin popped up in front of him. He nearly dropped the posthole digger on his foot. As it was, he knocked himself in the shin hard.

"What the hell are you doing? Trying to take a year off my life?"

The judge rubbed his belly with one pudgy hand. "Now, that's funny, boy, considering you was up on a horse three weeks ago fixing to lose all your lives."

Teague tightened his jaw. "What do you want?"

"I heard from Jackson that Miss Brewster has got a horde of goods in her house. Is that so?"

Teague nodded. "That's what I told him."

The judge leaned forward, and his watery eyes held nothing but malice.

"You'd best not be lying, or hanging will be the best thing to happen to you."

Teague straightened up and leaned toward the shorter man, angry and fed up with all this shit.

"Don't threaten me. I don't take kindly to it, and I told Webster that myself yesterday. I'm doing my job. You just need to keep your distance. I feel like a boy with two mothers trying to give me their teets."

The judge backed away with a frown. "You've got a smart mouth."

Teague slammed the post digger into the ground with enough force to make the posts shake in front of it. The judge jumped a good foot off and yelped like a little girl. Teague grinned deep inside.

"I've also got two big fists. So you best back off, fat man."

The judge backed up, stumbled over a gopher hole, and nearly fell on his considerable ass.

"You . . . you horse thief! You can't talk to me like that! Don't you know who I am?"

Teague raised one eyebrow. "Someone who thinks he can

force me. Believe me, fool, if you weren't paying me five hundred dollars, you couldn't make me budge an inch."

The judge's mouth opened and closed like a gasping fish. "Just remember where your place is." He tried to look officious as he said it. He smoothed the lapels down on his expensive-looking jacket and tugged on his vest, which probably hadn't moved in years.

"You just remember that you won't see or hear me coming."

"Don't you threaten me!"

"It's not a threat. It's a promise."

Madeline knew Matilda Webster was at her house by the fancy rig in front. Her servant, an elderly black man by the name of Orion, stood at the side in his fancy driving coat waiting for his mistress to need him. Madeline sighed long and hard about facing Matilda again so soon, but she was actually glad of it. Perhaps she could get some information from her.

"Good afternoon, Orion," Madeline said pleasantly as she reached the house.

"Good day, Miss Brewster," he replied. His smile was white and broad as he tipped his hat to her. Orion had worked for Matilda since she'd been born and was as polite and sweet as the day was long. Although he'd been freed seven years ago from true slavery, he had never truly escaped the bonds.

Madeline walked up the steps and into the house. Eppie was standing in the doorway to the kitchen with a hideous expression on her face and her arms crossed over her chest. She gestured to the parlor with a sharp jab and rolled her eyes dramatically.

Madeline smiled and mouthed, "It's okay," to her friend before she tugged off her gloves and entered the room.

Matilda was looking at the glass figurines on the mantel. Still perfect, still blond and beautiful in her forest-green day dress. She nearly knocked off the turtle when she noticed Madeline in the doorway. She jumped and tittered nervously.

"Oh, Madeline, I didn't hear you come in. I hope you don't

mind me stopping by to see you. Eppie was kind enough to allow me to wait in here."

Madeline nodded and walked toward the settee. As she sat, she gestured for her guest to do the same.

"You are always welcome in my home, Matilda. We've known each other for too long to stand on ceremony."

Take that! Madeline kept the smile on her face with effort.

Matilda had the grace to blush slightly. "I wanted to stop by to see how you were doing. I've been concerned about you and that . . . man being in the house alone."

"We're not in the house alone. Eppie is here, and another guest. Besides that, Mr. O'Neal sleeps in the carriage house."

Matilda waved her hand in dismissal. "Yes, but you're not married. None of you are, that is. It's just not proper."

"I haven't been concerned with proper for years. Now isn't any different."

Apparently her answer didn't surprise Matilda. She nodded and pursed her lips as though selecting her words carefully. Her eyes carefully surveyed Madeline's clothes. She had to bite her lip to keep the smile inside. Apparently the sheriff had shared his information with his wife.

"That's something I wanted to speak with you about."

"Oh, what is it?" Madeline sounded innocent to her own ears.

"Your, ah . . . clothing, Madeline. It doesn't fit the town's wealthiest resident. You must try to be more in fashion."

Madeline shrugged. "Clothing has never been one of my priorities."

"It should be. Your money is the backbone of this town. Your image reflects the town."

"What does it reflect now?"

Matilda grimaced. "It reflects a poor town. Madeline, please don't be offended, but you dress like a scullery maid, not a millionaire."

Now Madeline was getting angry. "How do you know how much money I have, Matilda?"

"Well, everyone knows how much money you have. It's no secret. Your father used to talk about how much money he had all the time."

Madeline was shocked but tried not to show it. "He most certainly did not."

"You may have been his hostess, Madeline, but while you were making sure all the hors d'oeuvres were arranged, he was boasting of his money. He loved to make everyone feel . . . beholden to him."

Matilda actually looked impassioned as she spoke. It was the first real emotion Madeline had ever seen from the petite blond.

"I'm sorry if it bothered you. I never heard him speak of it."

"I don't expect an apology, Madeline. I did hope that when he died you would bring the name Brewster back into the upper class of Plum Creek." She fiddled with her gloves as they lay on her lap. "I would be happy to help you select . . . more appropriate items from your wardrobe."

Madeline felt a little disoriented from the information about her father. She tried to focus on what Matilda was saying and mentally slapped herself.

"Most of my clothing is similar to this, Matilda. I'm afraid there isn't much of a choice."

Matilda looked unconvinced. "Are you certain? We could take a quick look."

Madeline was glad to hear the information Teague had planted in the sheriff's ear was already taking root. It meant she could put her plan to work and use their own greed against them.

"I don't think so, Matilda."

Matilda sighed. "Oh, Madeline, please. I just want to be your friend."

"I don't believe you have ever wanted to be my friend, today or any other day."

Matilda's blue eyes widened. "That's not very polite."

Madeline stood. "Neither is coming to my house, telling me my clothes are shameful, discussing my finances, or disparaging my father." She walked to the door and opened it wide. "I'm sure you can find your way to the door. Good day, Mrs. Webster."

Madeline waited until Matilda left the room before she slammed the door and leaned against it, trembling.

This was going to be harder than she'd thought.

Chapter Fourteen

Teague watched Matilda Webster as she stomped out of the house. Her nose was so high up in the air he was surprised she didn't fall over backward or have a bird perch on the end of it. Maddie must've really let her have it. He grinned widely as she fumbled with the front gate, but his grin faded when he heard her yelling at Orion to help her.

When Orion approached, she smacked him upside the head with her reticule for apparently moving too slowly and then continued to berate him as they walked back to her fancy carriage. Orion just accepted it without protest. Teague didn't like the way Matilda treated her servant more like a slave than a man. It stuck in his craw that he couldn't do anything about it.

Not that he would. It was doing something about it that had landed him in this hell he called life. Growing up, his best friend had been Joseph, a young Negro slave who worked on a farm in town. His master was good to him, and Joseph grew up attending the same school with Teague.

When they were both grown men, Joseph began to get very vocal about slavery and the brewing war between the states. He married a beautiful girl by the name of Camille. When President Lincoln freed the slaves, Camille was murdered within the week by someone who didn't like her husband and figured because she wasn't property anymore, she was fair game for a stray bullet.

Teague's wife begged them not to go to war, but he and Joseph wouldn't listen. They were both out for revenge and paid the ultimate sacrifice.

Joseph lost his life, while Teague lost his soul.

Teague shook off the ghosts dancing on his back and went back into the carriage house to finish the parson's bench he was working on for Maddie's front hall. It was a surprise, and he hoped she'd like it.

As he hunkered down to sand the sides a bit more, he heard someone approaching. He quickly threw a tarp over the bench and started fiddling with the carriage wheel he was supposed to be fixing. It leaned up against the post beside the carriage that was obviously not going very far.

"Teague?" He felt a shimmer move through him at the sound of Madeline's voice.

Ever since she'd told him she loved him, he'd been wrestling with his inner demons over it. The voices were screeching and clawing at him and howling madly. Another woman declaring her love for him. Another woman who would suffer because of his failings as a man.

"In here," he replied.

The sun silhouetted Madeline as she stepped through the door. He had a moment where it was Claire coming through instead of her, and he felt nauseous. He didn't need to be confusing the two women—they couldn't be more different.

"Did you see who just left?" Madeline was dressed in a god-awful outfit that looked like it belonged on a nun rather than a beautiful woman like her. But her face glowed with a light that shone from deep inside. His heart squeezed tightly within his chest as the depth of his feelings for her grew another foot.

"I did. Matilda had a bee in her bonnet."

Madeline laughed, a full-throated woman's laugh that never failed to make him smile. "I let her know what I thought of her and her nosy ways, and I didn't spare a word of what I was thinking."

He nodded. "Is that the first time?"

She looked a bit embarrassed. "Yes, unfortunately it is. I always tried to put on a face of politeness for the society ladies, but apparently it was all for my benefit. They were too busy watching my father push their faces in his money to pay attention to me. And since he died, they've only stopped by to get money for a fund-raiser or charity." Madeline grimaced. "And I gave it to them. Over and over."

Teague felt the overwhelming urge to comfort her but fought against it. She wasn't in the mood for comfort.

"What did she want this time?" he asked.

She clapped her hands together with a smack. "It worked! You telling Jackson about my secret stash of clothing and such worked! She suddenly decided my wardrobe was not fitting for the town's millionaire, so she wanted to look through my closet to help me pick out more appropriate items."

Millionaire?

"Of course I told her she was rude to discuss my money and my wardrobe and kicked her out!"

Millionaire? Did Madeline have *that* much money?

"If nothing else comes out of this, Teague, I'll have the satisfaction of telling Matilda Webster to stick it in her ear."

She nodded and then smiled and looked so damn pleased with herself. Teague was trying to assemble a thought that didn't start with the word *millionaire.*

"I'm glad to hear it, honey. Did you—that is, what else did you want me to do?"

She couldn't have that much money. It was impossible. She wouldn't be living in a bright blue house with ten-year-old clothes and only a mulatto for company.

Impossible.

"My next victim is going to be that weasel Mr. Cleeson at the bank. I'm going to start planting false information for him to find. Oh, and I need to telegraph someone in Denver."

Madeline grabbed him in a hug and kissed him hard on the lips. He stirred to life immediately, groaned, and captured her flush against him. She softened and started kissing him like he'd taught her to do. Her tongue dueled with his, dancing and twining in an ancient ritual.

Within moments, he was hard as a stone and anxious to drag Maddie upstairs for a little afternoon delight. All thoughts of money and scheming townspeople flew out of his head.

"Mmmm, you feel good. . . ."

"So do you."

He reached up and pulled out the pins holding her glorious hair. It tumbled down over his arms like a curtain of silk. He groaned, remembering how it felt on his chest when she rode him. Forget upstairs. He needed her. Now.

Teague backed her into the post and slowly pulled her skirt up. He yanked at her drawers until they puddled around her ankles. Her warm thighs were soft and delectable, inviting him to travel up to the ultimate goal. She gasped when his hands lightly brushed against her nether lips.

"Teague . . . we can't. . . ."

He suckled her ear, laving the lobe and then biting it. "Oh, yes, we can."

He ran his fingers back and forth in her wetness. She was hot and ready for him. So quickly. As quickly as he was hard and ready for her. As if they were two magnets drawn together, he couldn't stop himself.

He picked her up until she straddled his hips. He freed his cock from the confines of his britches and breathed a sigh of relief. It had been about to cut off his circulation. Her hands grabbed for him, and he held his breath.

Maddie's fingers gripped him tightly and then moved up and down. He pulsed against her, and she smiled up at him, her beautiful eyes wide with passion. While his fingers continued to rub her hot button, her fingernails lightly scraped his balls.

He shivered at the sensation, his control leaning toward nonexistent.

"I need you, Maddie."

"Yes, now."

Teague stepped closer to her and lifted her slightly while her legs wrapped around his waist. She leaned back against the pole as he slid inch by inch into her pussy. She was as tight as a fist. He had to close his eyes and grip her ass to stop himself from coming like a green kid in a whorehouse.

"Maddie, sweet Jesus, you feel like heaven."

When he was fully planted inside her, he took a deep breath and held it, dizzy with the pleasure ricocheting through his body.

"Please . . ." she whispered.

Teague held her in place against the wooden post while he started to thrust in and out. The door was open, it was broad daylight, and he didn't care. He was making love to the woman who owned his heart.

It was inevitable. As Teague's rhythm grew faster, his heart started beating faster again. His soul breathed for the first time in seven years. Faster and faster. She moaned and scrabbled at his back as he slammed into her deep, deep inside.

"Teague!" she whispered breathily as she started contracting around him.

He felt the orgasm building from somewhere near Shiloh, through Missouri, Texas, and all through the west, until it hit him, here in Plum Creek, Colorado. It roared through him with the force of an avalanche, grabbing him in a tumbling fall that stole his breath.

His legs felt like jelly, and his heart was quietly weeping inside him. Madeline had done the impossible. That stubborn spinster millionaire had just breathed life back into his long-slumbering soul.

She grabbed his face and kissed him until he finally set her back on her feet. She smiled and tried to adjust her clothes, but it was no use. Maddie looked like a woman who had been loved. Thoroughly. Her lips were red as berries, and her hair was a dark cloud of knots that might take days to unsnarl.

And damnit to hell, he loved her.

Madeline snuck into the house through the back door and tiptoed up the stairs. As she took her reticule from the front hall table, she could hear Eppie talking to someone in the dining room, probably Isaiah.

When she reached her room, she closed the door behind her and locked it. She grinned at the empty room and spun around in a circle with her arms wide, feeling like a little girl. She felt young. Young and in love.

Each time she was with Teague, her certainty that it was love grew. She flopped back on the bed and felt a twinge between her legs. Teague had been rough, and she resisted the urge to go back and ask for more.

Who knew she could be such a wanton?

She rolled over and felt paper crinkling beneath her. Her reticule. How could she forget? The evidence against the conspirators was in here. Each day, she made a copy of the transactions, and each day the original disappeared. She had to find a safe place to keep these with someone she could trust. The problem was she didn't think she could trust anyone in Plum Creek anymore except Eppie. She didn't know if she could trust Teague. He was in league with those who would hurt her. Her heart told her to trust him, but her head kicked that weepy organ aside and shouted at her for even thinking of trusting him.

Madeline carefully removed the papers from her reticule and gazed at the week's worth of entries. There must be something else she could gather. Some kind of evidence that would support her claims.

She knew where the evidence might be . . . Denver. For a woman of her advanced years, she was scared to death to travel to Denver alone. Perhaps she ought to take Eppie and

Teague with her. Of course, she had to leave someone at the house to watch it. God knew what those bastards would do if they knew she was out of town.

As Madeline tucked the ledgers back into the reticule, she thought of someone to ask. With a whoop, she ran to her dressing table to fix up her hair. Madeline had someone to go see.

Most folks in Plum Creek had given up Micah Spalding for dead. He was a mountain man who came to town but once a year for supplies. An entire year had passed without anyone seeing either hide or hair of him. Everyone assumed he had died. No one knew much about him other than his name. He was a tall man with a big beard and long brown hair he kept in a queue at the back of his head. He wore animal skins, and everyone figured he smelled a bit like he was a stranger to soap and water.

At the general store, Candice was polite to him and always filled his order. He paid with cash, a rarity for many. But he always made Candice nervous.

He'd visit the blacksmith for his needs there, and he always checked on the mail and with the telegraph operator, as though he was waiting on something.

No one knew where he came from or even how old he was. No one, that is, except Madeline.

Not long after her father died, she'd found him near death by the creek behind her house. Somehow she'd made a litter and dragged him to the house. Although suffering from hypothermia, he begged her not to call a doctor, said he'd pay her to take care of his needs.

Madeline saw kindness in his silver eyes along with a bit of desperation and a touch of madness. She agreed to his terms but refused payment. She wanted him to bathe and shave while he stayed at her house instead.

Micah had reluctantly agreed. He told her he'd been fishing in the swollen creek when he'd fallen in and cracked his head on a log. Miraculously he hadn't drowned and had ended up near her house when he was finally able to drag himself out of the river.

Micah stayed with her a month while he recuperated. They became friends, something neither one of them had an abundance of. Madeline was surprised to find that Micah was only a few years older than she and that he was originally from North Carolina. She never asked him why he lived alone in the mountains, and he never offered up a reason why. Underneath all the grime and hair, Micah was a handsome man. Madeline remembered being surprised by that fact but not surprised that she had no interest in him as anything other than a friend.

Before he went back to the mountain, he promised Madeline if she ever needed him, he would come back to Plum Creek and help her.

Today was the day. Madeline knew where his cabin was. He had drawn her a map so she could find it. It would take only an hour to get there if she took a horse. She contemplated renting one from town but decided not to. Teague might as well accompany her. She wasn't exactly a worldly traveler, and having him along would probably be a wise idea.

She changed into her sturdiest boots and went out to the carriage house. Teague threw a tarp over something and looked at her in surprise.

"Maddie! What are you doing back so soon?"

She frowned at his behavior. "I need to go up the mountain to a cabin about an hour's ride from here. Will you saddle the horses and go with me?"

Teague's eyebrows shot up nearly to his scalp. "Now? It will be dark in less than three hours. Shouldn't you wait until tomorrow?"

She shook her head. "No, I want to go today. It can't wait."

He opened his mouth as though to argue with her but closed it. He walked past her out of the carriage house and headed for the barn. Madeline looked at the tarp-covered item but decided she didn't have time to snoop right then.

She hurried after Teague and caught up with him as he was saddling the first horse.

"Who are we going to see?" he asked.

"A friend."

He cinched the saddle, put the bridle on the chestnut, and laid the reins on the saddle horn. He moved to the next stall and started saddling the bay mare.

"Does this friend know we're coming?"

"No."

Teague sighed and straightened the blanket on the horse's withers.

"What if this friend isn't there?"

Madeline hadn't thought of that but figured Micah would be within shouting distance of his cabin. From what she remembered, he never went too far from it, except his yearly trip into town.

"He'll be close by. Don't worry."

Teague scowled. "He will, huh? So we're going to see a man friend that lives an hour up a mountain?"

Madeline was delighted to see a spurt of jealousy from him. It was jealousy. She was sure of it. Jealous of Micah? Now, that was something! Madeline had never had any man jealous for her before. It made her heart go pitty-pat and a grin creep up her face.

"Are you jealous, Teague?"

"Hell, no! I just don't know if I like this idea of yours."

She straightened her shoulders and looked at him with narrowed eyes. "That's too damn bad, Teague O'Neal. You work for me, remember? We are going, and whether or not you like it doesn't change my mind."

He snorted and finished saddling the bay without another word. His handsome face wore a horrible scowl, and he kept shooting her glares from beneath his brows.

Madeline couldn't help but watch his body as his muscles moved and flexed. Her body, so recently sated, was humming again. Teague was as sour as a pickle, and yet her body was still reacting to him like he was bringing her fresh flowers and chocolates. Somehow she wasn't surprised.

Within ten minutes, Teague had filled two water skins, and they were on their way to Micah's cabin.

Madeline led them behind the house to the creek and started following it north. The trees grew thicker as the air grew a bit cooler. It had been ages since she'd simply stepped out of the yard and into the woods. It was quite beautiful and sorely neglected by people like her.

Teague was still pouting an hour later when they stopped to water the horses. As the air was thinner, they had to be sure everyone was hydrated and not pushing too hard.

He scowled as he filled his canteen in the creek. As she watched him, she wondered how she'd ever considered being a virgin spinster with men like him in the world. It was sheer stupidity. Of course, what she was doing with him was sheer madness.

They mounted their horses and continued. She consulted Micah's carefully drawn map every ten minutes or so, taking note of each landmark they passed. He'd been quite thorough with them to make sure she wouldn't get lost. After all, Madeline was a dyed-in-the-wool city girl.

"Are we getting closer?" Teague asked with a bit of a whine in his voice.

"Probably another half an hour or so, from what he told me."

Teague stopped and turned to glare at her. "What are you saying? You've never even been to this friend's cabin?"

"No, I haven't, but I have a map, and I know about where he is."

"Woman, are you crazy? The sun is going to set in less than two hours, and we're out here heading toward a cabin you've never even seen?"

A vein bulged in his head as he shouted. Madeline felt her own temper stir to life.

"You will not speak to me like that, Teague O'Neal! I am

not some dog you can order around. I have every faith in this map because Micah drew it, and I have faith that we will be safe because you are with me. Now stop complaining and whining, and let's keep going!"

Teague's mouth opened and closed as though he'd never had a woman speak to him like that. Too damn bad. Madeline never kept her tongue when there were words that needed speaking.

"You have faith in me?" His softly spoken question tugged at her heart. It sounded as if no one had ever told him that before.

"Of course I do. You're an intelligent, capable man, Teague. Why wouldn't I?"

He shrugged one big shoulder and stared off into the evergreens. "It's unusual to hear, is all. I mean . . . thanks."

"You're welcome. Now, let's keep going; we've got to be close."

Another five minutes passed before Teague said, "Micah?"

"Yes, that's his name. Haven't I mentioned that?"

"No, you didn't." Teague snapped a stick off an oak tree and started fiddling with the bark. "There's a lot you haven't told me."

Madeline felt a snort of laughter billow up her throat. "If that isn't the pot calling the kettle black!"

"What are you talking about?"

Madeline sighed. "Teague, I know absolutely two things about you. You had a wife and child, and you were in the war with a friend who died at Shiloh. Before three weeks ago, you had a past, but that's all you've shared with me."

"I reckon that's true," he admitted grudgingly.

Madeline watched his big hands play with the stick and couldn't help but remember how much she loved his hands playing on *her* body.

". . . so that's why it's hard for me."

Oops. He had been talking, and she certainly hadn't been listening. Damn her wanton hide.

"I'm sorry. Can you say that again?"

Teague frowned. "I said I lost everything in my life that I loved in that war. I wasn't much of a man, barely living a day-to-day existence until I stumbled on that blasted horse. There are a lot of things you don't know about me, and many of them I'm not proud of, so that's why it's hard for me."

Madeline could certainly understand that. There were quite a few things she wasn't proud of, and telling someone about them was not high on her list of fun things to do. However, she had to somehow drag him out of his shell and get him to talk to her. The fresh air must have been making her brave.

"Okay, I'll make you a deal. I will tell you something about me, and you tell me something about you."

One dark eyebrow went up. "Like what kind of something?"

She shrugged. "Whatever you want it to be. I'll go first." Madeline took a deep breath then let it out. "My mother was the light in my life and allowed me to be more like other children. Well, as much as she could, anyway, because we both lived under my father's thumb. When I was twelve years old, she died." Madeline paused to take a breath. "I tripped and nearly fell down the stairs, but my mother pushed me out of the way and then fell down the stairs and broke her neck. My father was furious. He pulled me out of school and hired a tutor for me. He basically locked me away in the house. He once told me . . ." She had to swallow hard to say it. "He once told me he wished it had been me who had fallen instead of her."

The steady *clop-clop* of the horses' hooves, the rush of the creek, a few birds chirping, and some squirrels chattering above them were the only sounds she heard. Madeline felt her heart weep within her for the little girl whose entire life had changed because she'd tripped over the carpet runner in the hallway.

"You blame yourself for her death."

Madeline actually gasped. She had never told a living soul

that, and here was Teague, three weeks after meeting her, and he could see down deep into her soul. To unearth the darkest, festering thing he could find.

"Yes," she whispered. It felt so good to say it out loud. So many nights she'd lain there and punished herself over and over with "what if" and "if only" scenarios until she thought she'd go mad. Perhaps she had—a little, anyway.

"How did you know?" she asked as she wiped a tear from the corner of her eye. Too many tears had been shed over the last twenty years to shed any now.

"I . . . I feel the same way about someone's death."

Madeline sat up and took notice. Teague was about to give her some kind of information—some crumb of insight into his heart.

Teague sighed long and deep. "I lied to you about my wife and son. They were alive when I came back from the war. They were barely scraping by on potatoes and pin money from the eggs they were selling in town. Folks were jealous of those hens but for the most part left her alone. She couldn't bear to look at me, couldn't bear my touch. It was like she had gone off to war instead of me. I don't know what happened while I was gone, but it was enough to turn Claire into a different person."

She could see his hands were tight on the reins, white-knuckled.

"When she did talk to me, we fought, long and hard. Christopher didn't even remember me. He was a wild thing, dirty and barefoot. I got angry one night and went into town to the saloon. Got stinking drunk and passed out. When I woke up in the hoosegow, the sheriff told me bushwhackers had raided my farm, killed Claire and Christopher, and stole the damn hens."

Madeline's stomach heaved at the thought of what the jay-hawkers had done after the war. People had been insane with bloodlust and had left their better judgment, if they had any, in the dirt behind them.

"I'm so sorry, Teague." Madeline moved her horse closer to his and touched his arm. It was like touching granite—cold and hard.

"Thank you kindly, Maddie. I don't know if I could have stopped them if I'd been home, but I'll never know, will I? So I blame myself for their deaths, just like you and your ma."

He turned his dark eyes on her, and she saw it. A light way back in those beautiful orbs. There it was. Hope.

Teague felt like a long-tailed cat in a room full of rocking chairs. They found the cabin with a bit of looking. This fella had it well hidden in the evergreens, so if you didn't look hard enough, you'd never know it was there.

Madeline smiled when she spotted the chimney. "There it is, Teague!"

The cocking of a rifle cut short his reply.

"You're on my land. Get." The hard voice came from somewhere to their left and behind them.

Shit.

"Micah?"

There was a moment of silence when even the birds stopped singing, and there surely wasn't a forest critter within ten miles.

"Madeline?"

He pronounced it with a long *I* in the middle. Made*i*ne. Like she was a dessert or something. Like a Southerner would.

A wave of blackness swept through Teague as long-buried memories pounded his mind. The sounds, the smells, the fear, the absolute misery.

Maddie had found herself a Johnny Reb.

"Yes, it's me."

"Who is that big fella yonder?"

"He . . . he's my friend, Teague. I've come to ask for your help. I'm in trouble."

Another moment of absolute silence. Teague swore he was

about to choke on his own vomit as he struggled against his past.

"All right, then. Y'all can come down from those horses and set a spell."

Teague dragged himself off his horse and fell to his knees. He vaguely heard Madeline call his name. His head dropped down to the dirt. The smell of pine needles and the loamy smell of the earth waved past his nose. He struggled for breath.

"Teague! What's the matter? Micah, help me!"

He felt her hands touching his back, but he couldn't lift his head up.

"It's okay, Madeline. You take the horses on back to my lean-to. I'll take care of your fella here."

He wanted to tell Micah to shut up each time he opened his mouth and that drawl emerged.

"She's gone now," Micah said quietly near his ear. "Just breathe, big man. Deep breath."

Teague started taking big, gulping breaths, each one deeper than the last, until finally the urge to curl up and die passed.

A tin ladle full of water appeared in front of him. He took it and swallowed it greedily. "Thanks."

A pair of well-worn boots stepped in front of him. He saw brown trousers and some oft-mended laces.

"I reckon we've got some things in common. Other things we could probably argue until we're old and wrinkled. You were Union Blue, right, Yank?"

Teague nodded and pushed himself up to his knees. He focused on keeping his dignity and pride in tact.

"Yeah, I was. You a Johnny Reb, right?"

"I fought for the South. The war's long since over. I moved out here to leave it behind. I expect you did, too."

A hand abruptly appeared in front of Teague. "Madeline cares about you, so I reckon you must be okay."

Teague took the proffered help and stood with a rush of blood to his head that nearly had him swaying.

"You're too big to pick up, so don't fall."

Teague turned and got a good look at Madeline's friend. The first thing he noticed was the scar. A very sharp blade had made it. Micah had a scar that ran down his jaw to his neck. Looked as if he was lucky to be alive and must've had a damn good surgeon patch him up.

Micah had long, wavy brown hair halfway down his back. He had a matching beard that hung down his chest. He was dressed in raggedy but relatively clean clothes. It was his eyes that captured Teague, though.

He had been prepared to be jealous of this man for being Madeline's friend, but one look in those silver eyes changed his mind. Micah had suffered as much, if not more, than Teague in the war. There was nothing left behind those cold eyes but the tiniest flame of respect for Madeline.

It seemed to Teague that he had lost his heart in the war, but Micah had lost his soul.

Teague stuck out his hand. "Teague O'Neal."

Micah nodded and shook his hand briefly. "Micah Spalding."

"Is he okay?" Madeline called as she came running back toward them.

One eyebrow rose on Micah's hairy face. "This is interesting."

Madeline reached Teague and cupped his face in her hands. Worry clearly showed in her dark eyes. "What happened?"

Teague shook his head. "Just felt lightheaded from the air being so damn thin up here."

She didn't look convinced.

"Let's have some coffee." Micah walked past them toward his cabin.

"I'm fine, Maddie. Let it go."

She nodded, and her hands dropped from his face.

"Coffee will help."

She threaded her arm through his, and they walked into the cabin.

Chapter Fifteen

Micah turned out to be quite a tidy housekeeper. Most of his belongings were neatly stacked on shelves, hung on hooks, or tucked under things. The floor was wooden and well swept. The potbellied stove sat relatively clean in the corner. On it, blissfully, was a pot of coffee, burbling away.

Madeline was not convinced that Teague was okay. She had no idea what had happened to him out there, but obviously Micah had. She resented that and felt a twinge of jealousy. Over what? Her lover and her friend understanding each other? She tried to kick her own fanny over that.

Teague flopped down in one of the two chairs in the room. Micah sat on the bed, so she took the other chair. Sturdily built out of logs, it matched the other chair and the table at which Micah obviously ate his meals.

There was a beautiful wall hanging made with beads of incredibly vibrant colors. It looked Indian-like, so she was hesitant to ask him where he'd gotten it.

"Coffee?" Micah asked after he and Teague shared another look.

Damnit! Stop it!

"That would be a godsend," Teague replied. It was all Madeline could do not to roll her eyes.

As Micah took two tin cups down from the shelf above the

dry sink, Madeline noticed there were two of a lot of things. Two towels, two chairs, two cups, two plates. And only one Micah. Another mystery she'd love to stick her nose into.

Today wasn't about Micah and his mysterious past, though; it was about her problem. After that mental pinch, she found her focus was back where it should be.

Micah offered her a cup of coffee, and she shook her head. He sat back down on the bed and looked at her intently with those fathomless silver eyes.

"What brought you all the way out here, Madeline?"

"I need your help."

"Of course. I am always at your service. You know that."

Madeline smiled at his gentlemanly ways. Most folks didn't see past the beard and the long hair, but Micah was a true Southern gentleman through and through.

"This is a very sticky situation, Micah, so I want to be sure you know what you're getting involved in before you say yes."

"I already said yes, but get to the information so you can stop fiddling like a kid at Sunday service."

Madeline frowned. She wasn't fiddling. She thrust her shoulders back and launched into the story. She explained how Teague was arrested and became her employee for a month (without mentioning the lover part of that), how the sheriff and the judge were conspiring against her, how information and money was missing from the bank, and finally why she needed his help.

"I'm going to Denver, and I need someone to stay at my house while I'm gone. Eppie can't be there alone—she's no match for these low-down snakes. I can trust only you to protect everything for me. I know you don't go to town much, but would you consider this for me?"

Micah took a big gulp of coffee and looked at the depths of his cup for a moment before looking up at her. He didn't look enthusiastic, but he did look determined.

"I'll do it for you, Madeline."

Madeline felt a great weight lift off her shoulders at Micah's agreement. She'd been afraid he'd say no.

"Does Eppie know I'm coming? You know that girl does not like me one smidgen."

The urge to laugh was almost too strong to resist. Apparently it *was* too strong for Teague. He burst out laughing and slapped his knee with one big palm. "Hell, Maddie, does that girl like anybody but you?"

Micah grinned at Teague. There it was again! That damn connection between them. What was it? Did they already know each other?

"Eppie is particular about whom she places her trust in, that's all."

Teague snorted, and Micah shook his head. Madeline allowed herself a small laugh. They were right. Eppie didn't like many people, but she was going to have to welcome Micah because without him, the plan wouldn't work.

"When do you want me there?"

Madeline glanced at Teague. "I've got only a week before Teague is . . . released from my custody. I need to leave tomorrow morning for Denver."

Madeline ignored the clench in her heart at the thought of having him for only another week.

"So, tonight?"

"If possible. If not, tomorrow morning. I think the stage leaves before nine, so it would have to be early."

Micah nodded. "I'll come tonight. Give me a few minutes."

"Thank you."

He held up his hand. "You don't need to thank me. I owe you my life. Guarding your house for how long, Madeline?"

"Two days, possibly four."

"Two to four days to sit at your house isn't going to even come close to what you did for me."

Teague set his cup down and looked Micah in the eye. "They don't play nice. You'd best bring a weapon with you."

Micah nodded. "I figured that was likely the case. Got a nice Colt forty-five and a Winchester."

"You might need them."

Madeline felt her heart drop to her feet. "Is Micah in danger?"

Teague cocked one eyebrow. "Not any more danger than what you or I are in right now, honey."

Honey.

He had called her that once before, and that word held a lot of meaning. Even Micah sensed it—he glanced at her with eyebrows raised and a question in his eyes.

"I just don't want him putting himself in danger to protect a house."

"I'm not doing it to protect a house, Madeline. From what you've told me, I'm protecting you and helping you kick them in the . . . well, helping you."

Teague grinned into his coffee.

"All right. I need a little bit of air. Teague, will you come out with me to get the horses ready?" she asked and stood. Teague swallowed the last of his coffee and rose. After only a split second of hesitation, he nodded at Micah and headed toward the door.

"I'll be there in ten minutes," said Micah as he, too, rose.

After Micah packed his belongings and they readied the horses, the three of them headed back down the mountain into Plum Creek. Micah led the way because he knew the path better than any of them. Madeline's stomach was fluttery, and her mouth dry.

This was really it. What happened in the next two days would steer the course for the rest of her life. It was frightening. It was exhilarating. It was amazing.

Madeline had never felt so alive. She was ready to battle.

*   *   *

"I cain't believe you let that man in your house again!"

Folks in Denver could probably hear Eppie's raised voice. She was standing in the kitchen with her hands on her hips and fire in her dark eyes. Isaiah was sitting at the table eating a biscuit and a glass of milk, watching the rest of them like a kid at a magic show.

Micah stood by the back door leaning against the door frame, his eyes shuttered in the lamplight. Teague was keeping out of it. He chose to stay in the carriage house.

"Eppie, Micah is my friend, and he's going to be staying here while I'm gone."

"Where are you going?" she demanded.

"I told you. Denver. I will be back in a few days. Micah is making sure you're safe."

Eppie snorted and stepped toward the sink, giving Micah a disdainful look.

"Safe? With him around? He cain't even find his way to a bar of soap. How is he going to protect me?"

Micah looked like he was biting back a grin.

"Eppie! That's not polite. Micah is a gentleman, and he will treat you with respect. He is staying while I'm gone, and it's not up for discussion."

Eppie opened her mouth as though to say something else but closed it. Her light cocoa skin was flushed with enough red to let Madeline know she was really upset.

"Why don't you and I talk a little more . . . privately?" Madeline suggested.

Eppie turned and sashayed out of the kitchen. She turned to look back at Madeline, her eyes lit from a fire within. "You coming or not?"

Madeline grimaced and followed her friend. Eppie could sure flay the skin off a body when she was angry. She found her pacing in the sitting room.

"Eppie, tell me what's wrong." Madeline sat down on the

wingback chair by the fireplace and waited. She didn't have to wait long.

"It's that man, Madeline! When he was here, he actually . . . That is, he . . ."

She trailed off and looked at Madeline as though she didn't know how to voice her thoughts.

"Did he hurt you, Eppie?"

Eppie shook her head so hard she nearly dislodged her bright blue scarf.

"No, he never done nothing like that. It's just . . . he sparked with me. Me! A Negress with scars on her heart and a history he don't want to even know about."

Madeline couldn't hide her shock. Micah had flirted with Eppie?

"Are you saying he's sweet on you?"

Eppie threw her hands up in the air. "No! I don't know what I'm saying. He smiled and talked to me and made me feel . . . special somehow. I cain't explain it better than that."

"That makes you angry?" Madeline was confused. Why would feeling special make Eppie so angry? Micah was a good man beneath the dirt and hair.

"Yes! He's a Southerner, Madeline! He fought for the South in the war. How could he . . . I mean, it feels . . . wrong."

Madeline finally understood. Eppie had never told her the details, but she was sure Eppie's former owner had taken liberties with her. More than likely treated her special, and then when he got what he wanted, used her as he wanted. Micah's attention had to bring back memories she wanted to keep buried.

"I'm sorry, Eppie. Micah isn't like that, you know. He might be a little rough around the edges, but his heart is golden."

She stood and hugged her friend, though at first it was like hugging a broomstick. Eppie was unbending until Madeline started rubbing her back; then she seemed to collapse like a house of cards. She snuggled into Madeline like a little girl. Madeline was surprised to feel tears soaking into her dress.

"Shhhh, it's okay. He would never hurt you."

"I know," came Eppie's muffled reply. "It's the fact that I liked it. The sparking, I mean. I liked it, and it scared me. Scared me something fierce."

Madeline rubbed her hand up and down Eppie's back and held her tightly, wishing the world hadn't been such a cruel place to a young girl.

Back from the carriage house, Teague helped himself to a cup of coffee and offered one to Micah. Micah shook his head, his gaze focused on the door Eppie and Maddie had passed through.

"Strong women."

Micah nodded.

"You like her, don't you?"

Micah looked at Teague with a raised eyebrow. "Madeline is my friend and nothing more. You don't need to worry any on that account."

His Southern drawl nipped up Teague's spine again. He would have to work on getting used to that.

"Nice try. You know I wasn't talking about Maddie."

Micah's gaze flew to Teague's again. His intense eyes studied him carefully for a full minute before he shifted back to the doorway again.

"What's not to like about Eppie? She's bossy, argumentative, mean, and pigheaded."

Teague took a big sip of the black brew and felt the warmth travel down into his stomach before he spoke again. "It's worse than I thought. You don't like her . . . you love her."

This time Micah truly looked startled. His mouth opened slightly as he gusted out a breath slowly. "Damn. Is it that obvious?"

Teague shook his head. "No. From all accounts, you look like she makes you laugh, and she looks like she wants to fit you for a wooden box."

Micah smiled, and Teague was surprised to see how white

and straight his teeth were. He'd expected something worse, he guessed. Hermits weren't the cleanest critters in the world.

"So what are you going to do about it?"

Micah shrugged. "There's nothing I can do about it. She's a Negro, and I'm a white boy from the South. There is no way it will ever go any further than here and now."

Privately Teague disagreed, but he didn't say anything more. There was a haunted look in the other man's eyes he knew too well.

Madeline didn't want to admit it to anyone, but she was nervous. Her first trip out of Plum Creek into a city. A big city, compared to the small town she grew up in. She had no idea what to expect. No idea at all. That made her nervous. Madeline didn't like the feeling.

She lay in her bed that night missing Teague and wondering how she could sneak past Micah and Eppie to get to the carriage house. She grinned at her own crazy impulses. A month ago she never would have even considered sneaking out in her nightgown to climb into her lover's bed.

Madeline knew she ought to be sleeping. Too many things were running through her head like the creek running behind her house. Flowing, moving, jumping. Her feet were moving back and forth like a metronome.

Finally she threw the covers back and gave up the fight. It was no use. She needed him. Madeline threw her legs over the side of the bed and stood. After she made her decision, it was as if a hundred pounds lifted from her shoulders. She snatched her robe from the chair by the fireplace and hurried to the door.

As she walked down the stairs, she pushed her arms into the sleeves, or at least tried to. The left arm would not go in; the sleeve was bunched funny or something. She came around the corner and realized there was someone in the kitchen sitting at the table.

She stopped short and stared at Micah. He was slouched

on the chair looking even less tidy than usual. A bottle of amber liquid sat on the table, an empty glass next to it. Madeline realized she was half dressed and obviously on her way out the back door in the middle of the night.

"Evenin', Madeline."

Madeline always loved the way Micah said her name— with the long "I" that hung in the air for a second. His drawl was refined and lazy, like hot honey on toast. Tonight that drawl was deeper, more pronounced.

She untangled her arm and succeeded in getting the robe completely on. As she buttoned it up, she thought about what to say to him.

Was she embarrassed? No.

Was she going back upstairs? Absolutely not.

"Good evening, Micah."

He reached for the bottle and poured himself a healthy splash of the amber liquid. Madeline was surprised to see his hand shaking. Micah was one of the strongest men she knew. Something must have been very wrong that he would drink enough to make him shake.

"Are you all right?"

He shrugged and took a big swallow. He held up the glass in the candlelight and regarded it as if he were reading a crystal ball. "I will be. Don't worry about me, Madeline."

Madeline sat down across from him and took his free hand. It was as cold as ice. She rubbed it between her hands to try to warm it up.

"I do worry about you. You're my friend."

The corner of Micah's mouth kicked up. "You're the only person who does."

"I find that hard to believe. Even if it is true, I will always be your friend."

Micah took another gulp and then burped softly. "Pardon me. My manners seem to be absent this evening. You were going someplace, right?"

Madeline wanted to talk to Micah about what was bothering him, but his question rekindled her need to get to Teague. She felt torn between helping her friend and quenching her own thirst.

"You best get to him. I'm sure he's waiting." Micah set his glass down and leaned forward to grab both her hands. He squeezed tightly enough to hurt just a bit. His eyes focused on her so intensely she felt the urge to pull back. He held fast and pulled her hands a bit closer.

"Seize it, Madeline. Seize it while you can. Don't let life go past without taking hold of it with both hands and running with it." He pulled both hands to his mouth and gently kissed the back of each one. His mouth was dry and warm against her skin. It felt a bit like a minister kissing her at her wedding. "Do you love him?"

She smiled. "Yes, I love him."

He smiled back at her. "Then don't keep him waiting."

Teague stared out the window toward the creek. Missing Maddie. Needing Maddie.

When the hell had that happened?

It had been so long since he'd felt anything, or perhaps he'd been feeling everything for too long that he'd turned off his emotions. When Claire and Christopher had died, he'd felt so much agony life had been a giant gaping wound with a never-ending sting. A scab that constantly kept getting ripped off anew. To bleed.

As Teague listened to a pair of squirrels chattering in the top of an evergreen tree, he came to the startling realization that the pain was gone.

Gone.

It was Maddie. Being with her had somehow healed that scab until it was a smooth scar. He would never forget what he went through; however, he was ready to forgive.

He loved her. Holy shit. He really did love her.

The touch of a hand on his back did not startle him. He somehow sensed she was near, as if his imagination had conjured her up. He closed his eyes as her hands ran up and down his back.

"I'm sorry. I couldn't—"

He cut her off by spinning around and clasping her face in his hands.

"Don't ever, *ever* be sorry, Maddie."

Her dark eyes were unreadable in the moonlight, but he thought he saw a tear in the corner. He couldn't stop himself from kissing her any more than he could stop the sun from rising.

"I love you, Maddie," he whispered before his mouth closed on hers.

The first touch of lips was soft, like a butterfly. But it was as powerful as good whiskey. Intoxicating. The second kiss was firmer. Then the control was lost, and his arms wrapped around her and pulled her flush against him.

As his mouth and tongue danced and tangled with hers, he could feel her body heating. He could smell her. Intoxicating.

Her nipples were hard, pressing against his chest like small pebbles waiting for him to touch and taste. Her hands continued to move up and down his back; then, with no hesitancy, they landed on his ass and squeezed.

He smiled against her lips. Maddie was beginning to learn how to spread her wings and take what she wanted. Now she needed to learn how to let go of that control.

Teague backed her toward the bed, never letting go of her lips. When the back of her legs hit the frame, he stopped and, with one last kiss, pulled away. Looking into her eyes in the gloom, he saw everything he wanted. And more.

He ran his hands down her shoulders and felt the nightclothes.

"Take them off."

With only a second of hesitation, she unbuttoned her bathrobe and dropped it to the ground. Her white nightdress shone brightly in the moonlight.

"I said take them off."

Teague could see the points of her nipples straining against the cotton covering. His hands itched to touch them. His mouth ached to possess them.

Maddie's beautiful hands reached up and pulled off her nightdress. It floated to the ground beside them like a ghostly apparition fleeing into the darkness below.

Maddie was naked. Deliciously naked.

"What about your clothes?" she whispered.

He placed his finger against her soft lips.

"Shhhh . . . no talking. You listen tonight and obey. Can you do that?"

A shudder ran through her from top to bottom. Her generous breasts shook with it. His cock grew another inch inside his tight pants.

Maddie.

She nodded, and his chest swelled with the breath he sucked in, albeit shakily. This was too important to make any mistakes. It had to be perfect. He had to earn Maddie's trust again.

Madeline's heart was singing the song of ages. *He loved her.* Nothing could ever be as perfect as that.

She nodded at his question. Control was his tonight.

"Lesson seven."

She was shaking inside and out. She had come to Teague because she had no other choice. Whatever it was between them had drawn her here, with or without the situation between her and the town.

Teague was like the other half of herself. The half that had been missing her entire life. She had always felt . . . incomplete. Until now. Until Teague.

The first touch of his calloused hands on her skin forced another shudder through her. She was already wet for him, ready and willing. Yes, she was willing. Ready to give him control.

"Sit," he said.

Madeline immediately sat on the bed, which put her at eye

level with his cock. Even though it was dark, she could clearly see the length and width of his erection. She felt herself pulse deep inside at the anticipation of his hardness plunging into her softness.

He pulled his shirt up and off in one swift movement. She wanted to reach up and caress his chest, but she waited. Impatient as she was, she waited.

"Take off my trousers, Maddie."

With a big grin deep inside, she reached for him. Her fingers trembled a bit, but she ignored them in favor of her hunger. As the last button was undone, she thought she heard him groan. She was happy to note he wasn't wearing drawers. His erection sprang free, literally into her hands. She immediately started caressing him, but he grabbed her wrists.

"Not yet, honey. Finish taking them off."

Madeline was surprised to find herself obeying him. She pushed his trousers down to his feet. She could feel the heat from his erection near her cheek. All she had to do was turn her head, and she would be able to kiss it. The thought should have shocked her, but it didn't. It excited her.

She leaned slightly as he lifted his foot to step out of the pants, and her cheek brushed him. He sucked in a breath. As he stepped out of the other leg, she brushed against him again.

"You're playing a game, but you don't know the rules, Maddie."

She didn't answer him. She just continued to rub her cheek against his velvet steel.

"Take down your hair."

Madeline immediately took apart the braid she'd made when she went to bed. She was aching to touch him, but she knew he would let her. Would tell her to. Oh, God, she wanted him to.

Teague's fingers threaded through her hair, and he tugged on it slightly. Her scalp tingled at the sensation. "Do you want to touch me, Maddie?"

She nodded against his hands, eager to touch him.

"Do you want to touch me with your mouth?"

Her imagination was running wild at the question. He'd touched her with his mouth on her pussy. Now he was asking her if she wanted to do the same.

"Yes," she answered without hesitation.

He tilted her chin up with his hand and looked down into her eyes. "Are you sure, honey?"

Her answer was to lean forward and kiss him on the hard part of him that was waiting for her. It jumped about a foot and smacked her in the cheek. He groaned, and she laughed.

Madeline wrapped one hand around his shaft and felt the breadth of him. Impressive, nearly the size of her wrist. He pulsed against her, and she kissed him again. This time she stuck out her tongue and tasted him, too.

"Jeeeesus," he mumbled.

She decided the taste of him was as intoxicating as the smell and feel of him. Her tongue and lips took over, following her instincts honed by thousands of years of women pleasuring men. The more she licked and suckled him, the more he groaned.

Finally he pushed her away forcibly with her shoulders.

"Hang on, I don't want to finish so soon."

"I—" She started to protest that she wasn't finished but stayed silent. He had said to obey him, so she did. Madeline wanted to take control, but Maddie knocked her aside and relinquished control to Teague.

"Kneel on the bed."

She did so in a few seconds. Her tail was up in the air like a bitch waiting for her hound. She could even smell her own arousal. The bed creaked under Teague's weight as he climbed behind her.

His large hands cupped her ass, and, to her surprise, he spanked her once. Hard. Instead of anger, she felt . . . well, she felt excited. Her nipples rubbed against the wool blanket beneath her, the cloth lightly scraping the hard peaks.

"I've wanted to do that for a month. Your ass is made for spanking."

Madeline thrust her fanny even farther in the air, waiting, hoping for more. Instead his hands dipped lower, and his fingers delved into her wetness, teasing her. She moaned and leaned into his hand, needing more.

He pulled his fingers out and rubbed up and down from her behind to her pleasure nubbin. She couldn't help it—she gasped but bit her tongue to keep the command to touch her more from escaping.

Teague replaced his fingers with his cock. He rubbed up and down, over and over. Before she even knew it had happened, he had entered her and withdrawn. Then he did the same thing on her other hole, the one in her fanny.

"What—?"

Teague slapped her skin again, and she moaned at the sensation that shot through her like a bullet.

"You are not to speak. Just feel and obey."

Madeline nodded, knowing he couldn't see her, but she figured he understood her silence for consent.

He teased her again in her other hole, this time a bit farther. In and out, in and out. Again. And again. She didn't understand it, but she began to crave it. Different pleasure, but equally exciting.

Yes.

He plunged into her without warning, right up as far as he could go. She was full, full, full . . . and incredibly close to having an orgasm. He withdrew and plunged again into the forbidden. His talented fingers started pinching her clit, pushing her pleasure even higher.

Madeline came so hard she saw stars and the moon and everything in between. She heard herself shouting Teague's name, and then he plunged into her deeply. She clenched around him, still rolling on her own pleasure.

It was like the current of the creek, flowing and twisting around her. It seemed like hours, but it was probably only a minute, perhaps two. Teague found his own peak with a groan and a thrust that had her peak beginning all over again.

It was incredible. It was amazing. It was too much. Along with her second peak, Madeline's breath disappeared. Teague withdrew; then, within seconds, she was lying beside him, and he had pulled her close to him.

Madeline closed her eyes and felt a peace steal over her. A peace she hadn't ever remembered feeling. Teague's warm, strong arm was around her waist.

It was indescribable, really. She knew then that she had forgiven him for his betrayal. But if he ever broke her trust again, it would destroy her.

Chapter Sixteen

Teague was readying the carriage for the trip to Denver when he felt a presence behind him.

"Be careful, Mr. Teague. The sheriff knows you're leaving."

Teague knew before he turned around that the speaker was gone. He knew who it was. Isaiah. Why was he warning him? Before he could even think about what he was doing, he turned and ran to follow Isaiah. He found him just rounding the corner of the barn. Teague grabbed the boy and had him pinned to the ground before he could even take a breath.

He stuck his knee into Isaiah's back and kept him helpless.

"All right, the way I see it, you've been spying on this house since you got here. You want to tell me what you're up to?"

Isaiah grunted and tried to dislodge the knee. No such luck. Teague outweighed him by probably sixty pounds.

"What was that? I didn't quite hear you, Isaiah."

"I said get offa me and I'll tell ya."

Teague eased the pressure on his knee but did not let him loose.

"That's all you're gonna get, so start talking, or I start pressing harder."

Teague was suddenly furious. He was tired of the whole fucking town watching Maddie, recording her every move, scrutinizing her. The first time he'd caught Isaiah, he'd figured it was Eppie the boy was looking at. Now he knew different. It was Maddie.

"Who are you?" he demanded.

"Orion is my grandfather."

That explained a lot. Matilda Webster had had Orion since she was a child. Although a free man, he was still under her control completely. Teague was surprised he'd had time to have a family.

"Why are you watching Miss Brewster?"

"Sheriff told me he'd kick my granddaddy out without a penny if I didn't do what he told me to. I didn't have no choice. I like Miss Madeline and Miss Eppie. . . . I'm sorry for what I done."

He did sound sorry. Even to Teague's cynical ears. In fact, he sounded like he was going to cry.

"Isaiah, you and me are going to have a chat."

He let Isaiah up and helped him stand. He looked the boy in the eye and was not surprised to see tears glistening in them.

"You help me, and we can help your granddaddy and get him away from the Websters."

A small spark of hope ignited in Isaiah's dark eyes.

"Truly?"

"Yeah, let's go into the carriage house. Might as well help me get this goddamn carriage ready while we talk."

As Teague and Isaiah headed back across the yard, he helped the boy wipe the dirt and grass from his shirt. He had a feeling he and Maddie had just found their ace in the hole.

Madeline found Teague in the carriage house sanding something. He looked up at her and smiled.

"I wanted to finish this before we left, but you might as well see what it is."

Madeline's natural curiosity roared, and she made her way quickly over to him. It was a beautiful bench made of a darkish wood, and in the middle was an inlay that wasn't quite finished.

"The color is mahogany, like your hair. I wanted to give you something your money couldn't buy."

Her heart sighed as she looked over the beautiful curves and lines of the bench.

"What is the inlay?" she asked as her hands felt the warm wood.

Teague touched the unfinished middle with his calloused fingertips. "A rose. Like you. Your skin smelled of roses the first time I touched you."

Madeline grabbed his hand and pulled him up. His blue eyes were so full of love she wanted to weep. "It's beautiful. Thank you."

She had just received the most incredible gift of her life, and he'd made it with his hands. *For her*. She hugged him close and thanked God all over again for bringing Teague into her life.

The trip to Denver seemed to take days, when in reality it took only hours. Madeline squirmed so much on the seat that Teague snapped at her. Twice. She was as fidgety as a sinner in church, which certainly wasn't a stretch. She was a sinner, through and through. Her sins were in plain sight for anyone to see. In fact, he was sitting right beside her, expertly handling the reins of the Brewster carriage. It had sat unused for two years until today. Her father had had it made by some fancy outfit in Kansas City, with plush velvet seats and gold handles. Just another way to rub his wealth into the noses of Plum Creek.

Madeline hated it, but she couldn't very well ride all the way to Denver. It would definitely defeat the purpose for going if she showed up with horse shit and trail dust on her.

"How long until we get there?"

Teague sighed and shook his head. "You're worse than a

kid at Christmas. Probably thirty more minutes, Maddie. Just relax."

"I can't. I'm . . . nervous."

That one word made her whole body clench. She hated admitting it to anyone, even Teague, who held her heart and soul in his big hands.

"I'm sure you are. You've never been anyplace before. Denver is a big city by Plum Creek standards. You're likely to see things you've only heard about. Don't worry. I'll be there with you, honey."

His deep voice reverberated through her chest, its echoes calming her heart and feeding her starving self-confidence.

"Are you going to tell me what we're going to do in Denver?"

Madeline thought it was safe to tell him now. There was no way anyone else would overhear it.

"We're going to find a lawyer and a judge, find evidence against Jackson Webster and Earl Martin, and put them in jail for embezzlement and fraud."

He turned to look at her with shrewd eyes. "You think we can do all that in two days?"

"We're damn well going to try."

The inspiration had hit her days earlier. She wanted to turn the tables on the very men trying to destroy her. She wanted to take away their lives, their future, and show them what it felt like to be an outcast, shunned and disrespected.

In short, she wanted revenge. She also didn't want them to know it was coming.

Madeline was about to become a Brewster and show her claws.

It was a bit overwhelming, but as Teague explained everything to her, Madeline learned. There were so many things that were different from what she knew. He was very patient with her, like he was teaching a small, inquisitive child with endless questions.

He took her to the Regency Hotel, an establishment he knew to be reputable. It was quite fancy inside, with velvet chairs, beautiful plants, and a sparkling chandelier that must have had a thousand candles in it. He explained it was electricity, not real candles, but, nevertheless, it looked like a star had come down from the sky.

"Stop gawking, Maddie." He nudged her with his elbow until she closed her mouth.

"I read newspapers and books, Teague, but this . . ." She couldn't help but look at the chandelier again. "It's real. Do you understand? Like being with you. It's not just words. It's *real*."

He smiled and shook his head. "Never thought I'd meet someone who was so book smart but didn't know a damn thing."

Madeline's pride stung a bit at that, but she knew he was right. It was a little sad that a thirty-two-year-old woman with enough money for two lifetimes was goggle-eyed at a chandelier. She smiled back at him and squared her shoulders. "Proceed, Professor O'Neal." She gestured to the desk that had a man behind it in a navy-blue jacket pressed with sharp creases. He eyed them with a neutral expression as they walked toward the desk.

Madeline was dressed in her brown serge traveling dress and matching hat, directly imported from New York three years ago. It wasn't new, but it was of the highest quality. One look at the man's eyes confirmed he knew it. His slicked-back hair shone from some kind of pomade; his eyes were small and set deep within his pale complexion.

"Good day, madam. May I help you?"

Madeline felt her confidence rush back like a warm drink on a cold winter day, filling her.

"Yes, you may. My name is Madeline Brewster. I need two rooms. One for me, and one for my brother."

He didn't even blink. He began writing on a piece of paper with a fountain pen. As he wrote, Madeline noticed his hands were perfect. Not just clean or neat. Perfect. With no calluses or scars or dirt deep down in the whorls.

She glanced at Teague's hands as they held her bags. Big, strong hands covered with calluses and a lifetime of experiences. She winked at him, and a spark down deep in his beautiful blue eyes rewarded her.

"How long will you be staying with us?"

Madeline turned her attention back to the desk clerk.

"I'm not certain. At least two days, possibly more."

Within a matter of moments, Madeline had paid for the rooms, and a man Teague called a bellhop took them upstairs to a room decorated in ivory silk, with two ornate chairs in front of a fireplace with a black marble hearth. The bed had a green bedspread and what seemed like a dozen pillows. Her room even had a private bath. Something she hadn't expected. The claw-foot tub was large, larger than her tub at home. The sheer size of it gave her ideas about Teague.

Her body responded immediately with a low hum deep down in her belly. The things Teague had done in the bathroom at her house were insistent memories her body couldn't forget. Especially the blindfold.

"Maddie?"

Teague's voice floated in from the room. With a sigh and a promise, Madeline went to meet him.

"Just what exactly does that mean, Mr. Robinson?" Madeline asked through clenched teeth. She was dressed beautifully again in an elegant gray worsted-wool suit, her hair up in a bun on the back of her head.

Teague sat beside her, anger burning and rolling in his gut at the way Maddie had been treated the past two days. They had visited at least a dozen attorneys, and every one of them, down to this little weasel, had told her no.

The little balding man (who probably was only as tall as Madeline's shoulder) adjusted his spectacles and tugged at his striped waistcoat. Teague could practically smell the distaste coming off him.

"I cannot assist you with your endeavor, Miss Brewster. No attorney in their right mind would assist you. What you're asking us to do borders on illegal."

Madeline clenched her fist as it rested on her knees and stuck her chin up in the air. "It is not illegal. Land transfers are a matter of public record, and so are the moneys paid to elected servants like judges and sheriffs. I can find that information myself. What I'm asking you to do is represent me in any legal proceedings when I sue them for embezzlement."

Every time Teague heard her plan, his stomach clenched. She was looking for a fight. No, not just a fight. A war. Maddie had brass balls to turn the sights from herself to them. It made him nervous. No, it scared the hell out of him. Teague hadn't fought for anything in many years. He had hidden behind apathy and recklessness.

Loving Madeline had dragged him from that pit and pushed him back to the front line. He wasn't at all sure he was comfortable holding a gun again, but for Maddie, he would do it. In fact, listening to this asshole was getting his back up good.

"Not possible. You will never get a judge to listen to you, Miss Brewster. You are an unmarried female meddling in business you have no right meddling in."

Teague could practically see the steam coming from Maddie's ears. She stood abruptly, her reticule clutched tightly in her hands.

"I pity your wife, Mr. Robinson, if anyone was stupid enough to marry you. You are ignorant, biased, and small-minded. I thank you for not accepting me as a client. It saved me from having to fire you."

With a regal grace, she swept out of the room, leaving a slack-jawed Mr. Robinson staring after her. Teague rose slowly. Staring down at the attorney, he made his intentions clear with just his eyes.

Come near her, and you'll deal with me.

"You ought to marry that woman and teach her how to respect men," Mr. Robinson huffed.

Teague shook his head and followed Madeline out the door.

She was standing on the street pacing in a little circle. The sounds of her boots clicking were like a woodpecker tapping frantically on a tree. He grabbed her hand.

"Slow down, honey."

She whipped her head around and stared at him with her dark eyes full of anger and worry. "There's only a handful of attorneys we haven't spoken to. We're running out of options, Teague. I'm tired of these men telling me to get back to the kitchen!" Her cheeks were flushed with passion, and Teague felt his body stir to life. Now wasn't exactly the time to think about *that*.

"Let's take a walk down to Confluence Park. You need to catch your breath and calm down before you deck the next one."

He saw a hint of a smile peeking from the corner of her lovely mouth.

"You don't want to bruise your knuckles."

Maddie smiled and took his proffered arm. "You are far too charming, Mr. O'Neal."

Teague never thought of himself as charming, but with Maddie, he felt charming. She brought it out of him just as naturally as rain from the sky. He didn't even try, because he didn't have to. It was just there.

It was love.

Micah heard the loud knock at the door as it echoed through the stillness of the early morning air. He was expecting it, but perhaps not so soon after they'd left. It had been only two days. He dropped the wood he'd been carrying into the bucket by the stove and ran toward the front of the house.

As he sprinted through the kitchen, he heard Eppie's voice. She was being her usual sassy self, a bad sign. He heard a man's voice responding in kind. Then he heard something that made his stomach drop to his feet.

The sound of a struggle.

He ran as fast as he could down the hallway toward the front door. The sun streaming in blinded him a bit, but he could see two people locked in combat in the threshold.

A split second before he reached them, the bigger one drew his arm back and hit the smaller one as hard as he could. Eppie fell to the floor, hissing and screeching.

A growl of rage burst from Micah's throat as he jumped on the man who dared hit Eppie. Sheriff Webster looked more than surprised to have Micah in his face. Although pretty evenly matched physically, Micah had fury on his side.

"Get out of this house!" Micah shouted.

"What the hell are you doing here? This isn't your house," Webster grunted through his teeth.

"Madeline is my friend, and I am watching her property for her while she's gone, you son of a bitch. Now get out!"

"I will not! I have a warrant—"

Micah snorted and pushed the sheriff back toward the door. The lawman's boots slid across the shiny wood floor. Bless Eppie for keeping it that way. "A fake warrant from a crooked judge is not recognized in this house!"

The sheriff tried to push back, but it was no use—he was nearly out the door. Micah tasted the need for revenge in the back of his mouth for the bastard who would hit Eppie. He brought his arm back to punch the son of a bitch.

That's when Webster pulled his gun.

That's when Eppie screamed, "No!" and threw herself into the fray. He felt her small body try to get between them.

That's when the gun went off and Eppie fell to the floor in a pool of her own blood.

Chapter Seventeen

Madeline turned to look at the assistant escorting them to the door of the attorney's office. He was a dark-haired young man with a brown-eyed expression that resembled a puppy dog that hated its master.

"My apologies, ma'am. Mr. Weaver, he isn't as . . . open as he could be to certain clients."

"Mr. Hawkins, right?" she asked.

"Yes, ma'am. Nate Hawkins."

She stuck out her gloved hand to shake his. Even though she was shaking with anger inside, this young man didn't deserve that poison. He was polite, well spoken, and obviously in the wrong job.

"Thank you for your assistance, Mr. Hawkins."

He glanced behind him quickly and then leaned toward her. She could feel Teague at her back as he stepped closer.

"Elizabeth Mitchell."

Madeline blinked. "Excuse me."

"Go see Elizabeth Mitchell."

With that, he closed the door, leaving her with her arm extended and a bit of confusion in her expression.

"What did he say?" Teague growled.

"He said to go see someone named Elizabeth Mitchell."

One of Teague's dark eyebrows rose in an arch. "Who the hell is Elizabeth Mitchell?"

She shrugged. "I don't know, but we're going to find out."

It took about two hours, but they found her. In a building on the wrong side of town, LoDo, near what Madeline suspected was a brothel. LoDo was Lower Downtown, the oldest part of Denver, now the darkest part of it, known for saloons and brothels.

The plain, whitewashed building sported a simple door and a lock that looked strong enough to stop a train. Miss Mitchell apparently didn't take any chances with her safety.

When Madeline read the small sign beside the door, she nearly gasped.

ELIZABETH MITCHELL, ATTORNEY AT LAW

A female attorney. A woman who had pursued her dream to become what Madeline had always aspired to be. Bless Nate Hawkins.

As she raised her hand to knock, the door was flung open, and a shotgun was pointed at her heart from less than six inches away. Before Madeline could even react, Teague had the barrel in his hand and had wrenched it from the grasp of whoever wielded it. He shoved the person back into the building and turned the shotgun at its owner.

"Go ahead, shoot me. I know somebody probably paid you to."

It was a woman. Madeline was impressed.

"I'm not going to shoot you, ma'am. But you can't stick a gun in a lady's face in front of her man and not expect him to stop you." Teague's soft voice held a menace Madeline hadn't heard before. It made her feel . . . protected.

"I didn't know it was a lady. I thought it was another one of those bastards from old man Wilkins trying to run me off. You might as well come in."

Madeline followed Teague into the building. Inside she was pleasantly surprised to find a cozy house with a small fire crackling in a fireplace, a wall crammed with books, and a well-used desk in the corner piled high with papers.

Madeline finally got a look at Elizabeth Mitchell. She was perhaps thirty-five or thirty-six, with blond hair streaked a bit with silver. Her brown eyes were sharp yet tired looking. She wasn't as tall as Madeline, but she had a sturdy build, with wide shoulders and strong hands.

"Sit down." Elizabeth gestured to a sofa that looked like she had salvaged it from a house fire. She looked at Teague and then at the sofa. "Perhaps not."

Teague grinned. "I'll stand."

Madeline, trying to be polite, sat gingerly on the sofa's edge.

"Who are you, and why are you here?" Miss Mitchell asked.

Madeline hadn't met a woman, aside from Eppie, who was as blunt as this woman attorney. It was refreshing in a way, yet annoying as well.

"My name is Madeline Brewster, and this is Teague O'Neal. We need an attorney."

She looked between them. "You and your . . . husband?"

Madeline felt her heart clench at the suggestion that Teague was her husband. If wishes were horses, beggars would ride. She slapped down the surge of hope that threatened to attack and got back to the business at hand.

"Mr. O'Neal is not my husband." She thought she heard Elizabeth mumble something about big Irishmen under her breath. "He is my friend, and he's helping me. I'm the one who truly needs an attorney."

Elizabeth held Madeline's gaze for what seemed like an hour before she nodded. "Tell me why you need me, and I'll tell you whether or not I can help you."

Madeline took a deep breath and launched into her tale. She explained how her father had died and left her in charge of a small fortune, of how she had spread her wings and changed her life for the better (without mentioning her recent sexual play with Teague). After the history, Madeline introduced the subject of Judge Martin and Sheriff Webster and the idea that someone was stealing money from the bank.

When she was finished, she looked at Teague to continue. The rest of the story was his to tell again. She didn't want to embarrass him or force him into revealing anything he didn't want told.

Teague's beautiful blue eyes looked at her with such respect and affection Madeline felt a sting of tears in her eyes.

"I was hired to spy on Madeline."

Elizabeth's brows rose nearly to her hairline. "Now, that is interesting. Continue."

"The sheriff and the judge hired me to watch her, gather information about her, and try to . . . discredit her in the town's eyes."

Elizabeth's mouth kicked up in a small smile. "Obviously the cat's out of that bag."

"Teague told me everything. That's when I decided to fight back."

Madeline pulled her ledger copies from her reticule and held them out to Elizabeth. "As far as I can tell, there is over five thousand dollars missing in the last two weeks alone. I'm not sure how long it's been going on, but someone has been stealing from the bank for some time. We could be talking about a hundred thousand or more missing. The blame is going to fall squarely on me because I own the bank."

Elizabeth nodded and waved her hand in a gesture to continue. Madeline swallowed her dislike for the other woman's bluntness and concentrated on the fact that she was an attorney. Something Madeline desperately needed.

"I need an attorney to help me access public records for land purchases in the past six months, to find out bank balances for both the sheriff and the judge."

"And?"

"And bring charges against them for embezzlement. I want to catch them at their own game."

Elizabeth finally smiled, and Madeline was surprised to

discover she was pretty when she smiled. Amazing what a simple smile could do.

"Now, that's a case worth working on. I'm yours if you want to hire me."

Elizabeth held out her hand for Madeline to shake it. She again felt the prick of tears behind her lids. She would beat them. She would regain her name. She would find a way to make them pay for what they'd done.

Elizabeth was going to help her.

"The first thing we need is a judge who will listen to you without laughing or kicking you out of his office. I think I know a likely candidate."

Madeline felt her tension begin to uncoil and turn into a thirst. A thirst for justice. She could nearly taste it.

"You and Mr. O'Neal are . . . together?"

Madeline couldn't help it. She looked at Teague and waited for his eyes to meet hers. It felt like a lifetime before she felt rather than saw him smile.

"Yes, we're together," said Teague.

"You do know the fact that you're not married is going to be a weapon you are handing to your enemies?" Elizabeth asked.

"Then we'll get married."

Teague's words dropped on her head like a bucket of ice water. Had he just said *married?* Before she could assimilate what he'd actually said, he was kneeling in front of her. He grabbed her hands in his and gripped tightly. She stared deep into his blue, blue eyes and waited.

Teague was nervous as hell. He'd been thinking about marrying Madeline in the back of his mind for a while. He refused to think how long. All he knew was he couldn't imagine spending the rest of his life without her. He'd always love Claire, but this . . . this feeling he had for Madeline was deeper, richer, and woven into his soul.

"Maddie," he began and then cleared his throat when it

came out as more croak than word. "I don't want you to think this has anything to do with anything but my heart. You grabbed it weeks ago when you saved my life and made your business proposition. This proposal is a little different and not the best timing. Damnit, I am not good with words."

Her dark eyes were brimming with emotion. She squeezed his hands. "I think you're doing just fine."

Teague let out a shaky breath and continued. "I want you to be my wife. I want to wake up with you every morning and go to sleep next to you every night. I want to be on the porch for you when you come home. I want to marry you, Maddie. . . . I love you." He saw a solitary tear slide down her soft cheek. He reached up and brushed it off, cupping her cheek. "I didn't mean to make you cry."

She shook her head. "You're the first person in twenty years who has told me they loved me. I . . . I love you, too, Teague."

His heart stopped beating, his breath stopped blowing, and time stopped ticking. "Does that mean yes?"

She nodded and threw her arms around his neck. "Yes!" He pulled her to him and felt her heart beating madly against his. Maddie would be his. *Forever.*

"I hate to interrupt this beautiful moment," Elizabeth said dryly. "But we need to talk business, too."

Teague drew back and looked Madeline in the eye. "Ready to fight?"

Madeline nodded. "Ready."

"Now that we have that out of the way, tomorrow we'll get you two hitched down at city hall and then head over to Judge Montgomery's. My fee is five hundred dollars. Is that acceptable?"

Madeline nodded. "Perfectly. Although I'd pay you ten times that. You're the first attorney who even really listened to me. I'm grateful."

Elizabeth looked at her shrewdly. "I gather money is not a problem for you?"

Madeline shook her head. "No, it's not."

Elizabeth's sharp eyes probed like blue knives. "Do you mind telling me how much money you do have? It's relevant to this case."

She squirmed a bit on the threadbare sofa and then glanced at Teague. He looked at her steadily, waiting for her answer. He had to admit he was more than curious.

"Approximately five million dollars in capital investments, cash, and land."

It was the first time he had heard that number, and it shocked him. He'd had no idea.

Elizabeth whistled. "Wow, I guess it's not a problem. I'll need to see the information on all your assets as well."

Madeline nodded. "I brought everything with me. Where do we start?"

"I'd be looking for vindication, too, Miss Brewster." She smiled again.

Madeline turned to Teague and looked at him with worried eyes. "Do you want to change your mind?"

Teague admitted to himself that it was enough to scare him but not enough to change his mind.

"Not a chance. You're stuck with me."

She kissed him quickly. "Same here."

"Let's get started, then," Elizabeth said as she stood. "We've got a lot of work to do."

After they agreed to meet Elizabeth first thing in the morning, Madeline and Teague went outside into the twilight air. It was cool and still, with a hint of moisture in the air, as if it were thinking about raining.

Teague wrapped his hand around hers as they walked down the street. It seemed like a good idea to leave this part of town before it was completely dark. Madeline matched Teague's strides, one advantage of being tall she did not mind in the least.

His hand felt good in hers, like her too large hand had finally found its mate.

"So we're getting hitched?" he said.

Madeline smiled. "Yes, I guess we are."

"Do you want to do it in a church? Or take Elizabeth's suggestion and go to city hall?" Teague asked.

Madeline squeezed his hand. "It's sweet of you to ask, but I haven't been to church in two years. The preacher and I . . . well, we had our differences."

They waited for a wagon of supplies to rumble past them and then continued across the street. Teague pulled her out of the way before she could step in horse droppings. It was a very gentlemanly thing to do. Beneath that rough exterior, Teague was a gentleman in everything he did.

"That doesn't answer the question, though, Maddie. Church or city hall?"

Deep down, Madeline heard her mother's voice encouraging her to follow her heart in all she did. Her heart told her she wanted God's blessing on her marriage because she intended it to be the only marriage she ever had.

"Church."

He smiled and stopped to kiss her. His lips were firm yet supple. Before she knew it, she was flush against him, his erection pushing into her, teasing her. She wanted him. Now.

"Whoa," he said as he pulled back. "We're gonna get arrested in a minute."

One more quick, hard kiss, and he let her go. She was pleased to see his pulse fluttering madly on his neck. It certainly matched how she felt inside.

"I know the perfect church."

Madeline knew Teague had traveled around the West quite a bit over the last seven years. She wasn't surprised to find out he knew a church for them to get married in. Plum Creek seemed a million miles away, and she couldn't be happier. Perhaps after all this was over, they might move to Denver.

Teague hailed a hansom cab. He spoke quietly to the young man driving, and then they climbed in. They rode for a little while, not speaking, just sitting thigh to thigh, holding hands.

Madeline's stomach was jumping, and she felt just slightly queasy.

They were getting married. Now. Today. How amazing the last month had been. Before she knew it, they stopped in front of a little stone church with ivy growing up the side. The sign outside read FIRST DENVER METHODIST CHURCH. Teague opened the heavy wooden door for her, and they went inside.

It took a moment for her eyes to adjust to the low light, but she was immediately enchanted. Eight rows of wooden pews, well used but clean, filled most of the room. The altar was a simple podium with a red velvet runner draped across it. There was a scent of cinnamon in the air.

"Can I help you?" came a voice from the right side of the church.

They both turned and found a preacher dressed in the normal black accoutrements. Only, where his left arm was, there was an empty sleeve. He had wavy brown hair clipped close to his scalp. One eyebrow seemed to have been burned off, along with a patch of skin on his forehead.

"You sure look as ugly as I remember, Raider," Teague said.

Madeline gasped.

"Reverend Raider to you, you old son of a bitch."

The preacher smiled and walked toward Teague. They clasped right hands and then embraced quickly.

"Teague O'Neal! I didn't know you were back in Denver!"

Teague smiled. "Just for a few days. I'm here with my bride-to-be, Madeline." He turned to her. "Come meet my old colonel, Mark Raider."

Madeline stepped toward them and held out her right hand to the stranger. "I'm happy to meet a friend of Teague's."

Mr. Raider smiled, and Madeline was immediately at ease. He had a peacefulness in his brown eyes that looked hard fought.

"Bride-to-be? You lucky dog! Congratulations!"

His sincerity was apparent, and Madeline found herself smiling back broadly.

"When is the wedding?"

Teague glanced at Madeline and winked. "Well, that's why we're here. . . . You see, we'd like to get married tonight. Now."

Mr. Raider's lone eyebrow nearly went up to his hairline. "Now? What's the hurry? I mean, you aren't . . . oh, shit, I mean, pardon me, Madeline . . . I, oh, hell. I'll stop talking now."

Teague laughed, and the sound echoed through Madeline's chest like the purr of a big cat.

"Raider, I'll save you some embarrassment. Maddie and I love each other and want to get married. The hurry is we're trying to beat some bastards who are trying to bury her."

Raider's countenance changed immediately. "You need help?"

Teague shook his head. "Nothing more than to marry us tonight. Can you do it?"

"Done," Raider said. "Give me a few minutes to get ready?"

"Of course," Madeline said. "Thank you for agreeing to help us."

Raider looked at her, and a curtain lifted briefly. She saw into his soul, his wounded soul. She felt a kinship with him over a lifetime's worth of pain and heartache.

"I owe Teague my life. There isn't anything I wouldn't do for him."

Whatever bond they had, it went bone deep, way down inside where humans are most vulnerable. She assumed it had been forged during the War Between the States, but she didn't feel it was her place to ask.

While Raider readied himself, Teague and Madeline walked around the church admiring the stained glass. When he was finished, he called them down to the altar.

An older couple appeared from the back of the church to serve as witnesses. They introduced themselves as the Blackmans and congratulated Teague and Madeline.

As Raider opened a well-worn Bible and began the ceremony, Madeline's heart was opening. Wider and wider until she felt like the entire world were pouring into her, giving her life. She breathed deeply and repeated, "I do," when prompted and then her wedding vows.

Teague replied with a conviction that made the simple ceremony perfect. He squeezed her hand in apology when he told Raider he had no ring.

"I have my mother's in my bag at the hotel. I would love to wear it," Madeline said.

Teague cocked one eyebrow. "Are you sure you don't want your own?"

Madeline shook her head. "No, it's a piece of my mother. The only other person who loved me, truly loved me."

Teague smiled and then leaned toward her. He stopped himself and glanced at Raider.

"May I kiss the bride?"

Raider grinned. "I now pronounce you husband and wife. You may kiss your bride."

Teague's lips were soft at first but grew firmer as the kiss progressed. Her arms snuck around his neck as she pulled herself against him. Her heart jumped as his hold tightened. She nearly forgot they were in a church. She nearly forgot that Raider was standing there.

She could hardly believe Teague was her *husband*.

Someone Madeline never thought to call her own. A husband to her wife, a partner.

After congratulations and a promise to spend more time with Raider before they left Denver, Teague and Madeline left the church to return to the hotel.

Teague felt like a young man about to bed his first woman. He was jittery and nervous. He was thirty-five years old, for Christ's sake!

It didn't help. He was just hoping he didn't embarrass himself on his wedding night. He'd never expected to ever have another one, much less be so excited he could barely control his urge to bed his wife.

Their locked hands separated as they walked through the hotel lobby, avoiding the front desk and anyone's eyes. He tried not to walk too quickly, but he couldn't help it. He wanted her beneath him. *Now.*

Within minutes, they were in her room. Teague didn't even remember locking the door. Maddie's scent filled him as her clothes melted off as easily as his. They walked toward the bed, locked in a full-body embrace. Their lips locked together, moving, sucking, licking.

His cock was as hard as he ever remembered it being. It pressed against her soft belly, hungry for his wife.

Jesus. *His wife.*

Teague shook off the enormity of the words and concentrated on the feel of her. Her hands were roaming up and down his back, caressing and squeezing.

"Is this . . ."—she kissed his jaw—". . . lesson eight?"

He grinned against her cheek as his mouth meandered across her cheek, planting little kisses. "Perhaps it's a lesson for both of us, Maddie."

She nipped his earlobe with her sharp little teeth. A shiver snaked down his spine, making the hairs on his arms stand up like flags. Then again, there wasn't much on him that wasn't standing at attention.

Her hand cupped his balls, and one finger lightly pressed on his sac. He groaned from somewhere near his feet.

"Did I do that right?" she whispered.

"If you do it any better, we won't make it to the bed."

She laughed huskily and stroked his cock with her firm hand. He leaned into her and forgot all about anything but her touch.

His hands found their ways to her breasts. The raspberry nipples were like little rubies begging for his touch. He flicked his thumbs back and forth across them, savoring the twin points of pleasure.

Her hand tightened on his firm flesh, and he knew he had to get inside her soon. Now, actually.

He picked her up in his arms, and she squeaked like a little girl. Teague looked at her in surprise.

Her cheeks a light pink, she shrugged.

"It's not the threshold, but I'm going to carry you anyway."

Maddie bit her lip and nodded jerkily. "That's awfully romantic for a farmer from Missouri."

He grinned. "You inspire me."

Her beautiful dark eyes grew a bit misty. "I love you, Teague."

He walked to the bed and set her down gently on the white coverlet. "I love you, too, Maddie." His hand cupped her cheek as he sat next to her, unmindful of their nakedness. "Do you believe me? Trust in me?"

She nodded. "I didn't, but I do now."

"I'm here beside you. I promise."

Maddie's hands pulled at his shoulders. "I want you inside me."

She didn't have to ask Teague twice. He covered her body with his, fitting into the niche between her warm thighs. It felt wonderful. It felt incredible. It felt like home.

"Hurry, Teague," she said into his mouth as he captured her lips.

He slid into her easily. She was tight, hot, and slick. Buried deep inside his new wife, he had to grit his teeth to stop himself from coming too quickly. Maddie pulled at his ass, urging him to move.

After he regained his self-control, he forced himself to move slowly, to savor his first experience with her as a married couple. She clenched around him and moved with him, making their rhythm go faster and faster. Soon he was slamming into her, and her legs came up around his waist, sending him deep, deep into her pussy. Touching her womb . . . making his heart fly and his soul soar.

"Teague!" she shouted as her body tightened and began to milk him.

The wave of pleasure must have started in his toes because by the time it hit him, it was the most powerful thing he'd ever felt. He was sure he shouted her name, but the rest of him was humming and buzzing.

Teague wasn't surprised to find he was breathing hard. He was surprised to find tears rolling down his cheeks.

His heart was finally whole again in Maddie's arms.

They fell asleep not long after and then woke again in the night to make slow, sweet love. When the morning came, Maddie smiled like the happiest woman in the world and headed out with him to Elizabeth's. They heard the desk clerk call them, but they walked quickly to avoid any questions. After all, Teague was registered as her brother.

They laughed like young kids as they emerged into the street. Then the smile disappeared, and the warrior queen emerged. It was time to do battle.

Chapter Eighteen

It was three days of nonstop work. Elizabeth was a bit of a slave driver who apparently didn't sleep. Teague constantly watched her with a frown on his face, one that made Madeline smile inside. They hadn't been back to the hotel since they had arrived on Elizabeth's doorstep the morning after their wedding.

They had combed city hall, the courthouse, sifted through county records, and visited every bank in the city.

They had made good progress. Elizabeth had finally stopped cursing, and the pile of papers was growing exponentially. Evidence. Lots of evidence.

Enough to put both of those bastards in jail. Elizabeth went through the papers again—it seemed like the hundredth time as Madeline and Teague waited.

She looked up at them and smiled with enough teeth to nearly frighten Madeline. "I think we're ready. Now all we need to do is visit Judge Carter."

"Who is Judge Carter?"

"He's the circuit-court judge. He'll be in town on Friday. I already sent a note to his clerk," Elizabeth said. "He's really hard, but he's honest."

"Does this mean we can take a day off?"

Elizabeth raised an eyebrow at Teague's dry question. "Are you saying you haven't enjoyed my company, Mr. O'Neal?"

He couldn't help but grin. "Not at all, Elizabeth. I'm just newly married, and, well . . . I'm missing my wife."

The smile he turned on Madeline was enough to turn her into a puddle. Her body instantly throbbed with need, and a constant thrum began between her legs. She was that ready for him, that quickly.

Madeline grinned wickedly and tried her best to imitate his eyebrow waggle. He chuckled and leaned forward to kiss her quickly.

"You are a tempting piece, Mrs. O'Neal."

Mrs. O'Neal.

It was the first time anyone had called her that. Her heart skipped a beat when she realized she was Mrs. O'Neal. She was a wife, and she had a husband.

"I do believe you two need some time by yourselves. Why don't you go back to the hotel and meet me back here Friday morning at eight?" Elizabeth winked at Madeline.

Madeline felt herself blush just a bit.

"Thank you, Elizabeth," she said and reached for the other woman's hands. "I can't even begin to tell you how grateful—"

Elizabeth cut her off with one swipe of her hand. "Don't spoil it by turning into a simpering miss, Madeline. That's not you, and you know it. I don't expect gratitude or any weepy moments. Let's just beat those bastards."

"Amen," Teague said.

Madeline had so much more she wanted to say to Elizabeth, but she kept it inside. Now was obviously not the time. The truth was she would be eternally grateful to the other woman for even attempting to help her. Madeline knew she had a chance of losing this battle, but she wasn't lying down and letting men take advantage of her.

She was fighting for what she believed was right. And Elizabeth was helping her. *Her.* Madeline Brewster, daughter of the infamously cruel Rufus Brewster, and embarrassment to the town of Plum Creek.

Madeline felt ten feet tall as she and Teague left Elizabeth's house.

Madeline tucked her arm into Teague's arm as they strolled down the street. They took their time heading back to the hotel so by the time they got there it would be dinner. They could eat in the restaurant and then head upstairs.

They talked of things they saw on the street, horses, people, even hats in a store window. Teague felt tense, anxious, and excited. Their lives would change again in the next two days. He wasn't sure if it was for better or worse. Whatever it was, it would be assuredly different.

When they walked through the doors of the hotel, Madeline headed straight for the front desk. The clerk behind the desk watched her with wary eyes and then cut his gaze to his left. Teague glanced over and saw two men sitting with their backs to him in the plush red velvet sofas in the lobby.

When he looked back at Madeline, she was already talking to the clerk, who handed her what looked like a telegram. The pit of his stomach bounced. Telegrams were always the harbingers of bad news. She read it, and all the color drained from her face. She looked up, and her gaze found him. In those dark eyes, he saw a familiar ghost from the past. Grief.

Teague sprinted to her side and enfolded her in his arms without a word. He didn't need to know what the news was to know it hit her like a train. Madeline's normally strong body was shaking like a leaf in a spring storm.

"Teague," she whispered. "It's from Candice."

Candice? The lady from the store?

"She s—s—said . . ." she gulped loudly, "that Jackson shot Eppie."

Now Teague had another emotion to deal with. Anger. How dare that pompous ass cross the line as soon as he and Maddie left town?

"Where the hell was Micah?" he asked tightly.

"She says he was fighting with Jackson at the time, and the gun went off. He's barricaded himself in the house and only let Candice in to bring him medical supplies. She doesn't know if Eppie is alive or not." She clutched his shirt. "I have to go."

He cupped the back of her head and held her close, willing his strength into her. "We'll leave right now."

"What about Elizabeth? And the judge?" Maddie started to pull away from him.

"Oh, I'm sure the judge will be waiting for you back in Plum Creek, Madeline." Jackson Webster's voice lashed Teague's ears like a whip.

Jackson was standing beside them sporting a blackened eye and a few scrapes on his face but otherwise looked hale and hearty.

Madeline looked at the sheriff in confusion while it was all Teague could do not to pound the son of a bitch into a pile of nothing on the pretty patterned carpet.

"How could you, Jackson? Eppie is an innocent girl."

Jackson chortled. "Well, she is a girl, but she sure as hell ain't no innocent. Especially staying in your house with that crazy Johnny Reb."

"How dare you!" Madeline's cheeks flushed with color. Anger was much better than despair.

"What the hell do you want, Webster?" Teague snarled.

The sheriff's eyes looked them up and down. "You are getting mighty close to Miss Brewster there, horse thief. Her reputation has been tarnished beyond measure by that. As a matter of fact, there's many tarnished things about Miss Brewster. Right here"—he pulled a folded piece of paper from his jacket pocket—"is a warrant for her arrest."

Teague grabbed her before she could fall. They'd been expecting it, just not so soon and not right after the news about Eppie.

"What are the charges?" Teague demanded.

"None of your concern, lawbreaker. I'm here to bring

Miss Brewster back to Plum Creek so she can stand for her crimes."

Teague tucked Madeline behind him and faced Webster down.

"Yes, it is my concern. You see, Maddie and I were married three days ago. She's my wife."

Teague had the satisfaction of seeing the sheriff's eyes widen and a brief look of shock flitter across his cold blue eyes.

"Makes no never mind to me if she married a tree stump. She is under arrest, and I am lawfully bringing her back to stand trial for her crimes."

Teague grabbed a fistful of the sheriff's fine chambray shirt and yanked the other man toward him. The hotel lobby was unnaturally quiet, and he figured they were making a fine spectacle of themselves.

"I'm going to ask you only one more time. What are the charges?" he asked through gritted teeth.

"Embezzlement, fraud, forgery, and indecent, lewd behavior." The sheriff spit them out like they were distasteful bites of meat.

"Bull. You're not taking her anywhere."

Webster nodded over her shoulder, and Teague found himself tightly held by two burly men while two equally burly men pulled Madeline away from him. Teague had never felt so helpless or so furious.

"Let her go!" he shouted.

Webster had the brass balls to laugh. "Nothing doing, drifter. You had your chance to make yourself a better life with some money in your pocket. Now you threw it all away on a dried-up old spinster with sticky fingers."

Teague perhaps would never remember the next two minutes very well. There was cursing, punching, kicking, and screaming. When things finally sorted themselves out, two men were bodily carrying Madeline toward the door, and Teague had three men holding him down.

"Go to Elizabeth!" she shouted. "Tell her everything!"

"I love you, Maddie!" he shouted back.

"I love you, too!" came her voice as it faded away from him.

With one boot planted on his chest, Webster looked down at him and spit. Teague had no doubt he'd make the other man pay for every word, every insult he'd given Maddie. He had to be patient, but, hell, all he wanted to do was kill him.

"Sweet, very sweet. Too bad by the time you make it back to Plum Creek she'll have already swung from the oak."

Swung from the oak? They were going to *hang* Maddie? His heart clenched so hard he couldn't breathe for a moment.

Hell, no.

"Never gonna happen."

Webster chuckled. "How are you going to stop me if you're in jail in Denver?"

Teague discovered that Denver's jail was no less dirty than any other jail. He'd certainly seen, and spent time in, worse. He paid a young boy a dollar to get a message to Elizabeth and then waited, impatiently, for her to arrive.

He had no doubt she would, but would it be in time to save Maddie's life? She had saved him from a hanging, which seemed a lifetime ago. Now she needed him to save her.

Chapter Nineteen

Madeline stared out the small window in the cell. All she could see were branches from evergreen trees. Occasionally a bird flew by, or a squirrel chattered somewhere. Other than that, she was completely alone.

She wondered if Teague had gone to Elizabeth and if they were working on helping her. Some little devil buried deep inside her was jumping up and down and cackling evilly. That little devil reminded her that Teague would have all her money if she died, that it was in his best interest to simply let her hang.

Her heart stood up to the little devil and hung on to the belief that Teague loved her. She knew there was absolutely nothing that would convince anyone he would save her. Up until a month ago, he had been a drifter. Madeline knew, deep down where her soul rested, that he would not abandon her, that he loved her. She trusted him, and that was all she needed.

Jackson thought it was his job to come by every hour and talk to her. He would tell her that Teague was not in town, that the judge was prepared to hang her if necessary, that they had brought in an attorney from Boulder to represent the town. A highly respected attorney named Matthew Worthington, a man who had never lost a case.

The mere mention of a hanging made her so sick she could

taste bile at the back of her throat. She didn't give Jackson the satisfaction of reacting where he could see. She waited until he left before she wept into her hands.

Matilda Webster came by with her meals "out of the goodness of her heart." She just wanted to be able to gossip to her little trio of witches that she saw the Black Widow in jail.

Madeline desperately tried to get news of Eppie, but Jackson told her nothing, and Matilda pretended like she hadn't heard her. She prayed for her friend and for Micah, the man who was apparently trying to save her friend's life.

It was near dark on Thursday evening. She had been in the cell for almost twenty-four hours, and it felt like twenty-four days.

"Psssst. Madeline," came a whisper near the window.

Madeline jumped up from the cot and stepped up to the bars that kept her imprisoned.

"Micah?"

"Yes, it's me. Candice told me what happened, so I asked her to sit with Eppie while I came down here."

Madeline felt tears stinging her eyes. "Micah, what happened to Eppie? How is she?"

There was a pregnant pause. "That bastard shot her and then ran. She was hit in the shoulder and—" his voice caught. "I tried to save her as best I could. She is hanging on, but only by a thread."

Madeline's hands gripped the bars. "Has she seen a doctor?"

A rusty laugh floated toward her. "The doctor is in Jackson Webster's pocket. He tried to get in the house with a shotgun, claimed he needed it to protect himself. I told him to go to hell. I had to learn to be a medic during the war, so I've used my healing skills. Candice helped me, too. That's a good friend you have there, Madeline."

"Oh, Micah, I'm so sorry. I want to be there to help you. I . . . All this is my fault. I should have never—"

"Stop it!" he cut her off. "You sure as hell should have. You can't let low-down skunks like Webster and that fat judge control your life. We'll get them in court, sweet girl. Did you get your attorney up there in Denver?"

Madeline sighed. "Yes, and she's wonderful. Teague and I got separated when Jackson arrested me. He . . . he's supposed to be here with her any time now."

There was another pause. "That's good. I'm sure he'll be here lickety split. Now . . . what happened in Denver?"

She stared at her bare hand, devoid of a ring. She regretted a million times not getting her mother's wedding band before leaving Denver.

"We got married."

After a moment, he spoke. "About damn time, too. That man loves you to distraction, Madeline, just as much as you love him."

Micah's simple words were exactly what she needed to hear. Confirmation that others saw what she felt. That it wasn't just her imagination. That he truly did love her.

"Thank you."

He snorted. "No need to thank me. I got your best friend shot and you arrested. I failed you . . . and Eppie."

Madeline could hear the grief in his voice, could almost see the regret and sadness in the air.

"You didn't fail me, friend. You did only what you could. Micah, you and Eppie were my first friends. Ever. Nothing you do would ever be wrong or a failure, because you do it as my friend."

She reached her hand through the bars, and after a moment or two, his hand clasped hers. Calloused, and smaller than Teague's, it infused her with what she needed. Hope.

"We'll beat them, Madeline. Don't you fret. Teague will be here with your attorney, and we'll beat them."

Teague stood behind Elizabeth in the judge's chambers and fisted his hands to keep from hitting the hard-ass son of a bitch. Elizabeth had pulled some of her magic strings to get an audience with Judge Montgomery because they couldn't wait until Friday for that Carter fellow. Raider had shown up to lend God's help, not that it was helping. It was Thursday, and time was slipping away like sand in an hourglass, and this man was refusing to help them. He was at least fifty, with mud-colored eyes, balding black-and-gray hair, and sagging jowls. His gaze was razor sharp, and his jaw seemed permanently set in granite.

Elizabeth, bless her, used every weapon she could think of. She had paperwork coming out her ears, arguments, precedents in legal texts, and her own persuasive manner (which Teague cottoned to more to bullying, but, hell, she was on their side, which was the only thing that mattered). Nothing worked. Judge Pain-in-the-Ass wasn't budging.

"I told you, Miss Mitchell, I will not prosecute this case against the men of Plum Creek. Now please remove yourself from my chambers."

Elizabeth opened her mouth to say something, and the judge waved his hand in a chopping motion. "I've heard enough. No more, Elizabeth, or I'll hold you in contempt."

That, as they say, was that.

Teague moved Elizabeth aside and leaned over the desk of Judge Wilson Montgomery and let the full force of his anger and frustration come forth.

"Listen to me, then. A bunch of men who don't like a woman holding the cards are persecuting my wife, Madeline. They have cheated her, stolen from her, smeared her good name, and treated her like shit. She believed in me, trusted me, and I betrayed her. She forgave me, and not only that, married my sorry ass. I love her, and I refuse to let her die because a windbag like you won't help her. She's one of the good people in this world, and if she dies because of you, there is no corner on this earth you can hide in that I won't find you. Now, Judge Montgomery, are you going to go with us to Plum Creek and shove the book up Sheriff Jackson Webster's and Judge Earl Martin's collective asses, or do I need to persuade you a bit more?"

Judge Montgomery didn't flinch from Teague's angry tirade; however, he did flush a bit. Teague could have bitten off a piece of his oak desk and spit it out. Too bad he couldn't control his emotions like this man of the law.

"Did you say Earl Martin?" Judge Montgomery asked.

A tiny, tiny flare of hope flickered to life inside Teague's chest. "Yes. Pompous son of a bitch with a belly that arrives in a room before he does. Paid me five hundred dollars to spy on Madeline."

Judge Montgomery's eyebrows rose. "You didn't mention him by name before. Earl and I—well, let's say that we go way back." He turned to look at Elizabeth. "Show me what you have against them."

Raider grinned. "You know God is on your side when there's a true lawbreaker at hand."

The flare of hope grew bigger. Teague stepped aside and let Elizabeth work.

Madeline shifted uncomfortably in the wooden chair behind the defense table. Spectators packed the courtroom to the rafters, and the buzzing behind her was like a swarm of bees waiting to sting her.

It was Friday morning at nine AM, and Teague had not arrived. *Yet.* Madeline refused to believe he wasn't coming. The space beside her was empty. No attorney, no husband, and no friend. She straightened her spine and her resolve. Her faith in those she loved was strong. They wouldn't let her down.

Jackson stood by the door to the side room where Judge Martin had his chambers. The smirk on his face was enough to make Madeline want to kick him in the balls. Pretentious windbag.

He announced Judge Martin with a lot of pomp and circumstance. The judge waddled out in his best Sunday suit and looked at the crowd with an official glower. His bald head gleamed in the sunlight streaming through the windows. He sat down with a grunt and an obnoxious throat-clearing episode that made Madeline's stomach turn.

"Ladies and gentlemen," he said in his officious tone. "During these proceedings, we will have no outbursts from the gallery. This is a serious trial with serious charges. You will show the court its due respect."

A few murmurs met his pronouncement. They were surprisingly quiet. Probably waiting to see how quickly they could slip a noose around her neck. She shuddered involuntarily.

Judge Martin looked down his nose at Madeline and then pointedly at the empty chair beside her.

"Miss Brewster, I see you have no attorney present."

"Mrs. O'Neal, your honor," she said firmly.

"Excuse me?"

Madeline straightened her shoulders. "My name is Mrs. O'Neal, not Miss Brewster."

His mouth opened and closed, and then he smirked. "Where is your husband, then, *Mrs.* O'Neal?"

"Right here."

Teague's deep voice echoed through the quiet courtroom. Madeline jumped up with her heart in her throat. She saw Teague at the door in his best clothes, his hair trimmed and combed. Beside him stood Elizabeth, her arms full of neatly stacked papers.

Teague's eyes sought hers, and she was immediately awash in the love she found there.

"You! You are a horse thief!" shouted Judge Martin. "Sheriff Webster, arrest that man!"

"You will not touch him," said another deep voice from behind Teague.

A tall, thin man with salt-and-pepper hair stepped forward.

"Montgomery!" Judge Martin looked decidedly paler than he had a minute ago.

The stranger grinned, although Madeline could swear there was no mirth in that show of teeth.

"I would say it's good to see you, but that would be a lie, Earl. I hear you've been a naughty boy."

"I have done nothing—"

"Don't interrupt me, Earl. I brought some marshals with me to make sure these proceedings are legal and stay that way." The stranger stepped in, followed by two rather burly looking men with silver stars on their leather vests. They were both sporting pistols strapped to their impressive thighs.

As they headed for the front of the courtroom, Teague and Elizabeth walked to the defense table. Teague had to push his way through the crowd that erupted when the strangers headed toward the front. It was like watching Madeline's life unfolding right in front of her.

When he finally reached her, he pulled her into his arms and held her so tightly she swore she felt a rib creak in protest. He whispered her name over and over. His big arms felt like home. She had finally found one where she belonged.

"Let her go, Goliath," Elizabeth said from behind them. "We've still got some work to do."

The crowd finally settled down after Judge Martin banged on his gavel so hard the wood cracked on his desk.

"That is enough! Everyone needs to shut the hell up. This is a court of law, you know!"

His face was flushed a beet red, and his forehead shone with perspiration. Oh, yes, the judge was nervous now.

Teague sat down on the chair next to Madeline and pulled her close enough to touch. Elizabeth cocked one blond eyebrow at him, and he blushed and then stood, offering her the chair. He stood behind Madeline with his hands on her shoulders. "Who is that man?" Madeline whispered.

"Just watch," Teague replied.

The stranger pulled a folded paper out of his pocket and read it aloud.

"By order of the superior court of Colorado, I hereby re-move Judge Earl Martin from presiding over the case of Plum Creek versus Madeline Brewster. A new judge is now hearing this case. Me." He grinned and showed his sharp teeth to Judge Martin again. "Remove yourself from the bench and take a seat by your fancy prosecuting attorney." He refolded the paper and tucked it back in his jacket pocket.

Like a gaping fish, Judge Martin stood, stomped down from the judge's bench, and walked toward the prosecution's table. He shot a malevolent glare at Teague before sitting down.

"Now, just so you all know, my name is Judge Wilson Montgomery. I am a superior-court judge in Boulder, and I am now presiding over this courtroom. Any outbursts, and I will remove you from this room. No exceptions." He glanced around the courtroom to be sure his message was received. Apparently satisfied, he gestured to the attorneys. "Speak your piece."

The prosecuting attorney stood. He was a well-dressed, fit man in his midforties with jet-black hair and a sprinkling of gray around the sideburns. He carried himself with self-confidence. He scared the bejesus out of Madeline.

"Matthew Worthington for the prosecution, sir."

Elizabeth stood.

"Elizabeth Mitchell for the defense, sir."

More than a few snickers and several gasps met her statement. No one had ever seen a female attorney in Plum Creek.

Judge Montgomery turned his stare onto Madeline. Unbelievably she squirmed in her seat. His gaze reminded her a bit of her tyrannical father.

"You are Madeline Brewster, now Madeline O'Neal?"

"Yes, sir," she managed to say through tight lips.

"The man behind you is your lawfully wedded husband, Teague O'Neal, a decorated captain in the Union Army?"

Madeline hid her surprise. She had no idea Teague was a war hero.

"Yes, sir. Teague is my husband."

"You married him willingly and without coercion?"

She had no idea where the questions were leading, and she had no choice but to answer honestly. "Yes, sir."

Judge Montgomery nodded, satisfied with her answers.

"Someone provide Mr. O'Neal with a chair. I don't want him standing in my courtroom all day."

There was some shuffling, and another chair was brought to the defense table.

"Let's proceed, then. Mr. Worthington, present your case."

Teague had never been so scared in his life. He knew they had the evidence to thwart anything the prosecution threw at her, but there was the possibility of failure. He didn't even want to contemplate it, but he couldn't help it. He had just found the one person who made his heart whole, and there was a threat to her. A big threat. An enormous threat. And he couldn't do a damn thing to stop it.

He listened to the fancy attorney from Boulder lay out the evidence against Madeline, and his stomach grew tighter and tighter. Over one hundred thousand dollars missing, properties seized illegally, and falsified bank records. Then there was the ugly lie about her moral character.

Elizabeth proceeded to lay out her case—brilliantly, in Teague's opinion. She spoke of jealousy, hate, and greed and named the true guilty parties.

Then the prosecution started in earnest. Witness after witness came up and testified. A little weasel named Cleeson from the bank told how Madeline acted strangely and stayed late or came in early, how the ledgers never seemed to stay the same. Then some pulpit pounder named Reverend Mathias—had to be the one Madeline couldn't stand—talked about her immortal soul's jeopardy. How she took in strays, Negroes, and single men into her house, which she painted blue like a harlot's residence.

Madeline watched everything without crying, but he saw her chin wobbling a few times. He just kept squeezing her hand and tried desperately to give her his strength.

Lousy bastards. So many times he wanted to jump up and shout at them or, better yet, pound them into a pulp. He didn't. He heeded Judge Montgomery's warning and stayed quiet. No way in hell he wanted to leave Maddie's side. By the time Mr. Fancy-Pants Worthington finished pontificating, it was nearly four o'clock.

Judge Montgomery looked at the clock. "We will pick up tomorrow morning with the defense at nine o'clock sharp. If you're not here by nine, the door gets shut and you don't get in." He pointed at Madeline. "You are still in custody, young lady, and will be remanded to the marshals for this evening."

He slammed the gavel, and everyone rose as he left the courtroom. The burly marshals walked to her table and waited patiently for her to stand.

The crowd chattered away as the room began to empty. Teague was hoping the judge would release Madeline into his custody, but he hadn't.

"Ma'am," said the dark-haired marshal. "My name is Watkins. This is Hoke. No harm will come to you, I promise you. It's time to go."

Teague turned her face to look at him. Her dark eyes were sad, scared, and resigned all at the same time.

"We'll beat them, honey. I promise," he said and then kissed her gently.

She nodded and stood. She hugged Elizabeth briefly. "Thank you, Elizabeth. I don't know what I would have done without you."

Elizabeth waved her hand in dismissal. "It's the most fun I've had in years. No need to thank me. I wouldn't be here if it wasn't for this bear of a husband of yours."

Madeline finally smiled. The pure love that shone at him was enough to knock him to his knees. Then, in front of God and all the people left in the room, she grabbed his face and kissed him senseless. Lord, Jesus, he wanted to spend the rest of his life with this woman.

"I have something for you," he said, reaching into his pocket.

He fished out the gold band he'd found in her belongings and held it up.

Her smile grew wider, and she nodded at him. With something like reverence, he slid the gold band on her finger. It fit perfectly, like it was made for her.

"Thank you," she whispered and then proceeded to kiss him all over again. His body's temperature was rising, right along with his erection.

Watkins interrupted with a cough. "Ma'am, we need to go."

With one last kiss, she pulled away and whispered, "I love you," and then walked away with the marshals beside her. She held herself like a queen as the people left in the room whispered and pointed at her.

"Helluva woman," Elizabeth mused.

"God, yes," Teague said. "I hope to hell you can keep her mine."

Chapter Twenty

Teague helped Elizabeth carry her things back to Madeline's house. Court was held in the meeting hall in the middle of town, so it was a short, ten-minute walk there. The air was still relatively warm, and there was a hint of spring flowers in the air.

"Lovely town," Elizabeth said.

"Appearances can be deceiving," Teague responded.

She nodded. "They surely can."

The rest of the walk was silent. Teague was afraid to express his worry over Madeline's fate. As if speaking it aloud would somehow make it come true.

As they walked up the front steps, he heard the distinct sound of a shotgun being cocked.

"Micah?" Teague called. "It's Teague."

"Teague?" came a voice from behind the door. "About damn time you showed up, Yank."

The door opened, and Teague tried not to let his shock show at Micah's condition. Barefoot, he wore torn, bloodstained clothes. His hair looked like a tumbleweed, and his beard was matted. But it was his eyes that really stood out. He knew that look. That soul-encompassing grief.

"How is she?" he asked.

Micah shook his head. "Alive."

He introduced Elizabeth to Micah, and they all went inside.

Teague walked upstairs while Micah and Elizabeth talked. He found a plump redheaded woman sitting with Eppie. She stood up when he came in.

"Oh, my! Hello, there, I'm Candice Merriweather, Madeline's friend. You must be Mr. O'Neal." She held out one hand, and Teague politely shook it.

"Nice to meet you, Miss Merriweather. How is she?"

Candice glanced down at Eppie, whose chest was barely moving. She was swathed in white bandages and white sheets and looked just like an angel.

"There's been no change. She ran a high fever the first two days, but it broke, thank God. Since then she's just been sleeping so deeply nothing seems to touch her." Candice glanced at the door. "Micah has been beside himself with worry. I think, perhaps, there's more than guilt involved."

Teague felt his back go up at her words. He waited for her to express her distaste.

"It's awful what happened to Eppie. I hope she wakes up and sees how much he cares for her."

Candice truly looked saddened, and Teague's defenses retreated back down. She obviously wasn't a closed-minded moron like the rest of the town.

"Oh, my goodness!" she exclaimed. "How is Madeline?"

Teague sat down and filled Candice in on what had happened that day. She tut-tutted about the marshals taking her away and looked decidedly aghast at what the other townspeople had had to say about Madeline.

"Why, I can't believe it! These are the same people she's helped for the last two years, throwing it back in her face. That is . . . a low-down, skunky thing to do!"

Teague chuckled at how she screwed up her face and then didn't even curse. She had a good heart. Madeline could rest easy about this friend of hers.

"Yes, ma'am, it surely was. Now, if you'll excuse me, I'm

going to go downstairs and see if I can convince Micah to take a bath, now that reinforcements have arrived." He bent down and kissed Eppie's still forehead and then whispered. "Get better, you little curmudgeon."

Teague talked, argued, and then finally bullied Micah into taking a bath. Elizabeth threw up her hands and said she was going to the sitting room to read. She didn't need any naked men in her line of vision.

While Micah heated the water for his bath, Teague went outside to sit on the front porch. As soon as his body touched the swing, he was awash in memories of Maddie. He closed his eyes and remembered holding her hand, breathing in her flowery scent, falling helplessly in love with her.

It had been only two days, but he missed her like hell. What he had felt for Claire was young love. What he had felt for Maddie was a deep, abiding love that carved out a niche inside him. Losing her would simply destroy him. He couldn't let that happen.

As twilight fell, he saw the lights of the buildings in town twinkle in the purple darkness. His sharp eyes picked out three figures walking toward the house as though they wanted to sneak up on it. Teague melted into the shadows of the front porch and waited to see what they would do. He wouldn't put it past that bastard Webster to send someone to kill them all as they slept.

When the three figures came closer, one of them started walking faster, so the other two kept pace. That's when Teague felt his heart thump loudly.

Maddie.

He vaulted off the porch and ran.

Madeline saw Teague appear from the shadows of the porch, and tears sprang to her eyes. As he ran toward her, she walked as quickly as she could to meet him halfway. When they finally met, she threw herself into his arms, and he twirled her around and around until she was dizzy. His lips sought hers, and they kissed and kissed until Madeline nearly forgot she was on trial for her life.

"I missed you," he said against her ear as he nibbled the lobe. Sharp shivers of want echoed through her body.

"I missed you, too." A tap on her shoulder reminded her that her guards were still there watching them. She pulled back and scanned Teague's eyes in the darkness. "I begged them to come. I had to see you and Eppie and Micah. I couldn't stay another night in that jail."

Teague looked behind her at the marshals. "You have my thanks."

They murmured politely, and then together the four of them walked back to Madeline's house. As she stepped over the threshold, she thought about how much her life had changed since she had left. How different everything was. Her shoes echoed on the wood floor, and she heard the past echoing at her.

It was echoes. Nothing more. The past was going to stay there. Madeline was going to focus on the future.

Micah looked absolutely horrible, though he was clean. His eyes were haunted, and his cheeks sunken. He hugged Madeline, and her guilt nearly overwhelmed her. She apologized over and over for putting him and Eppie in danger.

He frowned at her. "Don't you dare take credit for what that lousy son of a bitch did to you."

She hugged him one more time and then headed upstairs; each step was like a lead weight on her heart. Eppie. Her outspoken, funny, lovely friend. The first friend she'd ever had in her lonely world. God, she couldn't believe death hovered so near.

Madeline stepped into Eppie's room and found Candice keeping watch. They embraced, and Madeline thanked her profusely for helping Micah and for sending her the telegram. She hadn't looked at Eppie yet. She was afraid to. Candice seemed to understand, and her sad green eyes encouraged her to be brave.

Madeline finally turned to look. Her knees gave way, and she landed on the side of the bed. Good thing she had a significant rear end, or she would have ended up on the floor. Eppie looked like a ghost. Her normally cocoa-colored skin was a sallow gray, and she was all in white—white bandages, white sheets, white nightdress. Madeline half expected a pair of wings.

She picked up Eppie's hand, startled by how cold she was, and started talking. At some point, Candice left the room. Madeline talked to Eppie about everything that had happened in Denver, how she had married Teague, how he had told her he loved her. She spoke to her of the trial and everything the town was doing to ruin her. All along, tears rolled down her cheeks as grief for her friend poured through her.

Madeline talked until her throat grew hoarse and her eyes were dry. She felt a hand on her shoulder and knew immediately it was Teague.

"How about you take a rest and try to get some sleep?" he said softly.

She nodded and then leaned over to kiss her friend on the cheek and whisper in her ear, "Don't leave me, Eppie. I love you, my friend."

Madeline allowed Teague to lead her out of the room. She vaguely saw Micah head back into Eppie's room. They entered her bedroom, and Teague undressed her. Like a sleepwalker, Madeline watched him work and didn't move to help him. He lay her down in the cool, crisp sheets of her bed and pulled the blanket up around her. Teague shed his clothes quickly and climbed in beside her. Her back snuggled up against his chest, and his strong arm anchored her waist. Within moments, she fell into a deep slumber.

It was dark when she woke. Madeline felt the snug warmth of her husband behind her and smiled. She could definitely get used to this. She wiggled against him and felt his cock harden against her buttocks. She wiggled again, and it grew longer, harder.

"Maddie?"

"Love me, Teague."

The darkness surrounded them like a cocoon, and all she could do was feel. His breath fluttered across her neck as he kissed the exposed skin. His hands started caressing her breasts, slowly circling the nipples over and over until they were tight and aching. He lightly pinched them, and an answering throb went to her pussy. One big hand crept down her stomach, and her legs parted to give him better access.

Teague rolled her onto her back. His hot mouth clamped down on one breast, and his fingers began to weave their magic in her damp core. As his teeth grazed her nipple, two fingers slowly entered her as his thumb circled her hot button. Sensations battered her as her body begged for more.

He laved and nibbled her other breast while his chest hair slid against the wet nipple his mouth had just pleasured. Three fingers now were sliding in and out of her. She felt her climax rising like a wave, and she tried to hold it back. *Too soon.*

"Don't you dare hold back," he whispered. "Fly, Maddie."

He pinched her clit, and she came, bucking and twisting against his hand. His mouth suckled her breast, and his hand continued to fuck her, prolonging her orgasm. She floated, and he gentled his touch. With one last lick, he abandoned her breasts and moved away. He moved her seemingly boneless body to the center of the bed and spread her legs wide. Before she knew what he was about, he had tied her ankles to the bedposts with the sheet.

"Do you trust me?"

"Yes." Her answer was without hesitation. Whatever he was going to do filled her with excitement, where only moments before she had been satiated. She was now hungry again.

He straddled her waist, and his heavy cock rested between her breasts. He tied her wrists to the brass headboard, and Madeline barely noticed. She was trying desperately to see his erection. She wanted to lick it.

As he moved off her, she moaned in protest. He stopped in midswing.

"Maddie?"

"Please, Teague. I want to taste you."

She felt him twitch against her, and her hunger grew.

He straddled her again, and she felt his hot skin graze her lips. She stuck out her tongue and licked the tip. Salty. Enticing. She leaned her head forward as much as she could and licked all around the head and then took it in her mouth. It was the most exciting experience of her life.

She was tied to a bed and licking her husband's erection. Her pussy was throbbing in time with his pulse, which she could feel in her mouth. She licked and nibbled as he had to her, following her instincts. He started to move back and forth into her mouth, putting more and more of himself in. She sucked at him and licked as his rhythm grew faster.

"Oh, Jesus, Maddie," he said in a husky voice. "Your tongue . . ."

She stopped, embarrassed.

"Don't stop, please don't stop. You're going to make me come. That is so incredible. So amazing. God, I love you."

He started moving again, and she tasted him. Tasted his essence as it leaked from the tip onto her tongue. He suddenly withdrew and jumped off her.

"Teague?"

"I want this to last. Anticipation can heighten the pleasure."

She ached to taste him again. Her tongue ran around the seam of her lips, and she shuddered in hunger.

"I want . . ."

One finger touched her lips. "I've got the reins, Maddie. You do what I want. This is your final exam."

She nodded against his finger, ready to follow his lead.

Teague's hands started caressing her; then his tongue and lips followed them. Starting at her fingers, he explored and then licked and nibbled her. His mouth left a hot trail down each arm, around her neck and shoulders. He didn't kiss her lips, though. She wanted to ask him to but kept silent.

His teeth bit her nipples nearly to the point of pain, but she simply moaned as her excitement grew. His tongue licked the bites; then he continued his journey down her stomach, now biting and licking his way. Madeline was nearly feverish by the time he reached her legs.

She gasped as his mouth skipped her aching pussy and went down each leg to her feet. She wanted to scream in frustration; instead she throbbed in anticipation. As he suckled her toes, she wiggled on the bed, hungry for more.

"Be still. You will move when I tell you to."

Madeline immediately stopped her movements.

"Please . . ."

"Be quiet. You will speak when I tell you to."

Somehow having Teague tell her what to do was natural. In the darkness of their bedroom, he was master, and she was his to command. It was right. It was meant to be.

"Do you want me to touch you anyplace else?" he asked silkily as his hands tickled her inner thighs.

"Yes."

His thumbs brushed dangerously close to her nether lips. She had to exert all her concentration not to push up into his hands.

"Where, Maddie, girl? Where do you want me to touch you?"

"There, between my legs."

His thumbs brushed her again. "Do you know what I call this? It's your cunt. Say it."

"Cunt." The word made her clench and throb that much harder. He was right. The anticipation was heightening her pleasure, right along with her master's words.

"Do you want me to lick, suck, and bite it?"

"Oh, God, yes," she nearly sobbed.

"Tell me."

Maddie took a deep breath. "I want you to lick, suck, and bite my cunt."

"Mmmm, I think I will. You are so wet and ready, aren't you? I can smell you, Maddie."

As one finger lightly trailed up and down her wetness, she waited patiently. He stopped, and she could hear him suck her juices off the tip.

"Delicious. After I taste this sweet cunt of yours, then do you know what I'm going to do?"

Madeline hoped she knew. She wanted it more than anything.

"I'm going to fuck you, dear sweet Maddie, until neither one of us can see straight. You will lay there and not move, do you hear me?"

"Yes," she answered.

"Good girl. Now for my feast."

His thumbs spread her lips wide, and he licked her from top to bottom—one long lick of his wide tongue that nearly made her scream. She just barely didn't jump a foot off the bed. Teague proceeded to lick, nibble, and suckle her with his tongue while one thumb slid in and out of her pussy, and the second thumb out of her other hole. It was incredible. It was indescribable.

He sucked her clit like he had her nipples and then bit and licked it again. His thumbs moved faster and faster as his mouth kept pace. Madeline felt an enormous orgasm building, and she rode along, happy to give Teague control, ready for an intensity she'd never felt before.

As the pleasure reached its crescendo, he put two fingers, along with his thumb, inside both holes and sucked her clit hard. She heard herself scream his name hoarsely as he held her down and prolonged her orgasm. Wave after wave tumbled over and down her body. His mouth kept pulling and pulling at her until she saw stars behind her eyes.

Just when she thought she would lose consciousness, his

mouth was gone, and his cock filled her. Hard, fast, and deep. He slid in and out of her wetness easily. Her body clenched around him, hungry for more.

Madeline didn't think it was possible, but energy infused her again. She wanted to move with him, but she kept still as he pumped in and out, over and over, deeper, faster.

Oh, God, yes!

She reached another peak as he thrust inside her so deeply he touched her womb. She tumbled again and again, feeling his warm seed spilling inside her. Her body was slick with sweat, sliding against him as he stretched their pleasure out.

He rolled off her and lay beside her, breathing heavily. After a moment, he untied the sheets, releasing her from her binds. He pulled her against him, and she rested her head on his chest, giddy and more satisfied than she had ever thought possible.

"Teague?"

"Hmmm?"

"I love you."

"I love you, too, Maddie, girl."

He kissed her gently, his tongue swirling with hers slowly, exquisitely. Then they slept in each other's arms.

Chapter Twenty-one

The courtroom filled again. Neither a seat nor a space was available anywhere. Madeline had confidence that Elizabeth would present a solid defense, but still she was afraid. Afraid to lose all the wonderful things she had found with Teague.

He sat beside her, his big hand holding hers under the table, lending her the courage she needed.

Judge Montgomery walked in, and everyone sat.

"The same rules that applied yesterday apply today to everyone in this courtroom. Mouths shut and ears open." He gestured for Elizabeth to proceed. "Whenever you're ready, Miss Mitchell."

Elizabeth stood. "The defense calls Sheriff Jackson Webster."

A low murmur arose from the spectators.

"Quiet!" Judge Montgomery yelled.

The sheriff made his way up to the witness stand and with his usual smirk sat down in the witness chair. After the clerk swore him in, Elizabeth began.

"Sheriff Webster, did you enter into an agreement with Teague O'Neal to pay him five hundred dollars to spy on and gather evidence against Madeline Brewster?"

"No, I didn't." Jackson looked properly affronted.

"Did you and Judge Earl Martin conspire to siphon money from First Bank of Plum Creek and use that money for your own gain?" Elizabeth said as she walked toward the witness.

"Absolutely not!" Jackson's face flushed.

"According to records filed in Denver, you own over a hundred thousand acres of land hereabouts. How is it you can afford that on a sheriff's salary?" She pulled a sheaf of papers from behind her back and looked through it. "Defense exhibit A, your honor. Land sale records in the name of Jackson Ezra Webster. Seventeen sales in the past twelve months, totaling one hundred twenty-three thousand two hundred six dollars."

The crowd gasped, and Judge Montgomery frowned them into silence. "Sheriff Webster?" he asked. "How do you explain this?"

"I didn't buy those properties. She made that stuff up."

Madeline stopped herself from rolling her eyes.

"These are sealed by the deed office in Denver—very official, as far as I can tell."

"Not mine," Jackson said. "She's lying."

Judge Montgomery hmphed. "Proceed, Miss Mitchell."

She walked back to the defense table. "Can you also explain how you have six bank accounts in Denver alone with over five thousand dollars in each of them?"

Jackson's face was now bright red. "Why are you making up such lies about me?"

Elizabeth's eyebrows rose. "These are records from the six banks attesting to the fact that Jackson Ezra Webster deposited these funds over the past six months. I also have ledgers from the Plum Creek bank records from the past month, originals and forgeries, with funds missing in the exact amounts deposited into Mr. Webster's accounts. Defense exhibit B."

She handed the papers to Judge Montgomery.

"I think this proves, your honor, that the missing funds from Plum Creek were not taken nor spent by Madeline Brewster. They were in Sheriff Webster's hands."

"You're lying! Earl did all this! I didn't buy any of those properties! He did! It was him!" Webster jumped up and ran toward a very frightened Earl Martin, who cowered behind

Matthew Worthington. The attorney looked completely shocked.

The marshals stopped Webster from actually hurting Earl, but the damage from his outburst was clear. The marshals backed Webster into a corner, where they bodily restrained him. The room lay in silence until Elizabeth spoke.

"No more questions, your honor. The defense now calls Isaiah Harper to the stand."

Another murmur drifted through the crowd as the young black man entered the room and walked toward the witness chair on visibly shaking legs.

Elizabeth approached him with a smile after the swearing-in. "Mr. Harper, can you tell me what Sheriff Webster asked you to do?"

"The sheriff told me to spy on Mr. Teague and Miss Madeline and catch them up to no good, if'n you know what I mean," he finished with a loud gulp.

"Did he offer to pay you?" she asked.

"No, ma'am. He told me he would fire my granddaddy and leave him out in the cold with no job and make sure no one would hire him again." Isaiah seemed to be growing stronger as he spoke.

"Who is your granddaddy?"

"Orion. Mrs. Webster's servant."

"Did you find any evidence that Madeline and Teague were up to no good?" Elizabeth asked.

"No, ma'am. Mr. Teague was nice and kind to me. Miss Madeline gave me a room, food, and a job when no one else would. Two good people there. I hated to spy on them. Just hated it." He shook his head and frowned.

"Did you tell Sheriff Webster any falsehoods about what you saw?"

Isaiah grinned. "Yes, ma'am. I surely did. I told him some whoppers. It wasn't any of his business anyhow."

"Thank you, Isaiah. No more questions, your honor."

Matthew Worthington mumbled that he had no questions for the witness. His expression was that of a man kicked in the privates by a mule.

Elizabeth next called Judge Martin to the stand, but in the excitement, he seemed to have disappeared. Madeline hoped the marshals caught up with him before he could reach Wyoming.

Elizabeth recalled Mr. Cleeson and presented him with a bank record that indicated he had ten thousand dollars in Denver. He broke down in tears and sobbed about how they had bullied him into it. He wasted no time backstabbing Earl Martin and Jackson Webster, despite the clear evidence of his own involvement. Honor among thieves certainly wasn't holding true. More like rats deserting the sinking ship.

One by one, Elizabeth brought up witnesses to testify on behalf of Madeline and her kindness to them. People spoke of help during hard times, extensions on loans, and generosity that seemed to know no bounds. Candice tearily testified how she would have lost her store without Madeline's help.

As she heard herself praised and thanked, Madeline's faith in the town grew. It was heartening to know that not everyone thought her a bad person or an evil Black Widow.

As Elizabeth was about to call another witness, the judge held up his hand.

"Please, no more sunshine and puppies, Miss Mitchell. I've heard enough. I find the defendant, Madeline Brewster O'Neal, not guilty. All charges against Teague O'Neal are dismissed. I order the immediate arrest of Jackson Webster, Brady Cleeson, and Earl Martin, wherever that little weasel may be hiding. They are to be held in the Denver jail until such time as they can be tried for embezzlement and fraud. Their bank accounts are to be seized and returned to the bank in Plum Creek."

He banged the gavel, and Madeline's heart began beating again.

"This court is dismissed!"

Teague jumped up and kissed Elizabeth on the mouth. As she

plopped down in her chair in surprise, he picked up Madeline in his arms and tossed her in the air. No one had ever, ever done that, even as a child, and the experience was heady.

"Stop, Teague! You crazy man!" She laughed as he set her back on her feet and kissed her quickly.

"I love you, Mrs. O'Neal."

"I love you, too!" she cried and then hugged him, breathing in his scent, reveling in the fact that she was free! She turned to Elizabeth. "I don't know how to thank you."

"My fee is enough; besides, this was great fun. I love beating the bad guys." Elizabeth smiled and wiped her brow. "You'd better keep that husband of yours locked up. He's liable to have hordes of women chasing him. Kissing like that! I never!"

They all laughed and hugged as the crowd filed out of the room. Victory had never tasted so sweet.

Epilogue

Plum Creek returned to normal within a few weeks, and life went on as it had before. Some people continued to distrust Madeline. Others were glad to see her vindicated.

Madeline had a specialist come in from St. Louis to look at Eppie. He pronounced her in a "coma," a kind of sleeping death from which most patients never awoke. Madeline grieved for her friend and wished she could change what had happened.

The doctor told Madeline in confidence that Eppie was pregnant, probably three months gone. He didn't know if a baby would survive the coma. He also told her that Eppie's body would heal itself. Now her mind had to do the same.

Micah still refused to leave Eppie's side. Madeline told him about the baby, and he wept in her arms, confessing his love for the sleeping beauty.

Madeline and Teague decided to move to Denver. She gave the house to Micah, who would watch over Eppie and their child, praying for a miracle. Orion Harper moved into the house to help Micah care for the house and property. Isaiah visited often and helped with the heavier work.

Madeline and Teague promised to return every month to visit their friends. She left the bank with Mr. Finley. He was competent enough to run it and seemed eager for the challenge. The only thing she took from the house was the furniture from her mother's sitting room and the bench Teague had made her. As they drove away in her father's carriage from the Brewster house, Madeline said good-bye to the Black Widow, to her father, and, lastly, to her mother's spirit, which had guided and protected her.

Life had finally begun for Madeline O'Neal.

If you liked this book, pick up
KEPT,
the second book in Jami Alden's
Gemini Men series,
available now from Brava. . . .

"What's up with you going where you're not supposed to?"

The deep gruff voice slid around her, grabbed her, and wouldn't let go. Alyssa couldn't have held back her smile if she'd wanted to.

His eyes were hidden in shadow, but his mouth curved into a half smile, and a dimple creased the left corner of his mouth. His lips were firm and full, and she knew they'd be hot against her skin.

"Do I even want to know why you're hanging out at the servants' entrance looking like you're about to stick your thumb out?"

"I didn't want to have to deal with the crowd on my way out. And now my driver got into an accident, so it looks like I'm stranded for a while."

Derek was silent for several moments, and though his eyes were shadowed, she could feel him studying her.

Ask me.

"Can I give you a ride home?" He almost looked shocked that he'd asked.

She didn't let that stop her. "Sure," she said without hesitation.

A slight frown creased his forehead, but he gave her a curt nod and left without another word to get his car.

As she waited she shifted on her sky-high heels, restless, alive with anticipation. After so many months on her best behavior, a reckless urge was pulsing through her. Uncontrollable, unstoppable. She needed to forget the consequences and do something outrageous.

But this time it wouldn't be for attention, publicity, or her father's censure. This time it would be all for herself. She'd been so good, watching her every move for so long. Surely she deserved a little treat?

A silver Audi rumbled up to the driveway, and Alyssa wasted no time sliding into the passenger seat. The leather was cool against her bare thighs, and the interior of the car was full of his cedar and soap scent.

He backed out of the driveway and turned the corner, passing the snarl of limos and guests crowding the circular driveway of the Bancrofts' estate.

"Where to?"

Nerves warring with desire, Alyssa rummaged in her bag and dug out her lip gloss, slicking on a coat to give herself something to do.

Derek stopped at a stop sign. "Where are we going?"

She swallowed hard, her throat suddenly bone dry. What she was about to do was crazy. Stupid.

Necessary.

"You know, it's so early," she said, and turned to face him. She kept her eyes locked with his and placed her hand deliberately on his thigh. "And I'm not quite ready to go home."

He stared at her hard for what felt like an eternity. His thick, dark brows drew together in a harsh scowl.

Her stomach bottomed out as she realized he was about to turn her down.

"You want to get a drink somewhere?"

The moment of truth. She slid her hand farther up his thigh, delighting in the swells and ripples of rock-hard muscle hidden beneath wool gabardine. "I'm not much for crowds. Why don't you just take me back to your place?"

Don't miss Donna Kauffman's latest,
LET ME IN,
out this month from Brava. . . .

"I always found you to be an attractive woman, Tate."

Alarm filled her. But it didn't come close to matching the rush of . . . what? Anticipation? Surely she didn't want him to acknowledge, much less act on, the other kind of tension that was swirling around them.

"But, even in the most extreme situations, I never once considered doing what I can't seem to stop thinking about doing now."

She was the one hallucinating now, that was it. He was still in the bathroom and she'd come into the kitchen to get soup, and had somehow fallen down a rabbit hole or something, because surely he was not standing right in front of her, saying what she thought he was saying. It was wild enough that she was having any thoughts in his general direction, but at least she had the excuse of being retired and no longer the sharp professional.

He was still team leader, actively on the job. And the only person who'd been even more the consummate professional during their years working together than she'd been. All work, no wink. That was Derek Cole. Not ever. With her, or anyone else. At least not that anyone had ever known. CJ had made it her favorite topic of conversation on more than one occasion. So, if he ever had . . . flung, he'd been remarkably discreet about it, which was saying something around people whose job it was to know every damn thing. It was another aspect of his character that she'd admired. So, what the hell was this?

When she finally found her voice, it was damnably shaky. "You're injured, and recently injected with God knows what, so—"

"It's not the drugs talking, Tate."

"Well, it doesn't sound like you talking, either. At least not the you I worked for. We've got enough to deal with, without—"

"Oh, I know. Believe me. I came down the hall just now to see if I could sit in here and eat some soup. No ulterior motives. No skulking intended. Then I hear you commenting on my—"

"Must you repeat it?"

His lips quirked a little then. "See?"

"See what?"

"How is it I missed this?" he asked, sounding sincerely perplexed.

"Missed what?"

"You."

He was looking at her like he'd just discovered something amazing, and couldn't quite believe it.

"I'm the same me, I've—"

"No. You're not. I always admired your capable, no-nonsense work ethic. You and CJ were the best agents I ever had. Which, considering the talent I had assembled, is a high, but deserved, compliment. I said before that I found you attractive. I did. And do. But I always viewed that through the filter of being your team leader, looking at that as simply another attribute you possessed to be executed professionally, where and when best deployed."

"Just because I don't work for you now—"

"It's not just that. You're . . . more you now. Still everything you were, but there's so much more. I'm seeing the rest of you, probably the you you've always been, but whom I never had the pleasure of meeting. You're dry, sharp, outspoken, and surprisingly sarcastic."

"You're right, the professional filter is off, but maybe I'm not who I was before, either. I'm leading a very different life now. I'll pull it back together, focus, find my professional balance once again, but only because I have to. And believe me, no one is more motivated to get through this and make it go away as quickly as possible. To make you go away," she added truthfully. "To get back to the life I earned, the life I deserve. The life I *need*, Derek." If there was a quiet pleading in her tone, she wasn't going to apologize for it. Things were complicated enough without this sudden revelation from him. Especially considering she'd been thinking very similar things about him.

Which, if he hadn't known before, he did now, given her comment about his lack of clothing. Now he knew she was noticing him, too.

Which meant one of them had to get their act together, and get it together real quick. He moved closer and leaned his weight against the counter, along with the walking stick, so he could lift his free hand.

"Derek—" She broke off when he lightly brushed his fingertips across her cheek. His touch was gentler than she'd expected. She should be smacking his hand away, not wanting to lean into the unanticipated warmth she found there. She didn't need nurturing, or caretaking, but that's not what the look in his eyes was telegraphing. What she saw there was bold, unwavering, unapologetic want.

And what he wanted, was her.

Here's a peek at
IMMORTAL DANGER,
by Cynthia Eden,
coming next month!

His back teeth clenched as he glanced around the room. Doors led off in every direction. He already knew where all those doors would take him. To hell.

But he needed to find Maya, so he'd have to go—

"Don't screw with me, Armand!" A woman's voice, hard, ice cold. Maya.

He turned, found her leaning over the bar, her hand wrapped around the bartender's throat.

"I want to know who went after Sean, and I want to know *now*." He saw her fingernails stretch into claws, and he watched as those claws sank into the man's neck.

"I-I d-don't k-know—" The guy looked like he might faint at any moment. Definitely human. Vamps were always so pale, it looked like they might faint. But this guy, he'd looked pretty normal until Maya had clawed him.

"Find out!" She threw him against a wall of drinks.

Adam stalked toward her, reached her side just as she spun around, claws up.

He stilled.

She glared at him. "What the hell do you want?" she snarled, and he could see the faint edge of her fangs gleaming behind her plump lips.

It was his first time to get a good look at her face. He'd

seen her from a distance before, judged her to be pretty, hadn't bothered to think much beyond that.

He blinked as he stared at her. Damn, the woman looked like some kind of angel.

Her straight hair framed her perfect, heart-shaped face. Her cheeks were high, glass sharp. Her nose was small, straight. Her eyes wide and currently the black of a vampire in hunting mode. And her lips, well, she might have the face of an angel, but she had lips made for sin.

Adam felt his cock stir, *for a vampire*.

He shuddered in revulsion.

Oh, hell, no. The woman was so not his type.

Her scent surrounded him. Not the rancid, rotting stench of death he'd smelled around others of her kind. But a light, fragrant scent, almost like flowers.

What in the hell? How could she—

Maya growled and shoved him away from her, muttering something under her breath about idiots with death wishes.

Then she walked away from him.

For a moment, he just studied her. Maya wasn't exactly his idea of an uber-vamp. She was small, too damn small for his taste. The woman was barely five feet four. Her body was slender, with almost boyish hips. Her legs were encased in an old, faded pair of jeans, and the black T-shirt she wore clung gently to her small breasts.

He liked a woman with more meat on her bones. Liked a woman with curves. A woman with round, lush hips that he could hold while he thrust deep into her.

But, well, he wasn't interested in screwing Maya, anyway. Not with her too thin body. Her too pale skin. No, he didn't want to screw her.

He just planned to use her.

Adam took two quick strides forward, grabbed her arm, and swung her back toward him.

The eyes that had relaxed to a bright blue shade instantly

flashed black. Vamps' eyes always changed to black when they fought or when they fucked.

Sometimes folks made the mistake of confusing vamps with demons, because a demon's eyes, well, they could go black, too. Actually, Adam knew that a demon's eyes were *always* black. And for the demons, every damn part of their eyes went black. Cornea. Iris. Lens. With the vamps, just the iris changed.

Usually demons were smart enough to hide the true nature of their eyes. But the vamps, they didn't seem to give a flying shit who saw the change. 'Course, if a human happened to see the eye shift, it was generally too late for the poor bastard because, by then, he was prey.

Gazing into Maya's relentless black eyes, Adam had a true inkling of just how those poor bastards must have felt.

A growl rumbled in her throat, then she snarled, "Slick, you're screwing with the wrong woman tonight."

No, she was the right woman. Whether he liked the fact or not.

So he clenched his teeth, swallowed his pride and, in the midst of hell, admitted, "I need your help."

GREAT BOOKS, GREAT SAVINGS!

When You Visit Our Website:
www.kensingtonbooks.com

You Can Save Money Off The Retail Price
Of Any Book You Purchase!

- • **All Your Favorite Kensington Authors**
- • **New Releases & Timeless Classics**
- • **Overnight Shipping Available**
- • **eBooks Available For Many Titles**
- • **All Major Credit Cards Accepted**

Visit Us Today To Start Saving!
www.kensingtonbooks.com